All the Lost Souls:

Damnation

Cheyenne Kai

Order this book online at www.trafford.com
or email orders@trafford.com

Most Trafford titles are also available at major online book retailers.

Note for Librarians: A cataloguing record for this book is available from Library
and Archives Canada at www.collectionscanada.ca/amicus/index-e.html

Printed in Victoria, BC, Canada.

ISBN: 978-1-4251-9203-7 (soft)
ISBN: 978-1-4269-1559-8 (hard)
ISBN: 978-1-4251-9204-4 (ebook)

*Our mission is to efficiently provide the world's finest, most comprehensive
book publishing service, enabling every author to experience success.
To find out how to publish your book, your way, and have it available
worldwide, visit us online at www.trafford.com*

Trafford rev. 9/10/2009

 www.trafford.com

North America & international
toll-free: 1 888 232 4444 (USA & Canada)
phone: 250 383 6864 ♦ fax: 812 355 4082

ACKNOWLEGMENTS

Thank you to all the musicians, artists, actors, directors, dancers, choreographers, and writers who have inspired me. A special acknowledgment goes to Feeder: I doubt most of the story arcs in this novel would have been written without their inspirational songs.

To Clare for my wonderful front cover and for putting up with all my claims of this book being published soon; it finally happened.

Also thank you to Sara Muiño Carro for allowing us to use her stock.

And many thanks to Tavistock Printers in Fleet, Hampshire for formatting the front and back covers.

To my mother for giving me my love of literature, and her final edit.

To my father, for giving me my love of film. I am especially grateful for his editing, his believability in this project when I thought it was a hopeless cause, for putting up with my senseless ranting, and for naming Bethamy.

To everyone who criticised me and gave me encouragement along the way, especially 'Syaiz' for being the first to read the first full draft of this novel.

Thank you to everyone at work who urged me on to complete the final edit.

Another thank you I cannot miss out goes to my cats, for always being there when I needed a cuddle in my teenage years, and for understanding.

Thank you to all my teachers and lecturers who taught me how to improve my writing. Hopefully the prose in the sequel will be improved to show you in a better light.

Thank you to everyone for your patience and support.

And of course thank you to you, for reading these words.

FORWARD

Although it seems to me that she has always been writing this book my daughter tells me that she started writing it when she was just thirteen years of age, she is now 22. The text has been revised, changed, re-edited, and reconstructed many times as she went through the learning curve of taking her GCSE's, "A" levels" and then her Degree.

This long period, finally leading to this completed book, has resulted in a fascinating mix of her incredible imagination and colourful English as a young teenager, and her more mature writing later as a student taking her degree. Put the two together and you have this wonderfully creative, and I believe unique, novel.

She also wrote a number of short stories and poems during this time. I often wondered what her teachers thought of the stories she wrote for homework, they were somewhat of a grizzly nature. She was such a very quiet and petite girl and Chris, (her mum) and I were often told that she should ask more questions and be more interactive at school. Yet her imagination when writing was incredible.

When taking on the task of proof-reading the book I often found myself so carried away with the story that I forgot what I was supposed to be doing. I was very careful not to alter the unusual style of the writing which I thought would spoil her originality, whilst at the same time trying to correct what I thought was clearly wrong or misleading. The final judgement was always left to her of course and my recommendations were of a very minor nature.

I hope you will enjoy this book as much as I did and find yourself totally engulfed in the strange worlds of the Haukea, Keahi, and of course Earth.

Welcome to "All the Lost Souls: Damnation" – The story of a young man who inherits a destiny he did not want, but could not avoid.

Allan. G

Dedicated to my father, for taking me swimming every Sunday

CHAPTER ONE

Water dripped through the cracks in the bitter dungeon. Torches held mysterious blue flames that gave out a chilling freeze, numbing everything they touched. A musty smell of mould and cold shivered all around, lingering in the air like death.

Snakes littered the floor, tongues flicking from dark shadows, trying to find their prey.

In the middle of the cave was a table. Lying on top of it was a woman, panic-stricken and confused. Questions spread through her mind, all of which lead to the same man, the only one who possessed the answers: *Why would he do this? What was his intent?* The snakes coiled like ropes around her wrists and ankles, binding them. As she tried to move the serpents hissed, angry at being disturbed. Her blue eyes made contact with the infinite black eyes of the snakes, which pierced her soul with deadly hatred. The victim watched her breath escape, coming out like hurried gasps of smoke. She knew what they were, why they despised her: they were Keahi, and she was the reason why their master grieved. The woman dared not move for fear they would infect her with their deadly poison, despite the fact she was trying to tell herself he would never let anything harm her. It was hard not to squirm when the snakes wrapped around her with more intensity, their determination cutting off the blood supply to her hands and feet, restricting her sight, and forbidding her to hear anything above

1

the thumping of blood pulsating in her ears, so she didn't see as one of the snakes slithered along the floor towards the table. The woman couldn't hear as it made its way up the table leg.

Excitement from the sickly show was arousing the snakes that bound the prisoner: the time had come to dispel of their King's one weakness. They hissed eagerly in her ear. She breathed in and held it as the sensation of a serpent crawling along her body electrified her nerves. Its tongue smelled, tasted, her skin. It crept onto her face, its tongue licked her lips. Another snake slithered along her arm and bit down, hard, drawing blood and delivering poison as a substitute into her veins. The woman's veins and arteries throbbed as her heart beat venom around her system.

A voice slashed through her agony, broke through the barrier of blood still pounding in her ears. A voice which dripped in deceit.

"Aka," the woman said under her breath, finding her throat was sore and harsh. She felt a numbing sensation and again came to wonder why he was letting them do this to her.

It was no secret that he still loved her, they both knew that. The scar still glowed vibrantly where he had tried to cut it out of him, knowing for the sake of his people that he couldn't allow himself to give in to his feelings. Trouble was he already had, and in doing so Aka had caused great grief for all his family. They'd had a son together and - though she didn't want to believe it - him capturing her was surely a sign that Aka now relished the power that would be a marvellous asset to winning the war between their two people: the prospect his son had of near indestructibility. Kaelem would be twelve years old now. Aka needed his son before he came into his teens, to capture the unused mind of an innocent and the fragile imagination held at this age, before it crumbled.

2

Lily-Anna tried to swallow, but with fright she realised that her windpipe had narrowed. Torment filled her soul as a deprivation of oxygen spread through her body. Her breathing became shallow and started to haul out of her. She dimly noticed a man whose eyes shone intensely back as bottomless pools of darkness in deeply tanned skin. Threat and sorrow seemed to rise off him. He was tall, six foot four in fact, exactly half an inch higher than she was. He was dressed in a long black coat and trousers. His hair hung limply down just past his shoulders, and shone a dangerous black. She knew hidden beneath it, on the nape of his neck, was a tattoo of a circle with a dot in the middle. The symbol that represented his status in the Keahi land: the symbol of a King. Another tattoo was printed on the inside of his right wrist, which mirrored that of her pendant. His whole essence reeked of emotional turmoil.

Lily-Anna wheezed and averted her gaze, suffocating anguish in replacement of the inescapable knowledge that he was the cause of all this, someone who had been so gracious to her, so gentle. But the truth had given him away - he had used her as well as loved her. She wanted to cry as she thought back to all those times when it was just her and him. Alone and free in each others' arms.

"Please look at me." The sound was deep and entrancing, with a sharp edge. The same as it had been when they had first met. It reminded Lily-Anna of all the goodness that had once been so vivid and extraordinary. But now it also brought connotations of the deception that he had woven through her, using words to hypnotise. Look where they were now: It meant nothing. It meant everything. She moved her eyes as he passed his hand gently over her throat, a thin black-green smoke coming out of his palm, highlighted with sparkling bright white lights, and suddenly she could breathe properly again.

3

She drew in as much air as she could in one gulp, not caring that it tasted contaminated and vile with the stench of lies. She looked into the man's piercing black pupils. Sadness swept over her as she remembered how it had been when she was ignorant of his true identity. Aka saw Lily-Anna's sorrow reflected in her eyes, and put a finger delicately to her cold lips. He shivered slightly and whispered, "I need you."

Her lips began to tingle as the paralysis wore off them, and she managed a feeble word, "Why?"

"I *love* you. That is why."

She could smell his breath spilling out of him as he spoke, it had an aroma of mint, but then he continued, saying something that made her heart stop, made her throat feel as if it were closing up again, and she reeled upon hearing the unbearable:

"And I have to see my son. I cannot let him become associated with the Haukea."

Tears fell from Lily-Anna's eyes, drop by drop, welling up then falling, merging, into one another as they dripped down her cheeks. She felt them soften her lips as they came to her mouth. She tasted the salty sorrow, and knew their son would never have the life she sought for him if she granted this request. She wanted to scream at Aka, to shout, to cry out loud. She wanted to jump up and hit him, suffocate him so that her son wouldn't have the pressure of knowing what he was. She acknowledged that she was the liar now. But only a whisper could pass her lips, and so she focused her blurred vision onto Aka, expelling through her eyes all of the hate and anger she felt towards him at this point, and for a second the two pairs of eyes made contact. Then it was gone, lost forever, but it gave enough information to tell Aka that he would never get his true love back, and it was enough for Lily-Anna to see her forbidden love's secret unhappiness; to realise that Aka had lost someone who meant more to him than any war.

She felt ashamed of herself that she had thought otherwise. Her husband wanted their son to be detached from this war as much as she, the only difference was that he was not blinded enough to think this would be possible. When he spoke again, more softly, less compelling, she listened with more respect:

"You cannot keep his inheritance a secret forever Flower. You know what the Haukea are like, they will find his power and make him their own. I am sorry, but I intend to breach your trust by trying to find him. However I am afraid Flower: who knows what will become of our worlds with a power like Kaelem's... "

Lily-Anna gasped back her tears.

"What?" he asked.

She couldn't answer him, the truth was too painful for them both to have to handle; she dreaded his reaction to it, just as Aka would have been afraid of her reaction to his hidden life all those years ago. It killed her to think what she had to do, what she had done, but at the time she thought she had no choice in the matter; she was broken and fearful. The Haukea would execute her in their mission to get her son, and if Kaelem were taken to Hau Houna, her own world, without her, what protection and guidance would he have against building an allegiance with a group which brought so much misery to so many people? And with the information that Aka was to find and take her son she had to take action. So with sincere regret she began to whisper the spell that would allow her son to see her. Her eyes closed as she went into a comatose state. She saw her son, and reached out to him as he grabbed her. However, before she could finish, Aka quickly put his hand over her mouth, the uncertainty of what she was doing scaring him.

"I thought you were against them now!" he shouted in shock. Blackness seeped into Lily-Anna's mouth. She became half-conscious, but was determined to finish what she had started, there was no time to explain, and bit down hard into Aka's hand. He yelled at her, feeling the cold pain crystallising his hand. He clutched it to make the pain more bearable, and a drop of frozen blood fell from it to the floor, where it shattered next to one of the serpents. Its hiss was filled with the need to protect its master. The snakes that were scattering the floor started to crawl up the table legs surreptitiously and slide over Lily-Anna's body. One of them lunged at her skin, passing more venom into her system. Sharp pains erupted over her whole body as they pierced her flesh with deadly fangs. She saw the magic spilling out of her in great blue and purple lights. The snakes raised their heads, droplets of venom and blood descending from their drenched fangs, staining Lily-Anna's pure white skin crimson. She watched the connection fading between her and her son. Their hands unclenched, creeping away from each other through numerous unseen cracks. She felt him, her son, leaving, his soul full of emotion, could hear his frightened thoughts; Aka had done something to the connection when he had woken her, and something was not right. She knew her son would soon come into contact with the war he should never have been conscious of. The remaining lights floated above her, and disappeared through the ceiling, and she was gone as she joined them.

Aka cried, his scar still showing vibrantly where he had been told to cut out his love for her, but he couldn't, he just couldn't.

CHAPTER TWO

The music blared in an otherwise silent room. Light from a street lamp outside shone through the thin curtains. In the eerie glow of night the big room looked mysterious, seeming to bring life to the characters clinging to the walls.

With school seeming a million miles away, Kaelem was at last completely happy. The project, due for the first day back, lay crumpled in a pile and slowly slid down the back of the cherry wood desk, forgotten, ready for the twelve year old to run madly round the house, looking for it with anxiety flooding his mind at the thought that he had done nothing for the whole holiday. But this was a long time from now, and for all that Kaelem cared it would never come.

He spread out on his bed, blissfully thinking over all that he would do in the holidays, everything he and his best friend Jeb were going to explore. With the album continuously spinning round music that faded into the background, the boy silently drifted into a peaceful sleep, with nothing to wake him from his dreams.

A cold breeze swept over Kaelem. He breathed it in with closed eyes, finding the air salty. He stepped forwards, drawn toward something in front of him, like a magnet that was urging him on. A few steps later his toes touched clear water. But Kaelem quickly drew them back out as a sudden freezing sensation crawled over his foot. Breathless, he snapped his eyes open. A bright purple light shone into his blue eyes, nearly blinding him. Slowly a figure materialized out of the brightness, equipped with phenomenal expansive wings spreading out of its back. Feathers glittering white like snow, and highlighted with different hues of blue, rustled softly in the silent night as the cool wind caressed them. Their owner wore a magnificent dark purple dress, so long that the bottom was gradually becoming stained with the salt water, so astounding that the colour reflected light with every motion made. As the figure glided towards him it was almost uncomfortable to watch. But Kaelem carefully walked towards the figure, entranced by its beauty and grace, not wanting it to go away. As he approached a face became clearer, a woman's face, smiling gently at him. Nine slim blue earrings dangled delicately down from her left ear, a black pendant hung on a thick leather strap that was tied tightly round her neck. It was a symbol that the boy had never seen before. The black wood twisted and intertwined, creating the illusion that it was choking itself. He looked back up into her face and saw she had deep sorrow in her blue eyes. She reached out a delicate hand whilst her mouth formed whispering words that made no sense from dark blue lips. When Kaelem took her hand her chest heaved with sadness, regret, and love. He noticed a burn scar on her arm. The figure's presence seemed to seep inside him. He suddenly felt light and good, as if fear no longer existed, nor hate or anger. Everything was for once peaceful and perfect. He looked back up at the woman's face and smiled happily, almost laughing, as they floated above the world. But then it all went wrong.

He was suddenly standing on a cliff, with a harsh wind screaming terribly in his ears, making him cold and frightened. The woman looked back at him, sneering; her face horribly distorted. It scared him. Her pierced ears were ripped and her once wonderful wings had shrivelled and torn. As he watched they turned from a beautiful white and blue to a horrific black, as if they were slowly rotting. He tried to let go of her, but she held his hand tightly, her bony fingers curling painfully around his wrist, while sharp claws dug into his hand. A red rash slowly crept along it and continued crawling up his arm like an infection. He screamed, wanting to scratch the irritation, but the terrifying woman wouldn't let him, wouldn't let go. Then she jumped, pulling him down to his death.

Kaelem woke up rubbing his wrists. He looked down at the back of his hands to see a rash quickly fading before his eyes, until there was nothing left except for three drops of blood where the fingernails had dug into his skin most tightly.

It took him a while to shake off the nightmare. He found it was hard for him to breathe, as if his throat was slowly closing up. Beads of sweat trickled down his hot forehead as he tried to recollect what the dream was about. He could remember a women grabbing his arm, and then falling towards a fathomless sheet of water. He lay back down on his bed, wanting to get back to sleep, wanting to know the end of the dream, wanting to forget about it altogether, and still a woman's face kept reappearing in his mind. It was as though she were standing right in front of him, smiling. He knew he recognised her, as if she was an important part of his life, but he couldn't remember why; couldn't understand who she could be. He turned over and clutched his head, trying to take away the image of her, but it wouldn't leave. She appeared again, elegant and pretty. Blue eyes sparkling as tiny fragments of light radiated into them, her eyes full of relentless sorrow, her hand outstretched to him. But this time Kaelem didn't take it - thinking the dream was a warning, Perhaps even a premonition. A distant voice in his head told him that she was evil and he should stay away from her, but it wasn't his. He shut his eyes and put his hands over his ears to block out every last essence of her.

He must have eventually gone to sleep, because the next thing he was aware of was the morning light shining happily through his curtains, turning the mysterious room into his calm and familiar bedroom. He crawled carefully out of bed, and stopped abruptly on the landing; a curly haired tarantula was greeting him.

"Tika, you need to stop doing that to me." Kaelem sighed and picked her up. He then proceeded to put her carefully back in her house in Aolani's bedroom. Afterwards he sneaked downstairs.

The house was deadly silent. The only noise was the whisper of the second hand moving on the clock. It was eight-thirty. He went into the lounge and switched on the television. A random programme was on with singing animals and a meaning behind everything they did. He laughed silently to himself at how silly they all looked, hardly believing he actually used to like it. It wasn't long before he found himself quite enjoying the programme and laughing at their weird jokes. When it ended he began to sing along to the theme tune that played during the end credits, until the doorbell let out its shrill shriek.

Kaelem groaned as he crept to the window. He opened the curtain slightly so that he could see through a small gap. No one was visible at the door, but the bell continued to ring endlessly in his ears. His dad yelled to Kaelem from upstairs to see whom it was, but there wasn't anyone there. The doorbell was obviously broken or something. Grabbing the door keys he unlocked the front door and peered round to look at the doorbell. The button was pressed down, but there was nothing to keep it there. As he turned back to go upstairs and tell his dad a frighteningly cold hand touched Kaelem's shoulder. He shivered as a sudden wave of fatigue overcame him, before he fell into a soundless sleep.

CHAPTER THREE

Mya had been an official warrior against the Haukea for the past four years. It was her destiny to become one, due to the fact she was one of the few Keahi who had the ability to shape-shift. She did not resent this, but took it as a great privilege and honour. Now though, an envelope secured with the precious seal belonging to Aka, the Keahi's King, had been sent to her house. It contained a private invitation offering her to enter his home.

As she made her way closer to the door of his house, a wonderfully intense heat hit her. She closed her eyes and breathed in the suffocating fire. Its flames and smoke mingled into one another, reminding her of who she was, and what she must do. They spoke to her, the voice sounding like Aka's, his deep, careful words drifting into her head, examining her, making sure she was not an intruder, another shape-shifter in her form. At last he was satisfied and accepted Mya into his home. She opened the grand door and stepped bare-footed onto the hot black tiles. She looked around at the new surroundings. Candles glowed everywhere, creating warmth and light. Producing the most heat was a huge circular fire, blazing in the middle of the room. Flames reached up like hands towards the tall ceiling. She saw that numerous chairs were placed around it. A man sat in the biggest of these. The heavy wood was intricately engraved, reflecting the tree-like tattoos each Keahi had.

The man looked up when she entered the room, and stood. He glided through the fire to greet her. Taking Mya's hands in his, Aka led her to the left of the room and through one of the many doors that decorated the entrance hall. She found herself walking down a long corridor painted a striking orange, mirroring the bright flames of a fire that would never burn out. Steel doors ran endlessly along both sides of the corridor, each with it's own number, like a hotel. Behind them the occasional scream issued, or murmurs of the crazed and delusional. A loud bang to her left made Mya jump as someone started yelling curses at Aka. Putting his hands meaningfully onto the door Aka closed his eyes. A cry of pain came beating inside her ears, then nothing. Mya began to walk more swiftly, keeping as close as she dared behind Aka, her heart pumping fast and her breath quickening with the suspense of what they were doing down here.

Then, unexpectedly, Aka stopped. He turned to face a door on his right. The brass number told them it was room two hundred and six. Unlike the others there was only silence behind it. Aka tapped on the door, no answer. He brought out a key chain to this response; Mya saw that it was obviously heavy, carrying uncountable keys of different shapes, sizes and colours. Aka immediately knew which one he wanted, as if he had been in there more times than he would like to admit. He held up the key, letting the others fall weightily down, his arm giving way a little to take the shock of the sudden load. The lone key he held was one of the smallest, painted a dark purple, with an unusually large hole at the top, which allowed it to be joined onto the chain, forever. Aka slid it easily into the lock, and turned. Carefully, he circled round to face Mya and told her in a husky voice to wait, exactly where she stood, for him to return. He walked through the door and slammed it in her face, as if angry that she had done something terrible.

She waited, staring at the orange steel, as curiosity welled up inside; wanting to know what he was doing in there, why he had even stepped foot inside this corridor. It was no secret what lurked behind those steel doors: they were the crazed, those who didn't want their powers, who had never grasped how to control them. Many sat rocking back and forth, hot tears marking their faces as they wished it away. It was a lost cause; it would never leave them. Some threw themselves at the doors when they heard footsteps, screaming and shouting, telling stories that on their day of freedom from this endless torture they would show the Haukea how to penetrate Aki Houna's defences, and laugh as they witnessed the world turn to ice and the Keahi destroyed - for they also knew that certain Huakea had the power to bind their fire.

Now Aka had gone the corridor seemed more threatening. The sounds rose, searching for her weak spots, seeming to vibrate inside her. Some of the prisoners beckoned to her, asking in sickly sweet voices to let them out. Mya wished for Aka's return. She huddled up, frightened, listening to them with widened eyes, not understanding why they would rather be locked up in here than accept who they are, what they could never change, and become free, powerful. Finally the door to her right opened without a sound, and Aka came out, eyes red and cheeks stained with tear tracks. A strange coldness seemed to emanate from the open doorway before Aka shakily locked it again. He muttered to her in his usual dark voice to follow him. Silence crept over the corridor as he walked past each cell door. Only the sounds of sobbing, and people muttering for the others to be quiet in disturbed voices came out of them now.

Mya breathed in the fiery hot air of the entrance hall, glad to be out of the corridor.

She walked quietly in a trance, watching Aka's long dark cloak sweep the ground, raising tiny particles of ash with every step he took towards their destination. Fascinated she let her eyes gaze slowly upwards, watching the folds of material, seeing patches of bright light appear, and disappear like the flames in a fire as they moved through the shadows created by torches on the walls, swinging to the beat of his footsteps on the hot stone floor. The smell of faux leather rose off him like steam, mingling into the air.

Suddenly the atmosphere changed, Mya blinked as her hypnotised state dissolved into awareness. Looking around she found that they were making their way along another, darker corridor. Issuing from in front of her came the solitary light source. She noticed that Aka had somehow got hold of one of the torches from the wall of the previous room. The floor was now made of dirt, it was dry and dusty, she coughed, and rubbed her eyes as the soil disturbed under the feet of Aka rose up in protest and attacked her. The corridor seemed never ending, Mya was beginning to feel tired. Her legs felt weak, and her stomach growled with hunger. She looked at her watch, twisting it towards the light in Aka's hand. She saw that they had been walking for nearly two hours. She began to wonder how long these corridors went on for, if they ever stopped. She wondered where they were heading, and began to feel nervous about what her job would entail, if they had to go this far away from civilization, away from listening ears, and prying eyes. Perhaps it wasn't a job, who said it was? She had only assumed this, Perhaps she had followed him to her death. Down here anyone could get lost or go missing. No one would really know what happened, she doubted if anyone knew this place even existed, except for a select few in on the evil plans of their leader. She felt suddenly cold. She put her hand to her face, trying to warm herself.

They came to a dead end. Would this be where he would do the deed. Or leave her? It would be cleaner, she knew she could never find her way out with all the corridors that led off into smaller passages, some fake, leading to numerous dead ends, some so long she was sure she would die of starvation, or hyperventilate with claustrophobia before she reached the end of them. Mya took a step back, ready to run if she needed to, never letting her eyes wander away from Aka.

CHAPTER FOUR

Kaelem woke up feeling sick and dizzy with an oncoming headache. It was dark, a harsh wind wrapped itself around him, making the boy convulse into uncontrollable shivers. He lay down to ease the nausea and closed his eyes. The longer he stayed like this, the more wet his hair and back felt and so, unable to do much else due to the sickness enveloping him, Kaelem rolled over. When his eyes focused on what he saw a dull bolt ran through him: it was snow. But his illness overshadowed the full emotion of revelation and, instead of wondering what was happening, he moved his hand, picking a bit of it up, feeling the melting snow trickle between his fingers. He sniffed and held his hand to his head, letting the freezing sensation of the snow take his mind off the constant throbbing. He gave up and buried his face in the snow, not caring anymore about the cold, only of easing the pain and letting the sickness pass. He lay in the same position for a long time: eyes closed, breathing deeply, his hands pressed against his forehead, drifting in and out of reality as the aching subsided and came back again in the same motion. Finally he descended into a peaceful sleep and didn't wake for a long time.

***

The cold roused Kaelem from his slumber: it became too unbearable for him to sleep through. The first thing he noticed was that there was no more pain. He smiled. Kaelem pushed himself up with his arms and knelt in the snow. Snow? He looked up at the sky and witnessed an unusual blue sun emitting rays of light that felt cold upon his skin. He got a shock when his gaze reached the landscape: the magnificent snow combined with the sun to make a white so brilliant that he had to shield his eyes from the glare. He swallowed: something seemed to be stuck in his throat, and when he swallowed again he coughed painfully. Where was he? What had happened to him? In a tremendous shiver his body told him that the first thing he should worry about was primal survival: find shelter from the biting cold, then figure out what this all meant. With any luck, or perhaps misfortune, he would be able to do both at the same time.

He stood up slowly, eyes lowered, unsteady from shattered nerves and sinking feet - he watched as snow encased them. He looked up, his eyes attempting to adjust, and witnessed a place he never thought he would see first hand. His eyes found it hard to take it all in.

Standing there, open-mouthed, he saw a land covered in deep, sparkling, transcendent snow. He'd never seen it so pure, so infinite. Layer upon layer, never ending into the horizon, and beyond. Kaelem turned round until he spotted something in the distance which broke up the landscape. He screwed up his eyes and thought he saw the top of a building, light shining from it to merge into the sun's rays. Blue rays. He stood there, mouth agape, unsure what he should do, how he should react, knowing only the freezing cold around him. With a wind whipping at his clothes he began to make for the building, wrapping his arms around himself, hoping to find warmth, or at least shelter. The thought only now occurred to him that people must occupy this land - how else could a structure be here? Unless, of course, it had been deserted when the cold had suddenly come. No one could live in these weather conditions without at least some form of heat.

He wasn't watching where he was going as he ran towards the building, trying to heat up against the stinging pain of cold; breathless from the energy it took to stay upright. Suddenly he found his feet free of the snow and had to spread his arms out to keep his balance.

Kaelem looked down and saw that he was standing on a river that had been frozen over. Below the icy surface he could see motion. As he leaned down for a closer look he saw fish the like of which he had never seen before, swimming happily in clear water. They had huge gills and were the colour of the snow. Four blue stripes running horizontally across their backs patterned their scales. They had barbells around their mouth, like Catfish, but these were also blue, gradually turning white as the colour neared the tip. Their dorsal fin and tail also reflected a similar style. The fishs' eyes shone blue, with large black pupils in the centre. As Kaelem stared at them he saw that slowly, one by one, they were staring back at him. He could faintly see his reflection in each of their intense eyes. He gasped and stepped back, forgetting he was standing on slippery ice, and fell. He opened his eyes, the headache back. He saw a blurry figure leaning over him, concern in its face.

"You'll never reach it that way. It's miles from here."

"Reach what?" Kaelem whispered, rubbing his sore head.

"Hau hale ali'i. That is where you're going. Isn't it?"

"I - don't know. I'm frozen. I don't know where I am, or how I got here." He shivered, nevertheless the voice's tone reassured him, even if the words that came with it were confusing:

"We've been expecting you for so long. Now you're finally here. It's just a shame about the reason."

Kaelem looked up, his vision becoming clearer. He saw a girl, probably only a couple of years older than he was. She had short white hair with light blue highlights. Her face was also a startling white. She wore dark sunglasses that contrasted with her skin and blue lips. She offered her hand to his, and he took it. Almost immediately he drew his palm away. He had got a more biting shock of cold from her than he had from the weather.

"Sorry. I forgot that you're not yet..." She trailed off, anxiety coming over her face for a second. She saw his skin was turning blue and that he was shivering like mad. He was scared, and she knew why. But before Kaelem realised it her expression went back to a helpful smile. "Still. I'm here now. You'll grow to like this weather. Here," she took off her sunglasses to reveal clear blue eyes, "you can wear them, so you don't get blinded by the glare. My eyes are immune - they're really just a fashion statement for me."

Kaelem tensed up as her hands came closer to his face, he didn't want to feel that horrendous chill again: it was unnatural. She was careful this time though, and instead of putting them on herself, she decided to hand them to Kaelem. He began wondering what she was talking about, why she was here for him, how long they were going to keep him here. From the sound of it a long time was going to pass before he could go home.

"Well. I guess we should be going then, before you get pneumonia or something. Here. I'll help you on. Meet Siren." As the girl spoke she looked round. Her face fell and she sighed. She called out the name, and Kaelem saw a huge yellowish creature, which would have looked white had the snow not been the stark colour it was, bounding towards them. With sudden terror filling Kaelem's mind the thing became the form of a polar bear. He looked towards the strange girl for comfort. She was watching it, but her expression was relief. She sensed Kaelem's uneasiness, and turned round. She pointed at the bear, and explained, "That's

Siren. We're going to ride her. Don't worry she's friendly enough. Just hope she's in a good mood today. It'll probably take us about four hours to get there. She will have to rest every now and again. Polar bears don't like running for long distances."

She saw that the look of discomfort remained on Kaelem's face, and tried to make him feel more relaxed with the situation. "Don't worry, there are groups of houses every now and again where we can shelter and eat."

He didn't feel any less worried when Siren went up to Kaelem's saviour and nuzzled her head against the girl's arm. The girl approached Kaelem and lifted him onto the bear's back. She then heaved herself up and took the reins. She turned around to look at Kaelem. "It's okay. She'll only go about twenty miles an hour." She started laughing, and kicked Siren. Kaelem's body tensed up as he felt the harsh wind scratch his face and tears pricked his eyes. He stopped shivering with cold, but with fear instead. He clung onto the girl fiercely. Not daring to shift position, or even swallow away the dryness he felt in his throat.

After what seemed like hours the wind started to become less violent. They were slowing down. He saw they were heading towards a group of small houses. The girl tapped Siren behind the ear and the bear knelt down. They dismounted and walked amongst the houses. The girl was confident of where they were going and soon reached one particular house with ice sculptures surrounding the front door. They knocked and went in without waiting for an answer.

"It's really to warn them of our presence. We're very close here and tend to just wander in and out of other people's houses as we please."

There was a woman sitting in a chair. The chair, like everything, was created of ice. The woman looked at them, smiling. She stood up from the seeming comfort of her chair and walked into another small room. After awhile she came back, carrying a platter of food and drinks. She obviously knew they were coming. Kaelem felt very uncomfortable in her house as the two friends spoke rapidly together in whispers, occasionally looking at him with serious expressions. He gave a worried smile and looked into his drink for the rest of the time he was there. Eventually they left. He was glad to be back on Siren after that - at least she couldn't talk about him behind his back.

They stopped a few more times after that, until Siren was exhausted and Kaelem was tired. He only wanted to get warm, and although the building appeared to get closer, they never seemed to quite reach it. He closed his weary eyes, trying to comprehend how he got into this position, even though he was too cold to think clearly. Finally Siren halted again. Kaelem groaned: another house, more secrets. However, when he looked up from his reverie his breath caught in his throat as he saw a huge building: their final destination.

"This is Hau hale ali'i. That girl," his guide pointed to the person similar to his escort, but with long white hair, standing by their bear, 'is Opal. She'll take you in; I'm going to rest Siren and check on the other bears."

She tapped Siren behind the ear again and they both slid off her. Again the two people started whispering. Kaelem was tired of this, and wondered what the people of here were expecting of him. How did he get here? Why was he trusting these weird people who didn't seem to feel cold?

Opal came up to him as the other girl rode Siren away. "Come. She is waiting for you. We all are. I see you're cold. We must hurry." She seemed to have no emotion in her voice or expression, talking in the same, static sentences. He looked carefully up at the palace he was about to enter, and couldn't be mistaken it was made out of ice. Glittering in the blue sun's rays, cold and majestic, it towered above him seven large stories high, with its width giving the illusion of endlessness.

Upon entry the place seemed colder than outside. He couldn't stop shivering, and a numbness was creeping into his skin. He looked down at his hands and saw they were blue. His teeth chattered and his nose ran. He sniffed. Opal looked at him strangely. "You won't feel the cold anymore."

Kaelem snapped his gaze up at her, startled.

They came upon two large doors. Opal ordered him to stay where he was, and so he obliged, hoping that if he was obedient enough they'd treat him kindly. Opal opened the door and disappeared.

It was a while later when she came back to tell Kaelem to follow her. Kaelem shuffled into the throne room, and collapsed. The cold had got too much for him to bear any longer. The girl stopped and looked at his body. She then bent down next to him and picked him up. She began to walk towards two people, both sitting on their own elegantly sculptured ice-throne. They looked the same age as each other, even though the one on the left had a face that was much more tired and drawn, surrounded with dark blue hair, whilst the being sitting on the right-hand throne looked fresher, with many white highlights in her hair. Her expression told a different story though; through her eyes you could see the faintest spark of terror; however, was trained not to show emotion, and so she sat up poised and upright, making her mother proud.

Opal walked along the aisle that a hundred people had parted for her. Each of them looking intensely at Kaelem, faceless whispers lifting into the air, all asking the same thing, all anticipating what was to happen next, and each one of them had had their left ear pierced numerous times. When Opal got to the thrones the woman on the left spoke, "Is that him?"

"Yes," Opal replied, lifting Kaelem's shivering body higher for everyone in the room to see. They seemed to shift forward, trying to get a better look, some scared of what he could be, others excited. But all wanting to see him.

"We must do this quickly. He'll die soon." They quietened down as the Queen spoke again. "As Lily-Anna requested: fill up a bath with water and lay him in it."

"Yes." Opal walked away, confidently knowing what she was to do, having being prepared for this ever since Kaelem's powers had been stripped from his soul.

The Queen walked softly into the bathroom. She touched his frozen skin. She looked at Opal and nodded. "I want to do this, for Lily-Anna. I don't care about what his father may have infected him with. This must be done. If there is any trouble, we use him to find Lily-Anna, then we kill him. You understand me? If he won't co-operate we kill him. He could end up a major threat, only Lily-Anna knows what powers he possesses, and this is the only way of finding her."

Opal handed the Queen a small bottle filled with lights flittering inside, forcibly knocking against the sides, trying to get out. The nearer it got to Kaelem, the more energy the lights seemed to get, and the more they wanted to get inside Kaelem, to be whole with his soul again. Opal gave the Queen a needle, which she used to suck up the lights. With this the Queen pierced Kaelem's skin near his heart, then pulled it out with a squelch. Kaelem's eyes fluttered open, his body shaking and blue eyes, that were slowly turning to green, rolling, showing the intensity of his pain. He felt something like a thousand needles ripping through the skin on his legs, tearing apart his trousers. His elbows felt like they were extending; his spine twisting, both trying to force their way out of his body, but never fully succeeding. Instead, it felt like knitting needles were stabbing, one by one, through his

22

back. Nevertheless, the place where the most pain exulted was from the front of his body. Not only did it prickle, but it felt as though a knife was slashing him over and over…he looked down and gasped, tears in his eyes: six huge gashes had cut into his skin above his trembling lungs, following this there was only a great emptiness inside him where those lungs used to be. Then it happened. He arched back as sharp pain formed in his neck, as his pharyngeal pouch broke through to form more gills. He tried to swallow, but that was impossible. He looked around him with a panicked stance at the two women staring down at him. He couldn't breathe, he was suffocating. He couldn't breathe, he couldn't breathe…

CHAPTER FIVE

Aka had disappeared through the large doors that had carved themselves into the rock of the dead end at the sound of his voice. Mya stood before them, deciding whether to stay where she was and await her fate, or to try and find a way out of the caves. Aka should have returned by now, if everything that happened down here was legitimate. She chose, after much dithering, to stay where she was; realizing that she'd rather face whatever was about to happen to her in Aka's underground lair, than starve to death in darkness and confusion. Besides, Aka knew these caves better than she did, and when he found her he would be angry.

The doors creaking open made her jump. She felt her heart beating faster against her chest as the shadowy figure of her King stood in a bright fiery light. "You may now enter." He fell to the left of the door, leaving it open for Mya to step through. With agitation flowing through her she heard the door close behind her, clicking softly as it merged back into the wall. Mya took in a sharp breath of hot air and held it inside of her. Without a word, Aka moved forward, and she followed. Her eyes pierced into his back, knowing she was meant to be behind him all of her life. He had every one's best interests at heart, and if one of those was to kill her, then let it be so. Let it be quick. She held her head high and pretended it was nothing, whilst inside she was numb. Out of the corner of her eye she dared a look around her surroundings. She saw they were in a large room with long, elegant tables scattered randomly around. Balloons and streamers were hanging from the ceiling. It was bright, and the hint of a strange coldness similar to that in the dungeon wrapped around her. She noticed people holding glasses of wine. They were all laughing joyfully, silently, with each other, and to her. She looked sharply at Aka, feeling small and unsure. Aka faced her and smiled so briefly that Mya wondered whether it had existed. Perhaps it was a sneer?

"It is a welcome party for you. I am sending you on a most… personal mission, and trusting you will succeed. If not, exile is waiting for you behind those doors."

Mya turned to look where she had just walked in from, and swallowed the tears, fear and welcome relief taking over.

"Do not worry: great rewards will follow for the rest of your life when you succeed. This is inevitable. We must continue this conversation in private, the less people knowing about this the better: even the most trusted can be fooled. The party will wait for your return."

The people stood, as if time had slowed down. Their faces were full of eternal laughter, and their mouths were open, even though no sound was coming out as they moved their glasses of wine up to her in slow motion. Aka and Mya turned left and walked through oaken double doors. This time Mya didn't have time to look around her, for as soon as the door had closed Aka turned on the spot, twisting his black coat around with him. His speech came out emotionally, presenting to her the only weakness he possessed, "She has finally done it." He didn't waste time introducing her to the topic, for she soon sensed what it was about, and was amazed he was telling her. The thought that she was most likely the only person to know what he was about to say rushed through her mind, filling her with adrenaline as Aka continued, "He will soon obtain what he should have kept from

25

birth. Regrettably he has been incarcerated onto Hau Houna, fortunately though it also means I will be able to interpret where he is - once he is released. However, this time it is undeniable they will exploit his powers. The only thing we can hope is that they will not find out his other power, for if they do they will use it for their own gain, as usual, and not what the True Angel always meant for it: to help the humans live, to help others survive, not just their own race, not only their leaders but every race, every class.

"It has been ten long years since I last saw my son. As you know, he was taken away from me when he was only two years' old. He was stripped of his powers' essence in the hope I could not find him. This is why I have called you here, Mya," he took a breath, "to the depths of my kingdom, where only the most trusted and sacred may enter. It is where secrets are found, and truths told. When he arrives back on Earth I want you to befriend him. He must learn to accept and say openly that you are his friend. Then he will follow you when in trouble, and you are to lead him here, explaining it is an escape from the evil following him. If you do not befriend him, then he will be scared when you finally guide him to us, and probably end up hating our races as a result of this. Please be careful: he will be under the influence of the Haukea."

Mya's eyes looked in all directions, in awe of where she was, and a nervous, but privileged, smile started to form at the corners of her mouth. she wasn't led to her death then, she was here to perform a great deed, and one which her King would never forget. Her shoulders relaxed, she breathed out the air which she had been holding all this time, and continued to listen to what Aka was saying. "I chose you because you are the only shape shifter that is young enough to be a convincing friend to my son; the others may be able to transform into the body of a twelve year old, but they'd never be able to feel like one emotionally, and therefore will not be able to act or approach Kaelem accordingly. I will fix it purposely that you are in the same class as him. Be kind, hopefully he will like you instantly, if not it will just mean you will have to work harder to gain his *full* trust. Let's just hope that it is not too late, let us plead that the Haukea have not found what Kaelem has inherited from me. Inherited from a King." He sighed. Then silence. After a while he spoke again, making Mya jump - she'd been daydreaming again, thinking about what hushed thoughts were mentioned down here, thoughts which would never be heard by her ears. "Mya." The King stood upright, his face suddenly expressionless - a man whose inner thoughts and emotions could never be known by anyone but him. "You are free to go. I will contact you when I have found him, and we will begin your training."

She stood there for a second, shocked at how fast he could change from a father worrying about his son, to a King taking his throne. She left the room with him, noticing the party was still there, but the guests were now moving at normal speed. The cold had disappeared, the noise had quietened down, and only whispers were heard. She followed Aka out of the cave's seemingly endless maze, and remembered nothing more until she was lying in her scorching bed with a bright light shining lazily into her dazed eyes.

***

Hands pushed Kaelem down into the bath. He was too weak to resist their force, so he sank under the water, gasping hopelessly with fatigue in the aftermath of his transformation, trying to conserve as much air as possible. At first he squeezed his eyes shut, but being enclosed in an ignorant darkness petrified him more than the thought of the water stinging his eyes. Yet he was even more disturbed when he did lift his eyelids to find that the usual sensations did not come: he could see perfectly, and it felt comfortable, as did the freezing temperature of water that came from below miles of ice. He focused his eyes on the faces peering down on him, his eyes pleading desperately for help. He heard footsteps. A voice: "But I thought mermen were ugly. That's what it says in the fairy tales."

"Bethamy get out of here! You are not permitted to witness what is happening to this boy. Now go and prepare for your coronation. Stop being so immature." Footsteps walking out.

Kaelem knew he was about to faint if he did not get air, but when he tried a futile escape upwards he was blocked. He opened his mouth, expecting a mouthful of suppressing water, but shock ran through him: the slashes on his body and throat opened, and he found he was breathing. He was the... he couldn't bring himself to even think about it; that the stories he told his younger sister were real. That he was one of them.

Another voice, one he did not recognise, started asking questions, but the words blurred into each other as Kaelem closed his eyes, trying to contemplate what was happening to him. "Do you think what he inherited from his father is still in his veins? Maybe it was stripped along with his powers, and can't be put back in again. Do you think we should inject him with the Healers' vial?"

"No," the Queen replied. "We do not know whether Lily-Anna's blood, though it is not of royal descent, has affected his circularity system. The potion may allow for him to heal himself, as the Haukea do, or it may give him the ability of the Keahi, to heal others. Perhaps he even has the traits of both. We do not know, and that is dangerous. So no, he will go nowhere near the Healers' vial, unless I directly take him to it myself. Everyone understand? That could be the biggest mistake we execute."

Kaelem's eyes shifted beneath his eyelids as disturbing thoughts came to his mind of what powers he could possess. What had they turned him into against his will; who were these people; why kidnap him, and what was in that injection they gave him; why do this to him, then appear to be scared of what he had become? What was the point? He wanted to scream, but the people crowding around him didn't seem as if they wanted to go anywhere. They looked down at him with inquisitive faces, keeping a distance whilst Kaelem just lay there, feeling weak and drained.

"Is he glowing?" the same woman that had spoken before asked.

"No, Aka couldn't - how could he have? But that would mean he probably injected himself too. Go to the Healers' vial, see who has handled it recently. NOW." Footsteps running out. Silence. Then, quietly, the queen's voice again, "Someone get me a knife. Please."

When it came the Queen held it up and said, "Any volunteers? Don't be shy; it won't be a deep cut." They all took a step back, so she stepped forwards and pulled someone out from the few people there were. It was Opal. The Queen cut the girl's hand. Opal gave a tiny whimper and bit her lip. Blood seeped across her palm, contrasting against her skin. The Queen held the hand over the bath, and tiny droplets of the crimson liquid made ripples in the water.

Kaelem opened his eyes at this moment and looked up through the water, to see blood. He rose up, still keeping the gills on his chest below the water, and stretched out his arm. He was about to unfold his webbed hand when something grabbed him. "Let us see who he takes after."

A flash of light, then Kaelem realised his hand was bleeding; however he also noticed there was no pain. He sensed something wrong, and was drawn towards Opal. As Kaelem went to touch her he felt a warm glow flow through him, reaching into his uncurling fingertips. He saw the glow spill out of them, engulf the wound of the girl. He watched through half-closed, weary eyes, the wound healing rapidly. Afterwards nothing remained, not even the hint of a scar. He dropped his hand heavily into the water, his own blood diffusing scarlet around him. He felt as though the glow had been his energy, and Opal's cut had completely drained it out of him so it could be healed. He sank back under the water, exhausted and uncaring.

***

Aka yelled.

His rage erupted from him in the form of screams. He sat up straight in his bed, running his fingers through his straight black hair. He wiped his long, wet fringe from his sticky forehead.

"Damn it," he breathed, trying to calm himself down.

The dream had led him to where his son was staying, which meant his child had repossessed the powers he should have kept from birth. His spell had not been enough to stop Kaelem being transported to the Haukea, and now it couldn't stop his son from finding out his true identity, from releasing what was active inside him; from frightening him. Annabel-Acacia, the Haukea's queen, was not to be taken lightly, and would certainly use Kaelem as it suited her, with no thought as to his well-being.

Aka looked out of his window and up at the fiery stars in the light sky, pleading she would not discover that Kaelem held the power of life and death in his royal veins, for though being the power's vessel meant it was ultimately his decision whether the substance was used for good or evil, she was a strong manipulator.

This vial was what had first fuelled the war, what started the last two centuries of endless turmoil, and indefinitely into the future until the Haukea heard the true thoughts of their queen. There was no solution to the fighting, no way out, for no-one believed they were the ones using it wrongly. The Haukea had shaped death to the words that the Angel had spoken to their families two hundred years previously.

The only blood strong enough to absorb the substance inside the Healers' vial without making the host insane, then subsequently killing them, was royal, so when The Healers' vial had been taken back from the Haukea long enough to inject the contents into Kaelem, and then into himself, Aka had revealed his selfish secret to his wife: that he was her adversary's King. He still saw the wrinkles of a hurt and confused expression on her beautiful face, for they were forever stamped into his memory. But there were further consequences to this, because at that moment he had given away his previously esoteric identity to his enemy.

Aka stared out at his land and wondered how he could get Kaelem back, praying the Huakea hadn't fed him false information about the Keahi, and that his interference with Lily-Anna's spell had been enough to warn Kaelem not to trust the Haukea. Yet as much as he hoped his son had understood this, he would be sorrowed if Kaelem did not warm to his mother.

CHAPTER SIX

200 Years Earlier

It was the first day of July in seventeen sixty-five. Happiness flew in the air and in the souls of the Haukea and Keahi, for it was finally that time of year when the two united races celebrated in each others' company. The time of hate and separation was six hours into the future.

The field in which the festivities took place was an enchanted area of land on the Keahi's world.

Many decades ago all of the Haukea sorcerers came to the Keahi's land out of curiosity, to discover what kind of life could inhabit a place so opposite to their own. Finding the Keahi they formed an allegiance, and used their magic on the opposite side of the globe to the palace, where divides did not exist. Together they created a neutral temperature both races could survive in. The spell was stronger than anything anyone could have believed, and as time grew on it became even more unbinding, not that anyone wanted to reverse the power. Not at that time anyway.

The luscious field was thriving with life: red and blue flowers dotted the landscape amongst the green grass, snow covered some of the biggest hills, while dry sand filled the deepest ditches. Tables had been set up at regular intervals, loaded with mouth-watering food and delicious red and white wines that complemented it perfectly.

A smile invaded everyone's face, and excitement rose in the air like petals caught in the wind. It spread and evolved into every soul on the field.

Rarely seen friends rushed into each other's arms, while some shyly greeted the other race. As the celebrations got underway, and drinks were passed around, the talk and laughter increased in sound and enjoyment. But juxtaposing this, the yet unknown dread was drawing nearer.

It was two in the afternoon when they first noticed what would change both their lives, and their descendants' destinies, forever. It happened gradually, steadily, as if building up the anticipation and tension for dramatic effect, ready for the horrible climax.

It first appeared as an object in the sky, gliding carefully down through the yellow-tinted clouds. But even though the sun was glaring, a blackness surrounded the object like a shield. Each pair of eyes looked up to witness what their neighbours were focusing on, and soon all were squinting upwards, curiosity glistening from them.

The closer the object came to them, the more obscure it seemed to become. Though wings protruded from its back, the thing was unlike any animal they had ever seen before, because indeed it was some kind of being. The Haukea looked at the Keahi for an explanation, hoping it was part of the entertainment, but they were just as confused as the Haukea.

A huge breath erupted from the gathering when the entity finally came close enough for them to see what it was. Those that had been sitting down now stood up. Eyes glued to what was happening they began to make a clearing for the Angel to land in. The Keahi's leader at that time stepped apart from the congregation and the Haukea's Queen followed suit. They connected hands, and as they did electricity sparked from the combined elements. The Angel did not hesitate as he continued his slow progress down.

Twenty minutes later he stopped, hovering just above the earth, feet pointed above the grass, as if going any further would contaminate his being. His wings fluttered and he smiled slyly through full lips. He watched the two races through eyes that were such a deep brown the colour of the pupil seemed to have spilled into the iris. Yet the eyes were dreadful to look at: dull and lifeless, they made you forget to breathe. The Angel's figure was tall and lean. His features had an air about them that was similar to an eighteen-year-old's, though it was somehow obvious he was much older than this.

He spoke to his silent audience in a voice that was like a song: tuneful and clear. As the words left his mouth he held out his hand. A small vial, filled with multi-coloured lights, sat in the middle of his creaseless palm. "I call for all the royal descendents to come to me. You are to control the outcome of this day. Do so wisely, generations to come will be affected by your choices." The King, Queen and their children confidently approached the Angel, whilst internally they prepared themselves for whatever he asked of them. "Freewill is a major factor. You therefore have the choice in how to use this power. It is the vessel's decision. It is your blood. There is only one condition: the power the vial possesses can only be inserted into blood that has a gene originating from the first royalty. Those who do not have this gene will become maddened by the gift. It will consume them, resulting in the death of both them, and anyone else they decided to bring with them.

"So I am guessing you are wondering what is so special about these lights? They are unique because they allow those who hold them in their bloodstream certain healing powers, but as I have

said before, it is up to you to decide how to use them. I come to
you now because I think you are ready to do great things with it. I
will come back in two months' time to decide whom should have
possession over the vial. This decision will be based on whoever
uses it for the purposes I perceive as greatest."

The Angel departed, leaving the vial behind, knowing that they
were not meant for its power.

He had been exiled from the heavens. In revenge he had stolen
the vial, wanting to cause havoc between the two races to
highlight his own destructive power, and the mistake the gods
had committed in casting him out of paradise - he would bribe
his way back with the lives of these races by desensitising and
demoralising them. Those who banished him would see the
imbalance of evil and would agree to his deal of retracting the
war, in return for them allowing him back through the gates.

The lights reacted very differently in the Haukea's bloodstream to
the Keahi's. It made them live forever, never aging in appearance.
The only thing that gave them away was their hair, which like
all Haukea became bluer with age. As a result it meant that they
could not be harmed, and they were healed instantly if anything
happened to them physically. It also cured any illnesses and pains.
But it was all for the person who had the lights in their blood.
The Haukea believed it was the royalty who should be protected
and no-one else should benefit from it. Seeing as the Angel had
forbid it to be used in any bloodstream that was not royal, their
theory was backed up.

In contrast the Keahi wanted equality between the humans,
themselves, and the Haukea. But the Haukea did not like the
human race. At that time their leader's thoughts of them as
powerless evil beings that didn't respect the world they lived
on, and who were destroying their homes, had leaked in to the
general consensus of her people. The Keahi believed the power

should allow anyone to benefit from it, including the humans, as all life was precious. Being able to morph into anything with a soul had taught them this. The Haukea went against them, rebelling by threatening to take over the human race, to show them that they could use the power to restore the world to its original, wonderful, state. The Keahi tried to convince them that the Angel had talked to them about freewill: that taking over the human race would result in destruction, that people were now a part of the Earth's ecosystem. The Haukea had laughed in their faces.

Each race believing they were using it for the better purpose, both thinking their opponent wrong, and to some degree evil, the war began.

Two months after the 'celebration' had passed the Angel came down again.

The Angel asked to be handed the potion, and to it he added a new substance, making it stronger, more destructive, an essence of himself, something terrible that no entity should be burdened with. Born from a lost soul and built for evil he allowed the user to be able to bring people back from death or to take lives away - the key to life and death. Literally.

He then extended his wings to their full span, making himself look as magnificent as he could - taking advantage of his power, thinking that he was glorious. He opened his mouth to state whom should gain the vial, when he was struck down. His wings collapsed and he fell to the ground in a crumpled pile. Another angel came from above.

Unlike the first, her feet touched the grass of the Keahi's world. She looked gravely at the warring races, knowing it would not end for many centuries. The Angel's plan had worked: he had created his own hell in races that were once allies. But the races demanded to know who had rightful possession over the vial.

Unable to stop what had already begun, the new angel chose the Keahi. "Please, your athame," she said to the Keahi King. He gave it to her - the athames had certain healing powers, used by those Keahi whose powers had not yet fully formed. She dipped the knife into the vial. It lit up, but before she finished her operation the original Angel rose to his feet. He held out his hand and the knife was transported to him. "You'll regret this. You will beg me to come back, to relieve the pain of suffering as I torture the souls of these people. You won't be able to stand it." He turned round, and handed the knife to the Haukea. "This is now yours." He walked off into the distance, and as he went blue flowers died, dropping as ripples of death spread from his feet.

The Keahi looked in horror at the female Angel. "I am sorry. I can do nothing. He has prayed to a great evil, and has been rewarded with a power I do not want to understand. Its malevolence is so strong he was not able to transport the vial, because it held elements of kindness in it. I can't counteract what he has done, just as he can't counteract what I did to that athame." Her voice faltered as she said the last part, "I am afraid I have given them more ammunition now. I thought the Haukea would covet the vial so much they would not think about your athame, so I transferred part of the darkness he put into the vial into your knife: the power to take life away. I only realised he could gain possession of the things that had his power in them when he transported the knife. I guess this is why he did not stop me whilst I made the power transition, and why he didn't allow me to put both sinister powers into the athame. I guess he still owns the vial, even though he cannot assign it to anyone. I am only glad that I didn't give the athame the power of raising the dead.

"I am afraid a great darkness has befallen us all. You must protect yourselves. You must save the humans from whatever hell the Haukea will deal them.

"That Angel's soul is dark and disturbed. I warn you now not to use the extra power he put into that vial. It was born from evil and was meant for evil. Those who come back from the dead are not truly alive. They rise half-dead, forever tired yet never able to sleep, unless the one who did the deed wishes them back into the earth - releasing their soul once again into the ether. Otherwise the poor soul will have to wait until the day their resurrector dies, but alas, it cannot be by their hand, because if they kill the one who raised them they will be forever tied, forever damned, to them in hell.

"I will return only when I know for certain how this can be fixed, otherwise I fear to do even more harm." She rose into the air. "Be safe," were the last words she spoke as her form disappeared into the sun.

CHAPTER SEVEN

Aka walked gracefully down the steps to his dungeon. As he passed the familiar orange-doored quarters the yells started up again. As always, the same people, the same threats. It wasn't his fault they were locked up. Their virulent minds, their dangerous habits, kept them there. They refused themselves freedom. He had given them a chance to redeem themselves, but they hadn't taken it. None of them down here had. He knew the rumours the other Keahi were whispering behind his back, that he tortured the people, but he didn't. He'd never harm them, unless they pushed him past his limit, and each Keahi knew what that limit was. They had witnessed what would happen if he became too angry to control.

He didn't like their tone. They didn't know how lucky they were, if they had been born into a Haukea family and disrespected their powers they would be dead by now. If only they would just stop talking. He did not need this, especially not today. Every time he came down here, every single time. Do they never sleep?

'SHUT UP,' he screamed. There was silence, but it was more than just a lack of noise. Aka had never raised his voice before with such passion and frustration.

Fire erupted from their King, his whole body coming alight with combustion. It spread light through the dark dungeon, emphasising shadows of loss and fear on his face. As Aka glided towards a specific door the fire was sucked back inside him, and the dungeon was once again filled with a gloomy, dusty light.

He took out his keys, automatically reaching for the purple one, knowing exactly where it was and how it felt. What it unlocked. It was like literally holding the key to his soul. It felt cold, a fire of passion burnt out. The hole was too big.

He inserted it into the well-used lock and turned until he heard a click. He silently pushed open the door. Stepping inside he trembled and reached for the thermal clothing. It was always freezing in here.

The room was like all the others in size down in the dungeon. Quite big, considering it was his father who had commissioned the cells. But that was where the likeness ended. It was painted bitter, harsh colours, not the warm terracottas of the others. The temperature was below freezing, and the furniture was more luxurious - it looked uncomfortable though as most of it was beautifully sculptured out of ice.

Aka shivered uncontrollably. Even with the heated clothing the cold still managed to bite him.

A figure sat in one of the frozen chairs. Aka went up to her and she turned her head towards the sound of his delicate footsteps.

"Lily-Flower."

"Still on pet names are we? Aka."

Silence. Tension. Then Lily-Anna spoke again, "Why have you come today?"

Aka felt hot tears sting his eyes. They always came now, seeing her after what he had done. Knowing it was his blood the shapeshifters were protecting when they had killed her with their snake poison. He hadn't meant to cause this pain in his love.

"Don't cry. You know you can release me whenever you want."

"It is that easy is it?" Aka replied.

Lily-Anna stared at him. "You've already done worse you know. You resurrected me. I don't live. I have no purpose. I am nothing but a walking corpse waiting to go back into the soil and free my soul into the sky."

She stood. Aka looked down at the woman, her hair, her cold eyes, her lips, once smiling, now sad. He stepped forward, so did she.

"I can not give you up. I am not yet ready. You will know when I can let you go. I promise it will not be long...I promise. I just need to talk to you, about Kaelem's future."

"Ah, so that's why you came." A small smirk lit up her face.

"You know me too well to be surprised," Aka answered.

"I never said I was." There was a hint of laughter in the voice.

It was almost like before: chatting, smiling. Almost. The faces grew sombre again as Kaelem was discussed: "What are we going to do? Regardless of the fact that when the Haukea find out he has the power to heal they will guess that I must have injected myself with the lights as well, my concern lies mostly with Kaelem. Lily-Flower, you have to tell me what they are going to do with him."

Lily-Anna was silent for a while, before answering him, "They will use him to find me. Then, if he cooperates, they will teach him to be one of their warriors. Against you. He has great power and immunity in respect to fire and ice, as well as being a healer. He has the potential to defeat even you Aka."

"But what if he does not cooperate?"

Lily-Anna focused on the floor. "Let's just hope he does."

Aka tried to hide a flinch. "And he will kill my people. What can we do Flower? What have I done?"

Lily-Anna looked back up at him. "I lied to you too you know."

"But not after we got married. Not after we decided to have a child." Aka moved his head away from her, overcome by anger and regret. Then he shouted. For the first time he raised his voice towards Lily-Anna, with her being the cause, "Why did you transport him to *them*!"

"I didn't." Her voice was quiet with shock. "The spell: I spoke it to get Kaelem to trust the Haukea, that is true, but I only did it because they were the ones who had access to his powers. I didn't want him to be scared of his capabilities. The Haukea were getting anxious over the relationship between you and me.

"After they found out you were a Keahi I put on a charade, pretending to still believe in their cause, but they guessed I had turned against them when I kept returning without any souls. They came to the conclusion that I was a spy and would use Kaelem to win the war for the Keahi. They kept a close eye on me then. On the day they came for the vial I chose to give them Kaelem's powers to ease their suspicions, for they most likely would have killed me otherwise, and then...then they would have captured Kaelem. What chance would he have had disputing their claims without my guidance?" She paused, calming herself before carrying on. "I would never have brought him to the Haukea without me being there Aka. This is the worst stage in his life, to obtain his powers, to know who he really is. It's too much to understand, to handle, at the moment.

"He is too much of a gift, and I know that once they get a hold of him the Haukea won't let him go. I do not know what he is capable of. Maybe he has it in him to destroy both our worlds. Perhaps you know the horrific truth, for your power is a mystery to me as well, and I can see in your eyes that you are afraid of that additional power you carry yet refuse to tell. All I know is that he has the type of power the Haukea crave, it was therefore imperative to have a trust with him that was not built upon lies, and always will be. First and foremost he is our son Aka, but we must never forget what others covet him for."

"Even I am unsure of the extent of his power, and may someone help him if he is burdened with the same endowment as I - he already has too much to bear. Everything is my fault. If I had been honest with you in the first place, we would not be in this mess. Kaelem will lose his relationship with his biological father. He will fight against me, the Haukea will see to that, and I am sure I will fuel his response too. How stupid was I to expect it would all work out? I am a coward who should have explained himself to you when you told me you are of Haukea descent. Your race's law concerning identity may be born out of contempt, created for the wrong reasons, but at least it is truth." He sighed deeply. "All because of a love I could not expel." His hand subconsciously reached to his scar. He looked away from Lily-Anna, ashamed of himself. "What are we going to do?" he asked sadly.

"Bring him to me."

Aka focused back on the woman he loved.

"I may be able to understand. I am still a Haukea. As long as it isn't too late, as long as…" She stopped herself.

"Too late for what?" Aka dared query, not sure whether he wanted to know the answer. But Lily-Anna didn't reply. She said no more, and so Aka walked out of her room. The reason behind knowing when she did not want him anymore was too real for him.

43

CHAPTER EIGHT

Bethamy walked into the bathroom and viewed the somnolent boy emerging from underneath the water. But it wasn't a boy. His eyelids hid now green eyes, and behind them was a tiny opening: the spiracle, designed to pump oxygen to his eyes and brain. The skin of his upper body had turned a blue-grey in colour, and seemed to have a rubbery texture associated more with that of a dolphin's skin than a human's. A tail swayed instead of legs, covered in overlapping ctenoid scales, shimmering differing hues of blues, greens, oranges and greys. Even though his tail had the scales associated with fish, it was tipped by the fluke of a humpback whale, though in proportion to the boy's size.

The skin surrounding his gills and elbows were topped with blue, black and green placoid scales. She knew that if she rubbed them the wrong way her hand would bleed like Opal's. She resisted the temptation to see his powers at work on her. Looking more closely at his elbows she could see that small, fragile fins had extended from them. Unlike the rest of his body these were white in colour. They moved delicately in the gentle motion of the bathwater, as if feigning innocence.

Gills not only predominated the area on the front of his body his lungs had once been beneath, but there was also a set of gills on his neck. She saw his chest rising up and down in rhythmic breathing.

He turned slightly and Bethamy saw that placoid scales also ran along his spine, but this was a secondary shock to the great black and blue spikes that protruded from his back, similar in design to the dorsal fin of a lionfish. They were tinged orange at their deadly points. Bethamy flinched, both wondering and hating what the transformation must have felt like.

She was still standing there, contemplating about the power he could posses, if he was dangerous, and what the Haukea were going to do to him, when Kaelem opened his eyes and looked about the room. He saw that everyone had left except for one. She smiled when their eyes met. But Kaelem had learnt this meant nothing. The girl on the polar bear had smiled at him before leading him to this fate. Kaelem averted the gaze, not wanting anything to do with anyone else in this place. Bethamy's smile faded when she noticed Kaelem's open hand. A scar proved what her mother had done after she had left.

"I'm sorry. Does it hurt?" He recognized the voice as one which belonged to a girl, the one who had been made to leave the room. That meant she had nothing to do with this. It was not her fault.

Bethamy thought of her mother's words: *it was nothing to do with her.* Yet guilt still played on her mind, brought forth in a fit of apology.

Kaelem looked back at Bethamy, at the solitary face in this strange land that recognized he could feel pain. Perhaps even more alone in itself than previously, for even Kaelem was doubting that he could hurt now. The knife hadn't hurt when it scored his flesh. There hadn't even been a stinging sensation when he watched the blood seeping out of his skin. All he felt was the resistance of his skin against the pressure of the sharp blade, and then the sudden give when his body surrendered itself to the blade.

"Why don't you turn back?" She asked, wondering if he could.

Kaelem thought for a moment. Then, even though he was weak, he tried. He felt a slight change inside of him. He concentrated hard on becoming what he once was, until gradually the scales began to peel away to show legs, his gills healed over and his fins sucked back inside his body. The process was painless. Bethamy left the room blushing and came back with clean clothes.

"Here, these are for you."

Kaelem thankfully got out of the ice cold water and put them on. The cold did not bother him anymore, but the cut was starting to sting, making his eyes water. He felt reassured by this.

"What's the matter?" Bethamy inquired.

"It hurts."

Bethamy took his hand. "It didn't hurt before?"

Kaelem replied by shaking his head, swallowing back tears of pain and relief. "I-I don't understand." One determined tear slyly slid down his cheek.

"Oh, don't cry. It'll be okay." She felt both excited and scared at this news for a frightening realisation came to her memory: a woman named Lily-Anna, already suspected of having dealings with the Keahi, was stealing the Healers' vial. Bethamy had kept a promise to not tell anyone, she was too afraid of what the consequences would have been for both her and the woman. In compensation for the danger she had put her in, Lily-Anna had affirmed to return it as soon as she was able, and had reassured Bethamy's troubled mind that it was in no way an aid for the Keahi. Yet here he was: a mix of both species and injected with the Healers' vial. What great power had it given him? What other powers could he posses? Would fire be one of them? This worried her, for it proposed that he could be too dangerous to keep alive. If he joined alliances with the Keahi then what hope had they in surviving the war? She understood now: he had to stay here. He could never know anything apart from the Haukea side of their mission, even though it pained her to think he would become another pawn for her mother to play with, to corrupt. "Can you heal yourself?" What was she saying? If he found out he could the threat would be even higher. He could potentially be invincible. But Kaelem tried, and failed.

"I can heal others. I healed Opal." She nodded, feeling a wave of relief mixed with disappointment. "Will you help me escape?" Kaelem pleaded. She seemed nice, different from the others. But she stood there, and after a while she shook her head.

"I'm sorry, but you're needed for a very important reason." She couldn't tell him he had the power to destroy them all. However, her apology wasn't enough to stop another tear from betraying him. She felt guilty, but at the same time believed it was the safest thing to do for Kaelem, and the Haukea. She wanted to comfort him until his eyes dried, being kind to him was a good start towards Kaelem siding with them, although she knew deep down the real reason she wanted to stay with him had nothing to do with tactics. But she wasn't supposed to be here; her mother had already threatened her. Whether this was because she had concern for her daughter, or because of some other selfish thing, she wasn't sure. What she did know was that she didn't fancy being in this room when her mother came to check on him. Especially since Kaelem had now turned back into his human form. It just wasn't worth it, even though an adolescent voice told her it could be. "I'd better leave now," she said, and walked out of the bathroom, her heart beating wildly, fusing alarming emotions she had never experienced before.

No matter what she felt for Kaelem. Fear? Love? His uniqueness could get her into serious trouble if she didn't watch herself, and not just because of her mother's infatuation with his possible abilities.

***

The Queen unlocked the door and stepped into the room. She froze for a millisecond, drawn back by what she saw, but she was soon to reanimate herself, she could not show she was frightened or weak, that was one danger she preferred not to encounter.

What she found was the boy, now turned back into a human, wearing new, dry clothes that seemed to have appeared from nowhere. She certainly hadn't left them in that room. Obviously the boy had got his strength revived enough to change back.

She strode up to him, staring him in the eye so he looked away with uneasiness.

"Kaelem," she began softly, wanting him to gain her trust - the purposes behind this were by far greater than she had first thought. "I am sorry for that little adventure in the cold. I designed that to give you an idea what my people's essence is, to ease your mind into the full understanding of all that surrounds you here, and what you are; however there is no time to explain everything right at this minute. Though you no doubt just want answers to the many questions clouding your mind, your reason for being sent to us is of far greater importance. I'm certain you will think so too, because it involves someone I'm sure you want to meet: your mother."

"My mum? Is she here?" Kaelem was astounded, beyond amazed. For a second he did not care what creature he had become or who these people were: was he finally going to meet his mum? But Bethamy's tone told him this was not going to be so easy.

"That is why you are here. Do you remember anything about your father?" Kaelem looked down, and shook his head. "What about a vial of multicoloured light?" Kaelem shook his head again. The Queen nodded and walked out of the room, signalling for one of her guards to stay with Kaelem. "Just in case," she warned.

With the rest of her group she moved to the throne room. When the door was safely locked she began asking the questions, "How did he obtain what is only stored inside the Healers' vial?" she shouted.

"Calm down my Queen, we do not know. Shouting isn't going to bring the answers you desire. We checked the vial, it has not been tampered with, nor had the lock been forced. The glass hasn't been smashed or replaced either. We have no idea how Kaelem came into possession of that ability."

"Jadon. What is the power that Aka possesses?" their queen asked.

Her followers looked at one another, then the main speaker replied, "We do not know."

"We need to find Lily-Anna, to see if she is safe. With any luck Aka's love for her has prevented him from killing his wife, and hopefully Lily-Anna's love for her people is preventing her plotting against me. Still, Kaelem's training must start soon. He needs to be on our side, we can't afford for him to go against us. We need to adapt him to our advantage."

"Yes, of course. I will get him as comfortable as possible," another speaker answered.

"Good. I would like anyone who has to see Kaelem to go supervised: I do not want any casualties, or for him to feel threatened. I am especially worried in case he unlocks the Keahi side to his powers. If, of course, he has any. Perhaps we will be lucky enough to find that only Lily-Anna's gene dominated. But just in case, he is not to have any knowledge that he has Keahi blood in him. Is that understood?"

"Yes, of course."

"You may now go, I will train him personally. Only Saxton and myself may approach him without my prior consent."

"I will summon Saxton to see you now," a messenger replied.

"Good." Their Queen dismissed them, and her servants bowed their way out of the room.

CHAPTER NINE

Three months had passed since extreme white had first hit Kaelem's eyes. In a blink the Haukea had destroyed his life. He longed for ignorance to drown him, that same obliviousness he had come with, but it wouldn't enter his lungs. Whispers and frightened glances suffocated him instead. Talk of a powerful being, something that had immunity against both the powers of heat and freezing cold; A creature who could heal others, a trait only the dreaded Keahi King could perform. Yet underneath this fear hope brewed in the Haukea, an anticipation of a battle, with Kaelem fighting for them. A relief that the one captured by Aka would soon become freed. Kaelem covered his ears from the speech, refusing to believe it was about him; however, there was one thing he felt excitement about, and that was getting the opportunity to see his mother. He had been told that he would soon be able to sense her in his dreams, that his unconscious mind would allow him to communicate with her and lead him toward the knowledge of where she was. But so far nothing had happened, and all his nightmares brought were images of not being able to escape the Haukea's land for the rest of his life. He would wake up in a sweat of anxiety and apprehension that it would come true, and why not? How could he escape from somewhere if he didn't know how he came to be there? Was he even on Earth? Kaelem would then put his face onto his bed of ice and contemplate the incomprehensible.

The room in which the Haukea had locked Kaelem in was big, and constantly watched. It contained a bed, a chair, desk, wardrobe, and a toilet behind a dividing sheet of frosted ice. All was made of this same sparking material. He had to share the shower with the maids and butlers, and guards accompanied him wherever he went. The only place he felt freedom was by himself, bolted in his room. But there was one perk for this compromise: he was fed the best seafood he had ever tasted in his life. Or perhaps his taste-buds had changed.

Kaelem sensed the nervousness that was constantly emitting from the Haukea like a bad taste. He was growing tired of it, wishing for company that wasn't afraid of him, that wasn't making him scared of himself. He knew that there was another side to him, one that they hadn't told him, and were unwilling to. This made him as anxious as them, but at the same time, if he was honest with himself, he preferred to stay unaware of the secrets. The situation was becoming too bizarre, too unreal, too distant. He needed something to hold onto. With a desperation that hurt Kaelem to think about, he craved to see his sister. More than anything he wanted to speak to Aolani. He began to wonder what she thought of him leaving, what his stepfather had told her whilst questioning himself as to why his son had run away - or worse. Kaelem found himself hoping for a visit from Bethamy. She was kind. She treated him like a person. But he hadn't seen her since they had spoken that day in the bathroom.

Kaelem had long forgiven her for not helping him to escape. It was too dangerous, for both him and for her: she was the daughter of a Queen that coveted him.

A knock at the door startled Kaelem back to reality. Or what he thought was reality. He wondered how this abstract world could be true. The visitors didn't wait for an answer before they came in. Two servants grabbed his arms, saying he was to attend the Princess's coronation. They blindfolded Kaelem so that he couldn't find his way out again.

A memory got jogged in his mind. It seemed like years ago when he had first changed into a merman, and Bethamy had come into the bathroom. They had told her to get ready for her coronation. How could she have taken this long to get ready?

One day he was to know the truth, the horrible truth behind the Queen's past and why her age looked so close to her daughter's. What she was keeping from him would be revealed, ending a long and hard journey that had brought him loss, hate, and despair.

***

She was sitting on her throne, looking even more attractive than he first remembered her. Bethamy's hair was wound up into a bun, some strands had come loose and were corkscrewing delicately down her long, elegant neck. On top of her hair she wore a tiara. Opals dangled from it and encrusted turquoise jewels sparkled. She wore a long ice-blue dress that flowed to the floor. Thin straps, patterned with cyan beads, kept the attire from falling down.

Her lips were bluer than usual, a startling blue which you couldn't help noticing. It made her face even paler, highlighting her topaz eyes. They didn't shine.

Bethamy looked as if she had been crying, though she wasn't allowed to cry. It was as if emotion had been forbidden by her mother. Kaelem wanted to comfort her, to tell her that things were okay, but Bethamy looked unreal, like a doll, ready to come to life, eerily creepy without a reasonable explanation. She blinked slowly and her focus changed onto something else, indicating she was alive. A live doll. Except that soon her mother, the puppeteer, would be gone. Her strings would be cut. So were they tears of sadness, or tears of happiness?

The Queen stood. "You all know what happens now. I believe that Bethamy is at last capable of ruling our kingdom. She will lead us into war, and we will defeat the enemy. I will be with you, I will be a part of all of your souls." She looked at the sorcerers. "Once the Keahi have been destroyed we will have the freedom to take over the humans, to rule them, show them what life really is. We will be able to do what we like!"

The room erupted with roars of agreement.

The Queen focused on her daughter for a second. Bethamy stood up in response. With a jolt Kaelem realised that she was carrying a double-edged knife in her hand, and was approaching her mother with it. Bethamy gazed at her mum and her eyes softened for a second. A fragment of light passed between their pupils, an understanding full of love. Then the feeling got swept away, and as she raised the knife they went back to being dull and flat. Bethamy brought the knife down heavily into her mum's heart. Kaelem looked away, jumping at the shock of what she was doing, but the guard forced his head back, making him watch, not even allowing him to blink. A light came from the Queen and passed onto her daughter's hand, then seemed to get sucked inside the athame.

As Bethamy held up the knife her hair changed: the blue highlights faded and it became white all over. Her mother's body collapsed limply to the ground, waiting to be cleared away from the icy hall. "Her soul is free. She is resting peacefully!" Bethamy then took a vial of multicoloured light. She drew some of it up into a needle, and injected it into herself, showing no pain or fear. She then continued to speak, "My young soul is bound to your lives, it is yours until my daughter or my son grows up to become responsible and wise. Believe in me, believe that I will make the difference. I will be here to lead us into battle to take over the Earth. The souls we already possess are nearly ready to

be released from their prisons, they have understood our cause…
with a bit of help of course." She muttered the last part.

"With your help we can take over, we will make the difference.
Help me!"

They cried out again, raging with happiness.

Kaelem couldn't believe it, what had they turned her into? And
who were these Keahi? Did they hold the only power that could
stop the Haukea? What if they lost - what would happen to his
race? He was consumed with the thought that the only way to
save humanity was to stop the Haukea. He felt heat rise up inside,
boiling his blood. It overflowed and fire spurted from his hands.
People screamed bloodcurdling screams of pain as those nearest
to him caught fire. He loved the heat, but the Haukea couldn't
stand it. Some ran; some fell down, breathing hard, confused and
anxious.

The floor melted below his feet, as did the walls around him.
It was his chance of escape, the power he felt over them was
indescribable. He could stop their war, help whoever these Keahi
were.

But the fire wouldn't stop coming.

He tried to calm himself, yet still flames came, never wavering, out
of his hands. He couldn't stand the crying: the pain. Nonetheless
he knew it was somehow necessary for his own survival.

Through the panic and confusion he heard Bethamy's sweet,
sweet voice. It turned him icy, and the fire inside of him was
extinguished when the thought he had hurt her passed into his
twisted head. "Kaelem. It's all right, you'll see," she said gently.
"Come with me, I'll show you." She held out her hand. As he
grabbed it she drew in a sharp breath. It was still hot. She looked
at her hand: it was burnt.

"I'm sorry."

Bethamy contemplated the fact that he was saying sorry now. He was the one who had the power over them. She looked all around, at her melting palace the sorcerers were re-freezing, at the fires they were gradually dousing; this was the reason why Kaelem could not know about the Keahi side of him. He took Bethamy's hand again against her will. Thankfully it had cooled. His eyes reassured her as the pain eased itself and bright light engulfed her hand. He took his away, and the burn, the pain, was gone. "Thank you," she said.

He smiled: she wasn't angry with him. All of a sudden someone jumped him from behind. It was a trick - she knew what his reaction would be to her wound. He hadn't been able to control the fire coming out, and now he couldn't get it back. He was helpless as he fell unconscious, feeling the same shivering feeling as he had at home when looking at the doorbell. He hadn't hated the feel of cold in so long it felt unnatural to him now, as he fell into the inevitable sleep.

***

Kaelem woke up from his slumber in a small, dark room. He felt around for something, anything, but there was nothing. Not even ice. The walls and floor were made of something else, he supposed it was made to be fire resistant.

He tried to conjure the flames from his hands, to at least create a light. But to no avail. He thought of that anger again. The hate that they wanted death to his race, but it still didn't come. He sat down and placed his head in his hands, upset and tired.

A voice came from the other side. A woman's voice: Bethamy's voice, "Are you okay now?" She sounded sincere, but it enraged Kaelem.

"You know you're not one of them now, don't you?" she continued.

Kaelem was confused. "One of what?" he asked her, whilst bitterly understanding.

"A Human. You're one of us, on our side. You will be my King, and we can rule the humans together. You could be invincible Kaelem. Wouldn't you prefer that over bowing down to their weaknesses?"

"I don't know what you're talking about. I *am* a human. You already rule the Haukea, why take over them as well?!"

"You said 'them.'" She didn't say any more. Kaelem heard footsteps getting quieter and quieter. She was gone, leaving him to contemplate on what he actually was. But he wasn't a Haukea either, he didn't know! Maybe the Keahi did. He wanted to meet them, find out who they were, but most desperately he wanted to discover why these people were determined to take over the human race.

He heard a noise, a creak like a hinge that had not been oiled for some time. Then he saw a streak of light gradually getting bigger from one of the sides in the room. He blinked at it and stepped forward. The door to the room had been opened by someone.

He peered round and saw a line of Haukea looking back at him. He stepped out of his hold. They didn't move. He backed away from them, away from his room, and still they did not move. He turned around and began walking away. He heard no footsteps. Was this supposed to test how loyal he was to them? Or his stamina? He ran.

Without looking behind him, he ran. It seemed like hours before he stopped, exhausted, tired and hungry. He saw the lake and remembered the weird fish that were beneath it. He was just so hungry.

Kaelem touched his hand on the ice, imagined the heat, wanting it so badly, wanting to eat, wanting anything, and slowly the ice began to melt. He smiled: perhaps he could control it, if he concentrated hard enough. If he needed it badly enough. The fish swam quickly, frightened. They looked at him again with their huge eyes, intelligent, knowing. They tried to communicate with him, but Kaelem couldn't understand what.

He put his hand beneath the freezing water to capture one. He was quick, faster than them, catching his prey. The fish wriggled in his hand, desperate for life, suffocating.

"I wouldn't eat that."

He sighed. He hated her, she was no longer beautiful, she was deathly. "What are you going to do to stop me?"

"Tell you that is not a fish you hold in your hand. These creatures are people. Look closely at them Kaelem. I am not lying to you."

"What do you mean?" he asked, gently putting it back, just in case.

"It is where we keep the humans. We transport the souls from their dying bodies, into the athames and then into the fish's bodies, to keep them active, give them something to do."

Kaelem looked down at the fish he had just saved. He had always thought they were staring at him. Perhaps they were asking for his help, or warning him? "Why do they decide to fight for you?"

Bethamy laughed at his question. "They see that we are fighting *for* them, that taking over is in fact aiding their survival."

"Why do you take them? Why do you even care?"

"It's such a beautiful planet, we hate watching it become more and more disfigured with each passing year, but we care too much for the species to simply destroy them. Times have changed, the Haukea have seen beyond the destruction my ancestors once perceived. We have seen the beauty the race can achieve - if shown the right direction. Therefore I want to work with them now.

Some humans from their world have been transported to Hau Houna and have been given lectures on the ways they have been going wrong, and answers to how they can save their own planet. When they go back they will be able to put into practice our plans on a global scale, that is why only those strong of mind, will and body are educated.

We can't do this ourselves for we can't stay there long before the warmth of the planet is too much to cope with - just stationing in the Antarctic is not a practical solution. Plus, it may appear to be a malevolent alien invasion to some." She snickered. "That is why we get the sorcerers to bring them here, because they can keep casting spells on themselves to keep them cold enough."

Kaelem refused to look at her.

"Would you eat a human?" Bethamy asked.

That shocked Kaelem, forced him to look her in the eye, disgusted and sick. "No! Of course not."

"So, you're on our side then?"

"No."

"Think carefully Kaelem," she said, "why wouldn't you kill them? If you do you fight against the Haukea, you have to fight for what you believe is right, and doing that requires killing us when we are in combat, in battle. Is this not the same as taking the life of one of these fish? Is it because they were once human? Like you used to be? Kaelem…"

"Like I am! And yes, because they were human, and because I believe they still are. I wouldn't kill any of them." He knelt down, putting his hands over his head to stop her words getting into it.

"Interesting," Bethamy replied. "But you know, they are Haukea now. People can be manipulated so easily, don't you think?" she added, with a sick note in her tone. "You would have eaten them if they were fish. What's the difference now you've found out the truth? Don't they both breathe, feel? What's the difference Kaelem? They both have souls, don't they? How could you eat a breathing thing Kaelem? You were about to, you know, you were going to eat a human. What if I hadn't stopped you Kaelem? You would have still enjoyed it. I think I'm right. In fact…," she lent nearer to whisper in his ear, her breath tickling his neck, "I know I'm right. Eat it Kaelem, taste for yourself how nice it feels, how good the succulent meat is in your mouth."

Like a puppet he put his hand back into the cold water. She was the puppeteer now, and she held his strings. Like her mother had held hers, she had become the one in control of him. Where was the girl from the bathroom?

He picked a fish out forcefully and crammed it down his throat.

"You've just had your first kill Kaelem. How does it feel?"

He looked up at her as she walked away from him, his eyes showing the green of his merman form.

It felt disgustingly good.

"By the way," she shouted back to him. "They are fish!" She walked away from the scene, muttering to herself with silent laughter, "People can be manipulated so easily."

CHAPTER TEN

Looking down at the fish Kaelem sighed: once again it was time for him to go to his training session.

He didn't want to leave the ice lake yet; it had soon become his favourite place. Even the Haukea had come to accept that when he was here it meant that he was not to be disturbed. They feared him and so obeyed.

Each time he came here Kaelem apologised to the fish for devouring their friend. He didn't know how much they understood, but he liked to believe that there was forgiveness under the ice. In return he confided in them his thoughts and fears, although this was more to try and make sense of his feelings than to keep the fish company. Overall he liked these creatures, perhaps even to the point of being a little envious of them. He would watch them beneath the surface and have confidence that they knew who they were, that they realised their purpose in life, and understood where they could and couldn't go, where they stood in the grand scale of things.

Kaelem on the other hand was lost, he had no idea of who he was anymore, nor whom he was supposed to attach himself to: the human race, or the Haukea's?

Unfortunately this was not his only decision, if indeed he had a say in the matter, for there was also another, stronger, connection;

one that put him below with the fish, one that came from his fantasies about breaking through the ice and swimming with them, as a component of them, while the Wai hau loko lake quickly froze over above him, allowing him to be refreshed in the idea that there were no options other than to remain underwater, where nothing more would be expected of him. He would identify then where he belonged.

But Kaelem had been prohibited from transforming into a merman. Contradicting his own thoughts were ones of relief, for he didn't mind this restraint once he reminded himself of the excruciating pain of converting. His spine went funny just thinking about it. The Haukea had also disallowed him to use his fire power, but this did not bother him either: not only did he not understand where the fire power was from, and discovering another thing that questioned his identity was not in his plans, he had no idea how he conjured it in the first place. Confining the power was like suppressing the confusion that came with it, one less thing to worry about, and one less senseless thing to figure out. To just think that it had nothing to do with him: absolute bliss.

And so there it stayed, incarcerated inside him, ready to explode and destroy the ice that had been contaminating the mind of its master.

But for now Kaelem had to live with the fact that five people had funerals following the day the fire had rebelled out of him, and he would too if it happened again. There were now many vengeful and fearful Haukea that would find great satisfaction in 'disposing' of Kaelem, yet at the same time this fear was what was keeping him alive at the moment. Even though the Haukea would be happy to destroy him, they were afraid of his power, of what he could do to them if they attacked him. His level of value to their Queen was also an unfortunate factor. How powerful was his potential if he did decide to unleash its full force? More importantly would he be able to control this power? The day he had set the throne room alight proved that at the moment he couldn't. He couldn't even dominate the times or situations in which the fire would escape him. This scared him. He became even more convinced that leaving the fire inactive as long as possible without it taking over was the best option. If he *had* any options concerning the Keahi side of him.

Analysing this frightening change in himself, Kaelem's thoughts sidetracked to reflecting on the life the Haukea had made him leave. They had told him the faster he learned to control his power, the sooner he could find his mother and go home. He had asked them why he couldn't sense her here, and they had replied that Aka, his father, was very powerful and may interfere with the dream, the connection. This was very dangerous as Aka would then be able to see that his son was with the enemy. Not only would he then doubt Kaelem's loyalty, making it harder for Kaelem to infiltrate the Keahi's world and gain knowledge of their weaknesses and strategies in the war, Aka's hate towards the Haukea and their plans could then lead to Aka morphing the connection between Kaelem and his mother into something sinister, making her distrust her own son. If indeed Aka did have Lily-Anna, these two factors would make it almost impossible to save her from the hot hands of her captor.

The Haukea tried to put into him as much hostility towards his father that they could muster. They didn't want Kaelem to be able to trust his father, the risk was too high, and the result too disastrous to comprehend.

Kaelem's thoughts wandered towards his family and friends. When he considered what he was going to say when he did return, panic overtook him. Kaelem realised he had no idea how his friends, his stepfather, and half-sister had reacted to his sudden disappearance. Now he was going to reappear back into their lives - would it be relief greeting him, or anger? Could he tell them what he had learned, explain that he had become a weapon to take them over? He didn't believe they would see it as helping their race to survive. Then there was Alma; beautiful, wonderful, exquisite Alma…

The Haukea were trying to indoctrinate him into their thinking He knew that. He also knew it was working, that last thought proved it; he felt himself becoming more violent towards things and more attached towards the Haukea and their plans than for his own race. He looked down. "No, they are no longer my race," Kaelem whispered sadly to himself.

He didn't belong. There was something inside him, something even greater than all the Haukea. What frightened him was that this 'something' was more than they had expected of him, even had knowledge of.

He was connected to three elements, having immunity towards both ice and fire, and having the ability to breathe under water, but despite having the power that his circle of friends had always fantasised about, all he really wanted now was to be stripped of his abilities. However, like it or not, there was now no denying he was the key to the humans' freedom, which was becoming dimmer with each training session. As he became stronger Kaelem also came to trust, to know, that the Haukea were right. He couldn't fight for humanity anymore, because he no longer believed that they deserved the Earth. He no longer perceived them as harmless beings.

The Haukea were giving him more and more reasons against their rule, and as a result Kaelem was questioning himself as to why Homo sapiens should dominate the globe.

The Haukea had promised a better world, some deaths would have to be made for the better good, but they, the humans, were polluting the Earth, felling forests, massacring and desecrating wild animals, making them tame, disturbing nature's balance.

Humans had to be taken over if they were to live, if the Earth was to be saved.

They weren't murderers. Though it was true that people were being collected, the soul would remain alive; it wasn't transported into the bodies of fish, the only thing that changed would be that the shell the soul had once inhabited would become empty, but when the time was right the two pieces would be reunited. So what was the big deal?

Kaelem had doubts at first, but now he was starting to understand.

Not thinking of the hypocrisy of it all he smiled as some of the fish braved going up to him. He put his hand onto the frozen surface and felt it melt. The fire inside of him was seeping out, even if he did not want it to. The rush of cold water on his arm made him happy. He closed his eyes, the sensation in his fingers heightening as the fish brushed past them, their scales smooth and cold. Some nibbled on Kaelem's fingers. It tickled. He drew his hand out and sadly stood up, saying goodbye to them for now, as he climbed onto Siren.

***

He scoffed. Kaelem couldn't believe he used to fancy her, it made him sick to think of how 'pretty' he used to think Bethamy was.

"Kaelem, are you ready?"

He nodded. He hated training, it always took so much out of him, but gradually he felt himself becoming fitter and more agile, able to control his strength. Even though his power from the Haukea side to him wasn't useful - it only made his feet become colder - he was making a lot of progress.

He was to fight Bailey today, a strong sorcerer and the guard which had held his head at Bethamy's coronation.

They were to battle outside, so he would have plenty of room to show off his talents. But he was still nervous, he had never fought him before, and as a result he knew of neither his weaknesses, nor what type of strengths he possessed.

They tried to make these duelling sessions as realistic as possible in preparation for the war against the Keahi. They had told Kaelem that the Keahi were going to fight for the humans' freedom, and for the Healers' vial - a vial which contained the power to heal. But he was fighting for more than that: if the Keahi did have his mum, he had to be strong enough to find and save her.

Kaelem breathed in as Bailey came into view. Not only did he have to defeat the giant, he had to extract his soul, in preparation for capturing human souls.

Bailey looked more like a giant than anything else, standing over seven-and-a-half feet tall, with huge muscles in his arms and legs. As Kaelem prepared to fight, he promised himself he would defeat this opponent, knowing that if he was victorious he would be able to return home confident enough to avenge his mother's kidnapping. His training would be complete. But Kaelem stood shivering in fear: Bailey was the strongest sorcerer they had.

Each took a step towards one another, in the distance someone yelled something, and before Kaelem knew it Bailey had run at him with such a force that it knocked Kaelem down. Spitting out snow he kicked Bailey, aiming for his calf, but it didn't even budge the bulky presence. He saw his chance of freedom drifting away. Slowly Kaelem began to get up, but as he did something punched him hard in the face. Kaelem went down on all fours, discharging blood out of his mouth onto the white snow. He was becoming frustrated now. As he regained his balance he flung himself at Bailey, his athame held before him, but he didn't even get near enough to prick Bailey's skin as he flew backwards again from a sweep of Bailey's large hand. The pain no longer bothered

Kaelem, he had grown from when he'd first arrived here, he had got used to these fighting sessions. Anger was controlling him instead. Kaelem staggered upright and glared at Bailey, analysing what Bailey's actions consisted of, recognising the giant used strength rather than agility. Kaelem managed to rush behind Bailey and leap onto his back. Putting his arm round Bailey's throat Kaelem began to chock him. He tried to punch the athame into his neck, but Bailey prevailed as he threw Kaelem off with an arm reap. He grabbed Kaelem's right hand, almost numbing it as he pressed his fingers into Kaelem's pressure points. He then proceeded to twist the arm, pressing the hand onto his own body. Unless he wanted to break his arm Kaelem had no other choice than to let the athame go. He wasn't that uncaring, yet. Bailey followed suit and released the hand. But once Kaelem was standing again Bailey threw one more strike to Kaelem's head, and he fell down onto the snow with such force he remembered nothing more of that day. There Kaelem stayed, unconscious, his blood staining the snow beneath him.

***

"Kaelem, you are nearly ready." A voice woke him. He opened his eyes. At first what he saw was blurry, then Bethamy's evil face appeared before him. He turned his head away, hating her.

"Kaelem, don't be stupid. I'm letting you go home."

He looked back up at her. "But-but, I lost," he replied.

She laughed at him. "Kaelem, you couldn't win against Bailey. It would take decades for you to become like that. He is not only strong, he is smart too"

"Then why did you make me fight him?"

"I did it to see how long you would last, to see how strong you were, and believe me, you lasted much longer than I would have hoped you could. You lasted longer than anyone ever has. You're powerful, Kaelem, you know that. Perhaps too powerful. Even so, your physical strength isn't up to Bailey's standard. I have one more challenge for you Kaelem, and I promise you can go home when you have succeeded. I think you are ready for it. Meet me in the weapons room, and we will see how talented you really are." Bethamy left him to get changed.

***

Kaelem opened the door slowly, cautious of what Bethamy wanted him to do; what Bethamy was going to torture him with next. When the door was fully opened he walked into the room, and towards the waiting Queen. She was facing him, a sword in her hand. "You will not always be so lucky to have an opponent whom uses their powers Kaelem. Especially since they know you are immune to them. Now, fight me." Her stance was wide, back leg bent, and sword held before her, the point aiming at Kaelem obscured from sight by her left hand. Without further warning Bethamy swung at him, moving her sword to the left, then behind her by moving her arm over her head, and finally in one swift motion bringing it round to the right to hit Kaelem. Agility and grace oozed from her every movement. She was obviously skilled in sword art. Kaelem ducked and ran from her.

"Stop walking away from me Kaelem, " Bethamy commented, mocking him as she brought the sword back behind her. "You are not going to win that way." She pushed off with her back foot and let her front foot slide gracefully forwards while her arms extended towards Kaelem, striking him on his back. He arched for a second, then composed himself, breathing through the pain as he had been taught. *It means nothing to me.*

"I told you Kaelem: the only way to get out of this is to face me."

He turned round as she went to attack him again. He blocked her from hitting his face by putting his arm up. A red gash appeared, dribbling blood. He touched her face with his hand and she backed away sharply, a burn throbbing her skin. She smiled. "That's better. But your technique is awful." She raised her sword, circling it above her head, then brought it back behind her. She proceeded to bring the sword over her head, and down vertically. But instead of cowering at the inevitable impact, Kaelem went towards it. The sword came down, fast and firm, but before it could do damage Kaelem blocked Bethamy's arm with his forearm, circled it, then grabbed her wrist and didn't let go. He could see her face contort in agony, but she said nothing. He twisted her wrist into a lock position and she weakly dropped her sword. Kaelem picked it up, and in his emotion brought it to her neck. Bethamy smiled again. "I am not the only one on the field Kaelem. Remember that."

Kaelem ducked round as three Haukea leapt at him. "What do I do?" he asked in desperation.

"What I have been training you to do Kaelem. This is your last test."

Kaelem kicked out at one of them, but another held his arms. He made a small noise in his throat of defeat, although heat started to bubble though his skin. The grip on his arms loosened, allowing him to twist away. A flame burst through his hand for a second, and a silence swept through the room. But these people had been trained to keep going no matter what happened, and as they came at him again Kaelem forgot what the fire could do, and he jumped. Stretching his legs in the air he kicked at the chests of both his opponents. One of them went down, while the other staggered backwards. Using this loss of balance Kaelem hit him in the chest with the back of his hand, remembering to keep his hand limp. His attacker fell down. Behind Kaelem another Haukea grabbed his neck. Kaelem fell to his knees, trying to keep his chin under her arm. Bethamy's sword glinted in his eyes, and with a loss of breath he reached out for it, gradually pulling it towards him with his fingertips until he was able to get a firm grip. He managed to jab it behind him into the girl's side. At the split moment she lost her hold, Kaelem escaped and got quickly to his feet. He swung round, ripping her shirt, creating another wound on her previously flawless skin. Being untrained in sword fighting and unable to control his strikes Kaelem continued to swing the sword, and himself, randomly around. Through luck blood flew across the room from the face of the last Haukea standing. Kaelem stood for a second and dropped the sword. Then, whilst the Haukea was still in shock, Kaelem punched him in the solar plexus. He went down, winded. But in his triumph Kaelem had brought his guard down and something struck him on the back of his head. Once again he crashed down onto the floor, a resounding 'crack' reverberating through him.

***

"Remember Kaelem: you are not the only person in the battle," A distant voice. Kaelem looked up to see Bethamy. He was still in the weapons room. "I want to go home, normal," he said weakly, terrified.

"And you can now. We will do some more work on this nearer the time of the main battle. But I think you need a rest."

"Can't you take this power away from me first?"

"What?"

"I don't want this power when I go. I don't want things to be different."

"Kaelem, you are strange. What was the point of training you these last two years if we're just going to take your abilities back? You can control your power now, your strength. You don't need to be scared of it. After all, it is yours, it has always been there. The only difference is that now it has been awakened."

71

Kaelem didn't believe her, she was contradicting herself because she was scared of him, everyone here was, no-one understood him or tried to know him. They all saw him as nothing but a weapon. But he no longer cared; all that mattered was that he was finally going home.

That night they made their plans; he was to go in a fortnight. The Haukea had arranged a leaving ceremony, though he sensed relief emitting from everyone, not sadness. He sighed; soon he would be back with the people who loved him and wanted him.

"Could everyone please adjourn to the throne room please," Opal stated. There was chatter as people made their way there. A hand took hold of Kaelem, he swung round, Opal was standing before him. "It's for you Kaelem," she said.

"What do you mean?"

"You'll see," she replied, smiling.

She escorted him up to the throne, where Bethamy was sitting. Her hair was flowing down her back; her blue dress seemed to be sparkling more than ever. "It is Kaelem's last few days with us," she began. "He will aid us to complete our plan, he has been trained to help us collect souls and to fight in battle against the Keahi. He is immune against their fire power; he has become a strong fighter, our future is looking better than ever!"

Cheering erupted from the room.

"We will present him with his own athame to collect the souls." Bethamy produced the knife, it was new and beautiful. Three blue gems were incrusted into its handle, each of a different hue. The unworn blade shone and tempted Kaelem to touch it. He was mesmerised. As he took it he noticed that strange letters were engraved into its handle. He felt them with his finger, curious by how they disturbed the craftwork of the handle.

"The markings tell you it's yours. They represent your name," Bethamy explained, watching him.

"Thank you," Kaelem said to the crowd, and held it up for everyone to admire. "I will not let you down!"

Screaming and applause echoed round the room.

There was knocking at the door. Lily-Anna went to answer it, but her husband pulled her back. When she turned to face him he whispered for her to go into the kitchen with him.

"What's the matter?"

"Have you got the vial?"

Thoughts that had occurred frequently since Aka had first asked to borrow the vial ran wild through her: What purpose could he possibly have for it? She had told him he would find no use for what it held . Unless he knew how to destroy it; to stop successive Haukea monarchies from using its power.

"Yes, it's in the bathroom," she answered quietly, then ascended the stairs to get it. If there was any chance of demolishing the Haukea's dictatorship it was through stopping the royalty from having the power to regenerate, and the only way that could happen was through the eradication of the vial. The only trouble was no-one but the Angel knew this secret, and stealing the vial was a futile mission, for the Haukea had long ago got possession of the vial over the Keahi and had cast a spell on it so that they could detect whoever had hold of it. Additionally they had put a layer on the vial so bitterly cold that only the Haukea would be able to stand its touch. But Lily-Anna had a contact, an unlikely one that had been able to override these spells, a Haukea that would potentially be able to stop the totalitarian regime over the Haukea race, and save the human race. But they needed this safety net, in case she was brainwashed. Or worse. Lily-Anna felt numb at this prospect and erased the thought from her mind for now.

When she came back down she saw Aka holding their two-year-old son, and a needle. Aka recoiled slightly from her, shivering. "Could you please give me some of its contents?" Aka said handing Lily-Anna the needle.

"What are you talking about? What are you going to do?"

"You will see." He looked kindly and surely into her eyes, and she complied to his request; Aka was an amazing father who would rather face torture than expose his family to harm. He loved them dearly.

"It is beautiful, is it not?" Aka commented, looking at the vial's contents.

"Yes."

Inside the vial was a swirl of flittering multicoloured lights. Aka took the needle that now held some of the phenomena and injected part of it into Kaelem.

"What are you doing?" Lily-Anna screamed. "Only descendants of royal blood can handle what is in that vial, you'll make him mad! You'll kill him!"

The child squirmed as the light was pushed into him. Then it seemed to seep out of Kaelem's skin as he was engulfed with a multitude of colours. It sucked itself back inside the boy and he lay there, unharmed. Aka injected the rest of the lights into himself, whilst Lily-Anna stood there, helpless and crying. "Why are you doing this? Why are you leaving me?"

"I am not. It is not going to make me mad Flower. Or him. Trust me. Watch."

Aka handed Kaelem to Lily-Anna and she supported her son tightly in her arms. Her husband then took out an athame from a drawer. Lily-Anna looked at it in horror. "I thought you got rid of that."

"I kept it. So that we would be protected."

"It is bathed in the blood of the lost! How is an instrument like that supposed to protect us?"

Aka's response was to close his hand around the knife until he felt a sharp pain. He closed his eyes as blood oozed out of the wound and trickled between his fingers.

He took Kaelem's arm and grazed his boy's hand. Kaelem squirmed and began to cry. Lily-Anna gasped with terror and rage and held him close to her, instinctively protecting her son. But Aka still held onto his arm. "Please, Lily-Flower. This is important. It is something positive, I promise."

He closed his bloodied hand around Kaelem's. A tiny bright light emitted from their wounds. A bond soldered between them as Aka healed Kaelem and Kaelem healed Aka. The child stopped crying as the father uncurled his hand from his son's. Aka went to the sink and washed the blood from his hand. When he dried it nothing remained to show what he had just done.

Lily-Anna stared at his hand, then back up to him. "Who are you? Why are those people knocking on my door? Why don't you want me to answer them?"

He kissed her on the forehead and sighed. "I should have told you."

"What? Told me what?"

He took her hand. "About me. About...Kaelem."

"Kaelem? What do you mean? Tell me!"

"I will show you. You might understand better."

She looked towards the source of the knocking.

"Leave them Flower. You will know who they are soon enough."

Aka gently lead her upstairs, locked the door to the bathroom, and ran the bath. Once he had turned off the faucets he kissed his son on the forehead and submerged him beneath the water.

"What are you doing?" Lily-Anna screamed as she watched Aka hold Kaelem's head under.

"Watch," he whispered as she tried to grab Kaelem. "This is why I always bathed him."

As Lily-Anna saw Kaelem's appearance change, tears formed in her eyes.

"I...I don't understand. Tell me now. Who are you?"

"You know what I am, how Kaelem can be like this. The genes mixed. My royal blood enables him to keep sane with the contents of the Healers' Vial in him."

Aka held out his hand, took off the long gloves he always wore due to his sensitive skin, and released a ball of fire out from his palm. Its light highlighted the tattoo on his wrist. Lily-Anna stood her ground, knowing he wouldn't hurt her, not physically anyway. He adored her. Or was that a lie too? To get a son, the next in line to become Prince, a strong prince; half Keahi, half Haukea. Was all this just a sick plan? But the doubt disappeared when she saw the look in his eyes. They told her it was love. "They're Haukea, aren't they? They found out that you're a Keahi, and they've come to get you. Why did you leave it so long to tell me?'

"I am sorry. I tried, but I did not want to lose you."

"Do you love me? Or was it just to get someone to rule after you. Someone powerful, a hybrid?"

"I did not do it for the Keahi." There was a hint of anger in his voice. "You know that it was personal. I am devoted to you. I could not bear to lose you. When you told me who you were...I was going to state my origins, but I thought you would break off the engagement and we would never see each other again. I could not take that. I am ashamed that I was so selfish, so weak. The Keahi do not deserve a king like me."

"And you thought this was better?" Her eyes shone with tears, confusion and anger.

Aka looked away. "Please Lily-Flower. Please don't give me away. Bind Kaelem's powers if you wish. Bind them so that I cannot sense him. So I can not find him."

As Lily-Anna stood there she realised that the persistent knocking at the door had now ceased: they had broken it down. She heard footsteps coming up the stairs. Concerned voices were calling her name, anxious to get to Aka.

Her shoulders dropped into a relaxed posture. "I'm sorry Aka. I can't let you find Kaelem. It's too dangerous, I can't let him become prince of my opposed world. There are many innocent people there who have no choice but to go through with what our Queen demands. These are my family, my blood Aka. I am binding Kaelem's powers."

Aka nodded in agreement. "And what about me?" he asked.

The doorknob to the bathroom was turning - Would they break this door down too?

"Go back, Aka, to the Keahi. You can use your magic in front of me, I won't be scared." They shared a brief look of longing, of pain and of heartbreak before Aka saturated himself in flames and transported himself to his own world. Lily-Anna gasped as she felt

something brush against her right arm. She looked down to see a burn appearing. It reassured her, that he still loved her. A mark would remain there, reminding her for as long as she was present in this body, and then penetrate into her eternal soul Yes, he was Keahi, and she felt sick at the thought he had betrayed her, but this didn't change what her soul felt for him. He had changed her mind about the humans. Since they had created Kaelem she had no longer wanted the Haukea to rule, to take more lives and turn them into slaves. She had looked into her son's bright, intelligent eyes on his first day on Earth, and the thought of what would happen to him under the Haukea's government gave her fear for the first time of what the regime meant for Homo sapiens. She finally understood how all those who had gone against the Haukea felt. There was no freedom in the plans; the human souls were going to rot in bodies that had become drones to society. Maybe the Keahi were right to oppose them. Or was that just Aka brainwashing her mind?

Looking down at Kaelem, she whispered a binding spell to him. His powers drained out of him and floated in the air. As she watched them she felt ashamed yet determined that Aka would not know the reason she had taken her son's powers was because she was certain that, apart from being physically bound on Hau Houna, this boy, his son, was the only thing that could destroy her husband. She took her choker off, the one that Aka had given to her on their wedding day, and pressed the pendant to the special lock in the cabinet that Aka had made to keep her potions safe. When it opened she took an empty vial, pulled out the stopper and watched as Kaelem's powers went into it, then she put the stopper back in and locked the vial in the cabinet.

The Haukea were watching her.

"I bound his powers so that Aka can't find him. I couldn't stop Aka. I tried, but…" A sharp pain crossed her shoulder. "Look," she showed the burn to them, "I couldn't stop him," she repeated.

It was the perfect alibi, so they wouldn't know the truth about her love.

"You do know what this means don't you? Kaelem is a Keahi. We cannot risk one of them mingling with us. It is for the protection of our identity that he will have to stay here, on Earth."

"I know, and I'm staying with him."

"Are you sure? It's a big step."

"Yes. I want to stay with my son. Aka has given me some appreciation for the human race. I believe that this will be beneficial to us for I can observe them here closely and examine how best our plans will work for them."

"Don't worry, we'll punish Aka for doing this to you." Lily-Anna noted that they made it sound like what had happened to her had been a negative thing. Then…it was supposed to be, so how come she was glad? Glad she'd had a son with Aka.

In a blizzard of snow they left her. She was now on her own, with only Kaelem in her arms. He had started crying again. Her thoughts wandered to the repercussions of what had just played out. Not just for her and Aka, but also for both their worlds: the Keahi's King had finally revealed himself.

CHAPTER ELEVEN

Kaelem breathed in the fresh night air and savoured the familiar taste of home.

The night air surrounded Kaelem as he made his journey through the coastal town, smiling happily to himself with content and relief. Even though the cold wrapped itself around him like a blanket, he felt like he could combust with the warmth he felt at finally being here.

Out of habit Kaelem's gaze shifted to look up at the moon. It was full. Memories came to his mind of his little sister. He laughed gently to himself as he remembered the games they used to play. Once a month, when the moon was at its fullest, they would walk together along the pier, right up to the edge, to watch the sea. They would play tricks on each other, scaring themselves with strange stories about monsters and werewolves, pretending they were behind them, ready to jump out at any moment to catch their dinner. His sister thought it was so real that she would clutch him when she got scared, whilst at the same time giggled with joy and fear. When she got too tired to speak he would tell her about the unicorns, her favourite legend, then carry her back home at one in the morning. He loved his sister. He had missed her so much in the two years he'd been apart from her, and his friends.

He wondered what their father had told her, what he thought had happened to him when he had disappeared, without a word, when the doorbell had rung.

He moved his eyes to spot the pier, not expecting to see anything, but he did. A figure was sitting on the pier's edge looking up at the moon. Did she still come here alone? Maybe waiting for his return? He didn't want to see her yet, he didn't know what she would say, if she would be angry that he had not even sent a note. What would his alibi be? He walked towards home, towards his stepfather instead, perhaps he would think of an explanation.

***

Tears pricked Kaelem's eyes when he spotted the doorbell, his last memory of this place before he was taken from everything he had ever known. Instead of checking if it still worked he reached for the handle. He saw his hand was trembling with conflicting emotions of anticipation and anxiety.

The door had opened without his knowledge, and he found he was looking up at his stepfather. Kaelem began feeling dizzy, he needed to sit down or get out. He felt scared; the atmosphere had changed. He sensed his stepfather knew a lot more than what he had told Kaelem about his mother, and his biological father. "Sit down," he said, walking towards the lounge. "And shut the door after you."

Kaelem did as he was told. It felt good to be back in his house, though it didn't seem as bright and lively as when he had left it. He thankfully took a seat on the sofa as his father handed him a drink of hot chocolate. Kaelem secretly preferred to have salty water, but he wanted everything to remain, as much as possible, the same as when he had left.

"Have you spoken to Ali yet?"

Kaelem shook his head. "I saw her, on the pier. I guess she goes there by herself now."

"Yes." There was an awkward silence. Kaelem took a gulp of the chocolate, not knowing what to say or where he should start. "I know where you went. I wish I could have stopped the Haukea, but if I had tried, they would probably have killed me."

Kaelem looked at him quizzically, how did he know who they were? Did his stepfather know his son had Haukea blood in him?

"How…"

"I know because of your mother. I guess you also now know about her lineage, her power. I loved her very much, of course I wanted to marry her, but she was already married to a love that had gone 'sour'. I didn't probe her about it; I could see she wasn't ready for a divorce. I came to accept I would always come last in her heart. But one day I guess she realised I meant more to her than just protection and comfort. She said she had a confession to make - the Haukea law to tell the truth of their heritage was created as a way of deceit, in the hope of unbinding love. But, of course, I adored her too much to leave her. Of course I didn't like it at first, I was scared of her even, but when I was apart from her I couldn't stop thinking about her. I couldn't stand being away from Lily-Anna. I returned to her. A few months later she told me that she was pregnant. We had taken precautions, but obviously they had failed, but Aolani brought Lily-Anna even closer to me and there was not one day of regret. There was worry, of course, but it was in vain: it is impossible for Ali to carry any genes relating to her mother's power, due to the fact that human genes dominate over Haukea.

"Lily-Anna also explained to me about the Keahi, Aka, and, of course, what it all meant for the child from her previous marriage. She knew that one day Aka would find his wife and son, she warned me what I must do when this happened, that I was to take you two and move to a location which she did not know about, and leave her with Aka. He can access memories you might not remember from childhood, those engraved deep in the subconscious, therefore we had to eradicate them. I was to give our children a potion that would wipe their minds of their mother's identity, so that if Aka got into your head it would seem you were not the children separated from Lily-Anna. That is why there are no photographs of your mother. I had to protect you and your sister, if someone had recognised her, I don't know what would have happened. She said she would be safe with him." His voice became choked as he carried on, remembering his wife, "so when Aka visited our abode we ran our separate ways. I moved us here. I haven't seen or heard from Lily-Anna since. I don't even know if she's…" A look of horror covered his eyes, they pleaded to Kaelem.

"I did not see my mother." The Haukea had told him that Lily-Anna had stayed with them until she thought it safe enough to go back to find Dillon again. It was on her return trip to Earth that she had gone missing. Kaelem decided against informing his stepfather of this. It would worry him that she had gone back home, to a place that may have once again convinced her into taking souls.

"Why didn't you tell me about this?" asked Kaelem.

Dillon paused to compose himself before answering, "Afraid of you not believing me, or worse, that you did believe me and demand to see Aka."

There was another silence.

"Go see your sister, Kaelem. She's been waiting for you to return for two years." He smiled slightly.

"Where did you tell her I went?"

"To see your biological dad and mum."

"Was she angry? That I didn't take her to see her mum?"

"A bit, but more angry that you went without telling her.

"Kaelem, she has to know who you are, and it has to be you who tells her."

Kaelem nodded. "I've never kept anything from her, and I'm not going to start now." There was a slight glare towards Dillon before Kaelem drank the last bit of his hot chocolate and left to see his sister, going over and over in his mind what he was going to say.

As he climbed the steps up towards the pier he still did not know, and before he knew it he was at the pier's edge, sitting down next to his little sister. She'd grown a lot since he had been gone. She would be nine years old now. His heart jumped - he'd missed two of her birthdays. He supposed, to her, he had changed as well, though how dramatically was still to be deciphered.

Her blonde hair was still long, running loosely down her back. Her soft face was solemn. He felt nothing but love and sorrow for her.

Kaelem sighed heavily, hoping she would notice him before he had to say anything, unsure how else to break the silence. But she didn't move, she kept in the same position, as if she were playing his shadow. But there was no more time for games. Did she know? Was she doing this on purpose? But there was no change in her face, no glimpse of happiness or recognition.

"I'm sorry," he finally said, intentionally or not. Softly spoken she replied, choked, still looking up at the stars and planets, "Why did you leave me?"

"I'm sorry," Kaelem repeated stupidly.

"Did you see her?"

"No."

She nodded then collapsed heavily into his arms, as her sadness flowed out of her.

Kaelem didn't know how long they sat like that, but he knew if he didn't tell her what he was soon, he would loose his courage to.

"Ali, I have to tell you something."

She looked at him with curiosity. In the quiet that followed, Kaelem tried once more to devise a way to show her how he had changed without startling her. She would probably believe him; she used to be open-minded, but was she still?

He finally made the decision to show her instead, and so, not looking at her reaction, not wanting to know what she thought of him, he morphed. The ice power would come later, one step at a time. Taking off his trousers, remembering what had happened last time, he felt his body changing. Having not done this in such a long time the pain came at him with full force. But he didn't want to scare his sister, and so Kaelem kept his screams to himself; however he still couldn't help but keel over when the gills came, and falling with the coming of the scales on his legs that would turn into a tail. At last the transformation was complete, and he looked up at Aolani. Her eyes had turned glossy and were sparkling.

"I don't know you anymore, do I?" she asked, "How much have I missed in these last two years Kaelem?"

"Ali, I..." Unable to breathe Kaelem couldn't utter any more. He transformed back into his human form, once again looking away from her.

"You're not coming home, you're never coming home, because you're not Kaelem anymore. You're not my brother." The last phrase was said with such frustration that Kaelem felt as if he had been punched in the stomach. For a second he was paralysed, before realising it was his sister who was hurting the most, because of him, and this was her retaliation. Kaelem went to comfort her, like they used to when they were children if she got scared of the monsters. But she wasn't a child anymore, and he was the monster. Aolani pushed him away in anger and despair. Startled, he stumbled over the piers edge and into the cold sea of the night. The moons reflection quivered. For a moment Kaelem forgot everything; he was comforted by the water surrounding him, erasing all the bad memories. Until he realised he couldn't breathe. Wondering why he was not in his merman form he remembered his sister. He swam up to the surface and gasped cold air into his lungs. When Kaelem looked up to where his sister had been he witnessed a lonely shadow moving mournfully beneath the lights. Gradually, slowly, getting further and further away from his presence.

CHAPTER TWELVE

Kaelem swam out of the security of the water and trailed his way home. The seaside town hadn't changed that much since he'd left. In fact it hadn't changed that much in half a century. The tourists preferred it that way - to stay the same. They liked the old ice cream and sweet shops, the traditional pubs that littered the sea front as if frozen in time.

It was the high season at the moment, so it must have been late because not many people were around. It was normally less desolate than this, with students enjoying the night out with their friends, savouring the long summer break from school or college. Sometimes couples could be seen, walking hand in hand, bare-footed across the sand, listening to the sea beneath the night sky.

Kaelem's home was only a twenty-minute walk from the shore, but he wanted to remember, to feel, how he used to live, and bask in what was familiar to him. He loved the sensation of sturdy gravel beneath his feet which had replaced clumsy snow.

His house was only unique from the others down Dunmow Hill in the sense that he lived there. Instinctively he strolled up to his cracked, weather-beaten yellow door and tried to open it. It was locked. He let out a small scream of anger and hit it. After a few moments the light in the hallway came on and the door was opened. His stepfather dominated the doorway.

"Hi," Kaelem said in monotone.

"Your sister's very upset."

Kaelem bent his head down. "I know. I'm sorry."

"Don't apologise to me!" Dillon replied.

"Do you think she will be okay?"

"She's strong. But you're supposed to be the one she looks up to. She thinks that her guide, her friend, has gone."

"Will she see me, can I make it up to her?" Kaelem asked.

"I think it'll be better if you wait 'til morning. Of course it will ultimately be up to Ali whether she wants you to be her idol again." Kaelem nodded in sad agreement and began to walk away. "Come in," his stepfather said suddenly. Gratefully, Kaelem followed his instructions. "You still live here you funny thing."

Kaelem laughed and ran inside. At least he was still welcome here.

After another hot chocolate, drunk in silence, Kaelem went up to his room. He climbed the stairs, expecting things to have changed, but when he opened the door, the first on the right, it was the same as when he had left. The only thing out of place were the dirty clothes that used to splay themselves over his floor, these were now lying in eerie neatness in his drawers. Kaelem smiled to himself, happy that they hadn't touched anything else. Yet something was still missing. His stuffed toy that was kept on his bed, it was gone. He looked around his room, but to no avail. He breathed out in annoyance, but was too tired to go back downstairs and question his stepfather, and knew better than to disturb his sister from her sleep, especially with what had happened that night.

***

Aka was dreaming of a slither of continuous power, hanging in mid-air like a rope made of a billion tiny lights. The lights coursed in one direction. Aka knew that they flowed away from their owner, to which they were eventually joined, and that every time their owner moved the lights would come out of him, like a never-ending supply of handkerchiefs appearing from a conjuror's sleeve. Aka ran in the opposite direction to the current concentrating on his son, because if for one second his mind wandered from his quarry the path would be lost. He had no time yet to think of the repercussions this dream meant, only that it had finally come after twelve years of waiting and focusing.

***

Kaelem dreamt.

He was standing, surrounded by white, nothing else, just endless white. He looked down and saw he was floating in the blank space. He looked ahead and jumped: there was a person coming towards him. Kaelem backed away in fear when he realised whom it was: the woman from his dream. He had been only twelve years old when the nightmare had come - so horrible that it had invaded his memory, feeling like it would never leave his mind. He vividly remembered what she had become.

"Don't you want to know where I am Kaelem?" she asked. He shook his head. She continued looking at him and replied softly, sadly, "When the Haukea ask, let them know that Lily-Anna is safe. Say her soul will soon be free of her vessel, but she will be happy. Be strong Kaelem. Do not be afraid to stand up against what you know is wrong." The woman faded away, but Kaelem had no time to ponder on what she had said, for he sensed that someone else was still with him.

90

Kaelem turned around, and there was a man, tall and dark. "Where are you Kaelem?" He was overpowering. Kaelem had never felt so much dominance and force over him before. Certainly not from the Haukea - they all knew that he was the threat, even their Queen had been wary of his possibilities, but this man...he felt paralysed in comparison to him. Kaelem had no conscious will in what happened next, as the white around him disappeared and he found that he was in his bedroom, looking at himself sleeping, eyes moving behind his eyelids in REM sleep. Nothing else stirred. "Where is this Kaelem?" the man asked.

Kaelem breathed in harshly as they were transported to the outside of his house. The door number glowed vibrantly and the sea was heard clearly. Signs appeared before them: one bearing his road name and house number, one his town, and another his school.

"Thank you Kaelem. That's all I need."

They were back in the white room again. The man faded away as a deep voice whispered in Kaelem's mind, "I love you."

Kaelem awoke. Sweat drenched his T-Shirt.

Aka woke up laughing.

***

Aka knew the only way Kaelem could have sensed his mother was if he had got his abilities back, and that it would be harder to befriend his son now that the Haukea had spoken to him first. But Mya's training could be put to the test if need be. However, this proved that the Haukea were either worried about Lily-Anna or so desperate for power they would risk Aka being able to sense Kaelem's powers. He sighed, remembering the reason why Lily-Anna had bound his son's gifts in the first place. If he was able to get his son back, he promised that Kaelem would never be knighted. His heir would not rule the Keahi - his wife's adversary; it was the only thing he had left to give back to Lily-Anna. That and death.

He wondered again what lies the Haukea had fed his son, if they had already turned him into a killer for their own selfish wants. He ran his hand through his hair. He couldn't bear Kaelem having to carry a burden like that at such an early age, or any age for that matter. He would be fourteen now. So many years had passed, so many missed birthdays, so much missed time. "Sixty-four Dunmow Hill, Mowdon." Aka repeated it over and over.

CHAPTER THIRTEEN

Kaelem awoke to the sight of his cherry wood desk - a memory from long ago, yet still tangible. Something behind the desk caught his eye. Reaching out he felt a piece of paper that had been lodged there. Grabbing it between his fingers he pulled it out, and saw that it was the instructions to the project he was supposed to have done two years ago. He sighed; he didn't need to do it anymore. It could be thrown away. But the relief was juxtaposed with regret; for once he would have preferred to have done the work.

The floorboard creaked as Kaelem sneaked downstairs. He paused: something had changed. He proceeded down to the landing, and then right. Kaelem opened the door to the kitchen to find his stepfather and half sister looking around at him. "Morning Kaelem," his father greeted.

Kaelem didn't reply, but went to the cupboard to get some cereal, hoping it was still kept in the same place as when he had left. It was.

When he had got everything he sat down at the table opposite his sister. He smiled at her, but she looked gloomily down at her breakfast. "Sorry," was all Kaelem could say. Only the clanking of cutlery and chewing of food was heard for the rest of that morning.

Dillon came downstairs smiling after he had got changed for the day. He walked into the living room where Kaelem was watching television. "Why don't you take your sister out for a meal tonight. Just you two?"

"Because she hates me."

"Of course she doesn't, she's just confused. This will give you a chance to redeem yourself, to show her you haven't changed."

"Maybe tomorrow," Kaelem replied, concentrating more on what was on the screen.

"Look Kaelem, its hard for all of us. You two used to be so close, I'd hate to see you grow apart and lose each other. Please son."

"Fine. I'll take her to a restaurant tomorrow evening. I'll book up today." He began flicking through the channels, annoyed.

"Thanks. This means a lot to me." Kaelem watched his father walk out of the room. Dillon softly shut the door behind him.

The noise of the television faded into the background as Kaelem contemplated his sister. He felt sorry for her, he knew it was a shock, but he couldn't bear for them not to ever talk to each other again. He phoned up their favourite place and booked a reservation for half six the following night before telling his sister, to make sure he couldn't back out of it.

He knocked on Aolani's room. "Ali…Ali." There was no answer, but he heard shuffling behind the door. "We're going out tomorrow, leaving about five past six, is that okay?" Still nothing.

"I'll see you then." He paused. "Your dad would want you to come, he doesn't want to see us drift apart."

"My dad," Aolani breathed quietly to herself. Kaelem went to his room and sadly threw himself onto his bed. It was the first chance he'd had to contemplate what he was going to do now he was here. He remembered back to the night before, the sea. The rush he had got from falling into it. He wanted to feel like that again, free and exhilarated. Under the waves he had felt like he belonged somewhere. He sat up on his bed and listened closely to hear the distant water. He wanted to submerge himself in it, but the shore would be busy. He couldn't risk exposure, so instead he ran a bath, filling cold water up to the overflow.

He stepped in the water and changed. Although he let out small screams in reaction to the pain, his need to be in the water counteracted everything, and now he was out of the Haukea's hold he could finally change guilt-free. He could do this now, the Huakea no longer had a hold over him. He lay on his back and sank down. His fluke slopped over the side of the bath, the water rushed over his head. But it wasn't the same feeling that the sea gave him, it didn't have the same warmth, he couldn't swim, he was still restricted. He transformed and climbed out in annoyance, promising himself he would go down to the sea that night. He flung open the door to find Aolani greeting him. She gave a hint of a smile and walked round him into the bathroom. That was all Kaelem needed to feel happier: perhaps they were going to be okay.

CHAPTER FOURTEEN

Kaelem felt anticipation rising in him as he strolled across the beach, grains of sand rushing through his toes. The sea before him looked enticing, endearing, treacherous, waiting to swallow him up if he came too near to one of its precious secrets. Though he was no longer scared of what lurked beneath its uncertain surface, for he was now one of the things that lurked, that would kill to protect itself, that would cause harm to protect his identity.

He walked towards the icy depths, becoming excited, entranced, ensnared to do its will before it let him go. Kaelem took off his shirt and trousers and began to run, catching the memory of the previous night, the feeling of freedom. His emotion disturbed the sand under his frenzied feet, but as soon as the cold water touched his foot he stopped. He thought he saw something move out of the corner of his eye. Looking back it was too dark to tell. He didn't care, he'd waited too long, and so he glided carefully through the water until he was deep enough to completely immerse himself beneath the sea. The pain came once again. He cringed and let out a cry with sharpened breath. He collapsed under the water, and for a moment he couldn't breathe. He couldn't swim either. Panic took over from pain for the few seconds when his lungs disappeared, and the gills had yet to cut themselves into him. When the transition finally came he closed his eyes, and didn't open them until the hurt was gone.

Afterwards, he swam slowly and less frantically just below the surface, his head skimming fresh air as he savoured the calm. He hadn't gone too far out before he swam deeper, tail steering him vertically down towards the bottom. He liked the drop in temperature, the scenery of rock formations and coral. He watched as silver fish sped away from their predator, but it was too peaceful for death at the moment. It wasn't long before his fingers touched hard sand. He lay on his back, looking up towards the sky, towards the moon's light shimmering through the gentle waves. Silver touched his arm. He closed his eyes in paradise.

***

A soft drumming noise woke Kaelem up. For a second he wasn't sure whether or not he was still dreaming, though opening his eyes he saw the surface above had turned grey and disturbed, reflecting that of the sky. He swam up with curiosity, the melodious sound turning into a lion's roar. The sea beat him, rocked him; violent waves thrashed around Kaelem, throwing him vehemently back and forth, forcing him back down with a strong flow of rain. He dived deeper, where it was less turbulent, and swam towards the shore with sudden guilt. He had to see his sister, before her astraphobia got the better of her. Storms petrified Aolani, but he had always been there to comfort her, and she had always welcomed him with relief, using his warmth and protection to soothe herself, to bring down her heart rate.

Once in shallow water Kaelem morphed back to his human form and ran through the attacking waves. The rain continued to fall relentlessly in the dark. Droplets touched Kaelem's skin, making it tingle with pleasure. He picked up his clothes and put them on, the cold feeling of wet clothes sticking to his skin rushed through his body. It made him feel refreshed and alive. The rain came down hard, so strong his human eyes could hardly see through it.

Yet it was invigorating; he could feel every drop delicately touch his skin through the thousands descending.

After a dark walk home in the power-cut streets he pulled his door key from his trouser pocket and let himself in. Water drops gave away his path to the kitchen. They made tiny puddles, falling from his nose and clothes. He was drenched and happy. Kaelem fumbled around for a cup. He filled it with water once his eyes had adjusted enough to see, knowing that his sister's mouth would be dry. He then climbed the stairs and made for Aolani's bedroom. Her door was open, but when he crept inside he couldn't make her out. A flash of lightning revealed an empty bed. Tika was the only living thing occupying the room. Frowning he opened his own door. With a roll of thunder a shape moved below his bed. He walked up to it and knelt down. His lost toy peered back at him, cradled in the arms of his sister. "Ali," he whispered gently.

She trembled as she raised her head, her eyes wide. "You weren't there."

"I know," he replied. "I'm so sorry, I didn't know." He put the water beside Aolani and crawled under the bed to hug her.

"It's okay now though."

The rain thundered against the window, clawing its way down the pane. Aolani jumped, listening to it with fear, the stuffed toy still held in her arms, consoling her.

CHAPTER FIFTEEN

The restaurant was pretty. Serving the best seafood for miles around its reputation was high, as was the price to eat there. But it had been Kaelem and Aolani's favourite place since they could remember, and this was supposed to be a special day.

It was situated high up, stairs elegantly leading the customer up from the beach to a place decorated with delicate Japanese-style paintings of flowers and trees. Two boards of Japanese paintings stood proudly on each side of the doors leading people onto the outside area. There was a boardwalk running round the edge, with a large area for people to sit outside on hot days. Iron tables and chairs cluttered the decking, which jutted out to sea. If you were to lean over that would be all you would see: a deep rush of blue and turquoise, on good days. How ever romantic the premise it was still England, and normally a grey, cold, and forbidding water greeted the diners. Today it was dark. The smell of salt rose up around them, a soft lapping sound against the supports underneath them provided the music, a vain reminder from the sea of the power it held over their lives. The decking was still wet and slippery as the siblings followed the waiter to their seats. They ordered their drinks and waited for him to leave before talking again. Their faces were highlighted with candlelight as Kaelem smiled to break the awkward silence. But when it flickered shadows leapt across their faces, warning them of their fears and secrets. "How are you doing in school?" he asked.

"Okay." She looked away from him and towards the sea. She could make out the moon reflecting onto its calm surface, and the multi-coloured lights of the main pier.

"I don't understand why you couldn't have called me," she stated.

"I don't want to get into that. I'm really sorry, but there was nothing I could have done to change it."

She looked back at him. "If you ever do come up with an explanation, or want to talk, I'll be happy to listen to you," Aolani commented with anticipation.

"Thank you," Kaelem replied. He knew she was scared of what he had become, what he was. He promised his sister he would not show that side of himself to her again. He wanted to protect her.

The meal came after fifteen more minutes of waiting.

As they ate their conversation became more relaxed, they found themselves talking and laughing about their earlier childhood, anecdotes about previous embarrassing moments they had shared together.

Kaelem sat with a smile on his face, remembering his sister, her voice, her subconscious habits.

Aolani looked casually round at the sea and gasped. Kaelem saw her eyes widening and followed her gaze. A boy, probably no older than five, was climbing on top of the wooden barrier. He stood on top and called out to his mum to watch him, then began to walk unsteadily along it, his arms out to try and keep his balance. His foot slipped slightly on the damp surface the rain had provided it with the previous night. A gasp reverberated round the restaurant. A woman nearby let out a small scream and ran towards the boy, ordering him to get down, but as the boy moved his head towards the familiar voice he lost his balance and tumbled. His body disappeared as he fell off his balance beam and plummeted towards the waves breaking against the pier supports.

Kaelem stood up sharply, knocking his chair over with a clang, but no-one noticed as the consumers all rushed forwards. Someone cried out for a lifeguard, others took out their mobile phones and called for the ambulance service.

Kaelem looked at his sister - his eyes too were wide. Aolani's face was drained of colour as she nodded her head. 'Go,' she said. Kaelem didn't wait for anything else as he ran towards the edge of the pier. He pulled himself on top of the barrier. As people tugged at his clothes, telling him to come down, he jumped from them, his white shirt coming off in their hands. Moving his body in the air Kaelem changed to a diving position. The air hit his face as if it were trying to cut him. Kaelem closed his eyes in response, but that only made him feel sick from falling. His stomach reeled and he felt he was going to vomit. But Kaelem visualised the boy. He hit the water at such force it smacked him back. He fell below the waves, wasting no time before changing into the sea creature. He forgot about the pain as he opened his eyes to look for the boy, his nictitating membrane protecting his eyes as he hurtled through the water. Fish swam out of his way as Kaelem searched, panicking slightly that the boy would not survive this long without oxygen. His pupils dilated from the dark water, alert to any movement, until finally, through the murky depths, he perceived a limp shadow. Kaelem swam quickly towards it. Grabbing the body he rushed to the surface, transforming as he rose above the waves. He glided forwards, making sure the boy's head was above the cold, suffocating water. When it was shallow enough he stood. Walking through the waves he carried the boy in his arms. He found a frail pulse and willed that the child be okay. Kaelem drew in a breath as light erupted from his body and surged into the boy. It hurt his eyes as it came out, his vision still adjusting from that of the merman to that of the human, but Kaelem forced himself to concentrate on what was before him. The child's eyes opened, and he spat out water over Kaelem. Kaelem felt weak as he spotted a lifeguard and called out to her. He stumbled his way to shore, the boy suddenly heavier. The lifeguard looked at where the voice had come from. She exhaled a sigh of relief. Kaelem put the boy down gently on the soft sand as she came. Someone handed Kaelem a towel: his trousers must have come off from the force of diving into the water. The lifeguard saw that the boy was breathing heavily, though thankfully his eyes were open and focused. A crowd had now formed around them, and she ordered everyone to take a step back. They obeyed.

The sound of an ambulance rang out and they parted. The boy was carried off in a stretcher, trembling with cold and shock. His mother followed, her expression filled with worry and fear; nonetheless, she turned back to face Kaelem. "Thank you so much. Thank you." Her voice was shaky and genuine. "For a smart boy, Tarun sure can be stupid at times."

Kaelem smiled slightly, and he walked off alone. After a while he heard his sister calling behind him. "Kaelem," she panted. "Are you okay? I saw it Kaelem, a burst of light shining through the darkness; you are an Angel, you saved that boy's life!" Kaelem looked sombre. "What is the matter with you? You saved someone's life," Aolani said, agitated, wanting to punch some emotion into her brother.

"It wasn't me." Kaelem turned to face Aolani. "It was *them*. *They* gave these powers to me, and I used them. I didn't want to use them, but I did. Yet another thing I can't control. I used the thing they put into me, that they trusted me with, wrongly. The power is inside me so that I can bring hope, so I can collect souls, so that maybe the world can survive, so that perhaps the Haukea can live without the threat of the Keahi, not to save the life of one careless boy."

"Kaelem, I don't understand-"

"Did you not hear her? He's smart. I should have taken his soul instead of healing it. What good is that going to do the human race?" Aolani was horrified at the state her brother's mind was in. "Ali. I have to go. Please leave me."

"But Kae…"

"I'm sorry, I should have never come to see you again. It was stupid of me to think it was going to be the same. For the sake of your own life Aolani, please don't follow me."

"Are you threatening me?" Aolani threw his shirt at him. He caught it, smiled faintly, and left her.

Wandering alone back to the sea he knew he had let her down. She wanted him to prove her wrong, that nothing had changed; that he was still her older brother looking out for her.

The problem was everything was different now. She didn't think her big brother would ever come back from his trip. This was the thing that would never change. She wrapped her arms around herself.

CHAPTER SIXTEEN

Kaelem didn't notice the figure of a girl at first; he was still in a daze, walking aimlessly along the beach. He finally found himself at his usual spot and decided to take a swim to clear his head. He looked round out of habit, and that was when he saw her sitting on the sand in the shadow of an overhanging rock. He could distinguish very little about her in the dark. He wished that she would leave, but she seemed set to stay. Kaelem considered waiting until the following night to surrender to the sweet seduction of the sea, but soon the desperation for it overpowered his insecurity. A car drove by, but he hardly acknowledged it as he turned, uncaring, towards the water. No one would believe her anyway if she confessed to what she was about to witness. Reaching the edge of the sea Kaelem broke into a silent, exhilarated run, leaving only soft ripples in his wake. When the water was deep enough he descended flawlessly below the waves.

Even though he was used to being harmed now, and his transformation no longer scared him, the pain was still vibrant, coursing through every morphing bone, making his skin cells scream, and concentrating in each gash —every gill. He hoped that one day he would be strong enough to override the sensation, but even if he couldn't, the beauty of the sea, and his love for its freedom and wonders, would overcome his reluctance for the distressing change.

Tonight was not the same as last night though. It felt different; it felt colder.

***

Mya watched the boy called Kaelem move towards the sea. This was the second night she had observed him, and she wasn't too impressed by what she saw. From the headlights of a passing car she noticed that his hair was a dull blonde, windswept and dry. His blue eyes looked longingly out to sea, as if reflecting the colour they saw, and although he was of medium height he seemed small compared to his father. Then again, he hadn't finished growing yet. She saw him walk slowly up to the water, then run. He didn't splash - only ripples were left to illustrate he had been there - neither did he slow as he got deeper, he travelled through the sea with such an ease that he might well have been running through air. Suddenly he went under, never to resurface again that night, lost to the world with no one realising it.

She sat there for a while longer, contemplating the day when she would meet him in person, face to face.

***

The next thing Kaelem knew he was back, fully dressed, in his human form and looking up at Bethamy. A smile crept along her features. "Had a nice sleep?"

He stood up, confused and annoyed at finding himself here rather than his sanctuary. "Why can't you just leave me alone?!"

"Aw, Kaelem, that's not very nice. I like seeing you."

He looked away from her. "So, why have you brought me back?" he asked regretfully.

"Don't you remember? We gave you time to sense Lily-Anna, and then you had to report back to us. Well, your time is up."

"I'm sorry to disappoint you…"

"No, Kaelem, no. I know you haven't disappointed us. You probably just didn't know what you were looking for. Let's try to get into that mind of yours, find the right memory I need." Kaelem was silent. "Had any dreams lately?"

"Amazingly enough I have!" he replied sarcastically.

Bethamy sighed and tried again, "Vivid dreams Kaelem, lucid dreams. Dreams where you can feel your surroundings, control what your body does."

Kaelem thought, then nodded. "A woman was in it, she made me feel uneasy, but not as much as the man who came after she had gone."

"A man?" Bethamy tried not to show anxiety in her voice, "what did he look like?"

"I don't remember, I think he had black hair. I can still feel his presence though, it was so strong, so powerful." he laughed nervously, trying not to show fragility in front of Bethamy.

She looked around. "We'll deal with him later. Do you know where this woman was?"

"She was in a white place, endless white."

"Are you sure?" This time Bethamy found it harder to control her emotion, and a little concern crept into her words.

Kaelem had a spark of thought. "She said something, she said to tell you that Lily-Anna is safe, and." Kaelem thought hard, trying to remember her words. "And that, and that her soul is free of her vessel, or something. She said she was happy."

Bethamy stepped away from him; she looked as if she were about to cry. "Then we're too late. I hate him so much that bastard.

He will suffer for what he did to her." She stared Kaelem in the eye, intimidating him to make sure he did what she was about to plan. "And you will help us. This is no longer just about the humans. He has made it so much more than that." She raised her voice, calling for her followers. "I want everyone to meet in the throne room, and be prepared for battle."

"Bethamy…"

"Lily-Anna's dead. Aka killed her, and she will never be able to repent, to come back to us. She is damned, now we will fight for her justice."

They looked shocked. "Yes, my Queen." One man turned around before leaving the room, showing his sympathy and sadness at this news. For a second he made contact with Kaelem, and shivered.

Kaelem stared at Bethamy, wanting answers. "Does this mean that, my mum's dead?" Bethamy nodded. Kaelem broke down, trying to make sense of what he had just heard. For once Bethamy hugged Kaelem with no alternative in her mind, she shared his grief and tried to comfort him - though the arms that wrapped around him were tense, as if they wanted to draw away, but were being kept there by a powerful force acting against them. In a cracked voice Kaelem spoke, no longer thinking about what Bethamy thought of his weaknesses, "I never even got to see her."

***

The next morning Kaelem awoke to a guard knocking on his door. He hadn't gone home that night and at first he didn't know where he was. He groggily went to answer the call, his eyes stinging where he had been rubbing tears from them. As he tried to come to his senses the guard informed him that the Queen apparently wanted to speak to Kaelem. He groaned: what did she want this time?

***

It was the first time that Kaelem had seen the throne room this empty. He was surprised by how huge it really was, as well as being captivated by the way it sparkled with gleaming ice and snow. Bethamy was sitting on her throne as usual, waiting for Kaelem to come to her. "Good morning," she greeted cheerfully.

"Hi." Kaelem was a little surprised: she wasn't usually this nice. Perhaps it was compassion towards him due to the stinging news he had received yesterday? Whatever it was it didn't last long, for as soon as she smiled Kaelem could see that glint of selfishness, which now so often dominated her once pretty eyes.

"Your athame Kaelem," she said bluntly, reaching out her hand towards him. For a second Kaelem had to think what she meant, then remembered back to his leaving ceremony and the present they had awarded him with. A surge of guilt rushed through his body. "I haven't obtained any souls yet."

Bethamy nodded. "I guessed that. Once you get back to the humans I will give you some more time before seeing you again, and I will expect your athame to be carrying some. Remember the purpose for this Kaelem: the greater good." Her voice seemed to sneer on the last two words, but she was sly enough so that Kaelem wouldn't question it or understand why. His soul was too peaceful to know the truth about her real plans at the moment, but ignorance was bliss as they say. Hopefully if they kept their eye on Kaelem he would grow to understand the Haukea, and want them to succeed in dominating the human race. If he became her king he would have power, and then both the humans and Keahi would bow weakly before him, and Kaelem will love it.

"There is another reason you are here," she stated, standing up as three more Haukea walked into the room at the sound of her footsteps on the icy floor. Discomforted, Kaelem looked back and forth between the Queen and her three followers.

"Why. What is the other purpose?" Kaelem asked, feeling weak and helpless.

"The proof that you are Haukea, that you believe in us, what we are trying to achieve."

"How are you going to do that?" He was feeling increasingly concerned with the closing distances between him and the others.

"Your ears," she enlightened.

"What?"

"Have you not noticed, we all have our left ear pierced nine times?"

"You can't!" Kaelem protested.

"Why not? You are one of *us* now. Or do you not want to be? Do you want to be an outsider, exiled?" she added with a sinister tone.

"No. But what will people say? I'm only fourteen."

"Don't worry. You'll look 'cool'." They grabbed him and pulled him to the throne on the left. The one that had belonged to Bethamy when her mother was in power. They held him down as he heard another pair of footsteps enter the room. Something came up close to his face. He jumped as a needle pricked his ear, accompanied soon after by a throbbing sensation. This happened again and again. Kaelem closed his eyes, wishing it were all a dream.

"It's done," a voice concluded. Then footsteps faded away from him and the others let him go. Aware of the studs against his skin he felt a wealth of depression and sadness rage through him at the fact that they had branded him like this; like livestock.

"That wasn't so bad, was it?" Bethamy said to him. Kaelem put his hand to his stinging ear. "Don't take them out Kaelem, or I promise you will be exiled, and I will make you an enemy to the Haukea." There was a slight wavering in her voice, but as tears pricked Kaelem's eyes he was concentrating more on how heavy his left ear seemed to feel now, compared to how free his right ear was.

"Now," Bethamy continued. "This still leaves us with a slight problem: the Keahi will know now that you want to be one of us, yet we still want them to believe you are on their side. It will be easier this way once the war starts, having a spy." She paused. Kaelem didn't move. Still shocked at what they had done to him, her voice drifted in and out of Kaelem's consciousness. "So. You will have to dye your hair black, like theirs, to look like you are rebelling against us. Do you hear me Kaelem? Kaelem!" He moved his head slowly towards her and nodded. "Yes," he replied weakly.

"Good. Now go home." She went back to sitting on the throne to his left. The three Haukea had now gone, but Kaelem was a lifeless marionette, lying on the throne next to her, not seeing the smile of triumph that crossed her features.

"Your throne is ready my Prince," she whispered.

CHAPTER SEVENTEEN

The alarm shattered through Kaelem's sleep, bringing him rudely back to reality and the first day of school in two years. His father had re-enrolled him and Kaelem had proved that he could manage the harder work of year ten.

Kaelem groaned. Sliding under the covers his hand reached out to stop the piercing ringing. After ten dozy minutes he shuffled into the bathroom, intending, once again, to fulfil the Haukea's orders.

"I can't stand her," he muttered as he exited the room forty-five minutes later, flinging the plastic gloves into the bin and leaving black water to drain down the bath. Entering the kitchen he took a banana. Dillon and Aolani stared after him. "What?" Kaelem asked irritably, subconsciously running his fingers through his hair and wishing he were in the alternative realities of his dreams. Things seemed clearer there, more serene; he could think and he didn't have to worry about how his actions would affect a whole race's existence.

He left the house in a bad mood, and wasn't expecting it to get any brighter. Everything was supposed to be okay once he got back home, but echoes of the Haukea were still there, constantly reminding him of his duties, his loyalties. They floated round him, flooding his mind with confusion over what was expected of him. He wondered if he would be able to fulfil their wishes.

He still hadn't had the chance of obtaining a single soul yet. He took a deep breath and tried to concentrate on school.

In the dull light of the morning the building looked exactly the same as it had fifty years ago.

"Nothing ever changes around here," Kaelem said wistfully under his breath. He was surprised to find that he was beginning to like the stability of his town. He felt comforted, because even though his life was going in a dramatic direction, and who knew where it would lead to? He saw that he could always come home and bask in the unchanging glory of Mowdon.

His tutorial room smelt of sweat, and an uncomfortable stuffiness hit him as soon as he entered. But this was immediately put into the background when he found himself staring at the plump form of Jeb. He tensed. With sudden guilt Kaelem realised he hadn't told his best friend that he was back. Heck, he felt guilty that he hadn't told Jeb he was leaving in the first place, even though he'd had no warning that he was going anywhere. What must Jebediah have thought of his friend going away for two years without a word then turning up back in class one day? He should have phoned him; he should have seen him before now. He was just so entranced with everything else around him that he had forgotten about the one person who would probably have made everything seem like normal again. Kaelem began to heat up, angry with himself. He swallowed, thinking of cold, that there was no fire inside him, that his heart was frozen. It helped. Slightly.

Kaelem flicked a sorrowful grin at Jeb and headed to the back of the room to sit next to him. His classmates looked at him, whispering, but Kaelem ignored them. He'd grown used to things being told in secret about his existence, and was no longer fazed by adolescent rumours. *Either that, or I'm about to snap from the overload of denial,* Kaelem thought.

Jebediah's familiar round face stared accusingly at Kaelem's.

"Hi Jeb."

They were silent for a moment, but it was Jeb who spoke into the void first, "Your dad said you ran away to look for your mother. I understand if you didn't want to tell me, but you could have at least said that you were going away for a while. It hurt. I thought you were ditching me.

Kaelem was startled for a second before finding his voice, "I should have said something. Truth is, I didn't tell anyone Jeb. It was kind of a last minute thing."

There was another awkward silence.

"You never even told me you were back Jag. What am I meant to think? I was…worried."

"I really am sorry Jeb. There are no excuses for treating you like that, but I honestly didn't have any control over my disappearance. I should have phoned though, it's just…everything has been so hectic since I got back, trying to get my head around things."

"Did you find anything out about your mum then?" Jeb asked. His ignorance touched Kaelem, and it pained him to think of all that he had learned, all that he had become, was churning under the surface, unbeknownst to his best friend. Kaelem took a steadying breath before replying, choosing carefully what he revealed from the information he knew. "I went to where she was last seen: her birthplace. I saw an insight into her life. The occupants of that place were looking for her too. They were worried and so aided my quest to find her, but - something happened Jeb. She isn't - I mean - I can never get to see her." Jeb looked at his friend with sympathy, not knowing what to say. Kaelem wanted to cry, but couldn't, not while everyone was still looking at him: they too were wondering where he had been for so long. "It's okay, you don't need to say anything," Kaelem commented. Something had tautened between them now, unspeakable, unforgivable.

The thick atmosphere was lightened when a teacher flew into the room, hair in a mess, scurrying to her desk. Folders were dropping out of her arms as she heaved them onto the worktop with a loud bang.

"Sorry class," she announced breathlessly, trying to organize the piles of clutter in front of her, "I've had a lot to do this morning." She sat down, ordering silence. "Okay. We have two more people joining us this year. One, whom you already know, and has once more graced us with his presence: Kaelem Yaegar…" The form all turned towards him once again and he smiled sarcastically back at them. "…and a new student, Mya …" A girl stood up from one of the front tables. Kaelem looked at her with indifference, unsuspecting how close he was to the girl who sat watching him on the beach every night, not knowing how deadly his naïve perception of where she came from could be.

"She's cute," Jebediah commented.

"I guess."

"You're still blinded by Alma aren't you?" Jeb smiled. Kaelem pulled a face at him; a taste of normality had come back to his life.

"I don't know what you're talking about Jebediah," he replied airily. Jeb laughed.

Alma wasn't the most popular girl in their school, not even close. She wasn't thin, she didn't stand out in her looks, on either side of the spectrum, and wasn't exactly someone who liked to socialise too much. Kaelem had had a crush on her since she first held the door open for him in year seven, and his spirit had sung to her beautiful soul. Too bad this was as far as their relationship

114

had gone, for the only words he had ever spoken to her were his crumbling staccato Spanish in answer to her clear and perfect questions. He felt like a fool around her, yet he was always cheerier when he sensed that she was in the room with him.

The morning dragged on, filled with first-day-back gossip and depression. He hated the classes he had been put in, made worse by Mya being in three of them; she kept glancing at him, and it put him on edge. Once they had made eye contact, and her look was so filled with intense resentment that he found it hard to breathe. The only thing illuminating his day was the fact that Alma was once again in the same Spanish class as he.

When the bell rang dully for the end of the school day, Kaelem waited by the gates for Jebediah, keeping a wary eye out for Mya, hoping she wouldn't look at him again with those huge, amber eyes. He didn't know what he had done to deserve the emotion that came from them, and in fact wasn't in a rush to find out. People passed him, walking sluggishly home, some complaining about the amount of work, some angry, a lot just glad it was over for the time being. But Mya wasn't to be seen. Kaelem felt his anxiety ease when he spotted his best friend emerge from the crowd.

"Want to do something?" Jeb asked.

Kaelem smiled and nodded.

He hadn't realised how much he missed hanging out with his friends until now, how he missed their sarcastic jokes, their anecdotes with hilarious endings. They clambered onto the bus and rode it to the beach.

Not many people were here now the tourist season was over. Only a few older people, and some teenagers, waiting for college or university to start, were taking advantage of cheap off-season tickets. But a lot of the shops had now shut, so the place looked eerily deserted.

The September cold had settled in to dampen the mood even more, and a soft drizzle began to come down as the bus screeched to a halt. Kaelem and Jebediah clambered off the bus along with a few others and walked onto the cold sand. They took off their trainers and socks, leaving their feet bare to walk across the cold, hard sand.

Kaelem had decided he wouldn't tell Jeb what had happened to him. At least not yet. He liked Jeb's ignorance about him too much to let it go. He felt cruel doing this, but it had to be done. Kaelem walked closer to the water, close enough so that it lapped at his feet like an excited dog.

"Isn't that cold?" Jeb shivered involuntarily.

"Yes," Kaelem replied.

"Jag!" A shout of one of Kaelem's nicknames behind them forced the pair to turn round. Three boys were coming towards them. "Hey, haven't seen you in ages. You okay mate?" it was Ben who asked.

"Hi," Kaelem answered enthusiastically. The boy was slightly smaller than him, with brown hair, and fair skin. "I'm fine. I just needed to get away for a bit. You know how this town is never changing. It was driving me insane."

The three nodded in agreement. "So what you doing now, at the beach and stuff?"

"Dunno," Jeb replied. "Just walking."

"We'll come with you," Ben stated. The boys followed the sea line for a while, catching up on what had been happening in

Mowdon since Kaelem had disappeared, unsurprisingly it wasn't much, and what new trends they were all into now.

It was a while before any of them realised what they were seeing, and once one of them did, they all understood.

"Hey Jag, isn't that your sister?" All five boys were looking at the same spot, where four girls were taunting Aolani. She was trying her best to stand up to them, to show them she didn't care, but her true emotions were leaking through.

"I think I'll go. I'll meet you later," Kaelem commented, continuing to move in the direction of his sister.

"Okay Jag. You sure you don't want us to beat them up?"

"No," Kaelem answered in monotone, leaving his friends behind as he went to see what the problem was. "I'll see you tomorrow."

He kept his distance from the gang, making a conscious effort for them not to see him. The last thing she needed was her brother there, creating another excuse for the girls to bully her, to accuse and hate her for getting someone else involved.

The tallest of the group was smirking. Aolani tried to talk back to them, but her voice caught in her throat, and it came out as a pathetic whine. The girl burst out laughing, Aolani's eyes glistened in fear and dismay as the noise reverberated around her. She had nowhere to go and no one to save her, but Kaelem still decided it was better to stay back. This was her battle. She was never going to win if he stepped in, for once he was gone they would be all over Aolani like hyenas. He couldn't stay with her forever, and it wouldn't teach her how to be strong and stand up for her wellbeing. A silenced voice told Kaelem that if this had happened before his 'trip' those girls wouldn't be standing, but it was a sense beyond his range.

Reluctantly Kaelem walked home - she wouldn't appreciate knowing he had seen what he had. When she felt comfortable, safe, she would tell him.

An hour after Kaelem had gone stomping up to his room Aolani came in. She too headed for the haven of her bedroom.

Kaelem knocked lightly on the door after giving her some time and space to calm down. He heard sniffing on the other side. "Ali…" he started.

"Go away!" she yelled, frustrated and sad. Kaelem flinched and walked in. She was lying on her bed watching Tika burrowing in the dirt through the glass walls of her cage. Aolani's body was trembling as she twisted away from her brother, but he sat by her. He pulled her gently into a seated position and hugged her. After resisting she gave in and put her arms round him tightly. She cried.

"It's okay Aolani. It will be all right, you don't have to worry okay?" It didn't matter if she heard his words or not.

CHAPTER EIGHTEEN

The week passed at a lumbering pace. Kaelem tried as much as he could to avoid Mya, but she seemed resolute on following him. She had tried to converse with him, but it was forced talk spoken with a strained accent. Her eyes gave her away again, revealing a deep bitterness, extinguishing the thought that she was hanging around Kaelem because she liked him. There was an agenda behind all this that made Kaelem wary, but any fears Kaelem may have had were eroded away with the thought of seeing Alma. He loved to listen to her. She had a wonderful soul; she had a beautiful body. He could look into her eyes forever and be in heaven. They were a clear blue, tinted perfectly with a tiny hint of green. Her hair was a dull blonde, which now included brunette streaks. He listened to her laughing with her friends, and sighed.

"Jag," Ben said in his ear. Kaelem jumped at the voice. "You've got it bad. You need to find a new interest mate." Kaelem pulled a face at him and carried on working.

Friday afternoon finally came with a much livelier atmosphere.

Kaelem went to the beach and once again witnessed the girls taunting his sister. He went to bed angry, his mind wondering again how he would have handled this a couple of years ago.

The next morning carried an unusual heat for mid-September. Aolani was quivering as she watched the weather report. Kaelem recognised this behaviour and went to her. "It's okay Ali. I'm here now; I won't leave you again. The lightning can't hurt you." She looked up at her brother. "Promise me Kaelem."

"I promise," he replied. "Let's enjoy the sun while it's here and tackle the storm when it comes."

She took Kaelem's hand, but refused to go to the beach with him. "It's too exposed."

Kaelem nodded in understanding. The doorbell went and Aolani jumped.

"It's alright," Kaelem comforted. Then nervously opened the door. Jebediah was standing before him.

"Hey. Want to go to the beach?"

"I can't, my sister…"

"Kaelem, I'll be fine."

"Are you sure?" Kaelem asked.

"Yes. You promised me you will be here when the thunder comes, so I know that once the storm breaks out, you will make me safe."

Kaelem nodded with certainty and walked out the door with Jeb.

Upon reaching Mowdon's beach the friends saw that a large crowd of people had already taken advantage of the anomaly. Babies had joy exploding from their features as adults lifted them over the coming waves, strangers who were gingerly testing the water were splashed by teenagers bobbing in the sea, they turned from the sea in distaste. Children climbed rocks as their parents looked on anxiously, yelling at them to get off. Jeb went straight to sun bathing in his trunks, not paranoid for once about his large form. Kaelem smiled, glad.

"Weird isn't it?" Jeb commentated. Kaelem was silent.

After a while of lying in the sweltering heat, listening to senseless talk, Jeb suggested they should go into the water. For a moment Kaelem was unsure - he didn't know if he would be able to resist going under the surface, going deeper and deeper until suspicion or fear would surly cloud Jeb's mind. In the end he agreed, mentally telling himself to keep above the surface.

As they walked into the sea, Jeb glancing once at the position of the lifeguard, Kaelem felt energised, and the further out they got the stronger he felt. Sinking down to swim with Jeb he thought of all that lay below them. A zephyr swept his body.

"You okay?" his friend asked.

"Yeah. I was just thinking." Kaelem lay back, floating on the waves, and looked at the sun. He closed his eyes and felt the heat on his body. Suddenly he was below the surface. He trod water, spluttering, afraid that his body was automatically trying to pull him below, as if magnetised. What would happen if it changed too? But then he heard a laugh, and knew that things were normal and secure when he was around Jebediah.

"Hey!" he called, and laughed too. They threw water at each other, sparkling in the sunlight, Kaelem forgetting all of his worries, forgetting who he was and what he was sent to do. For one glorious moment he went back in time, he was his twelve year old self again with nothing to interfere with his friendship or playing. He had no alternative life - he was ignorant and happy.

CHAPTER NINETEEN

Kaelem ran across the pier, his bare feet hitting the wooden floorboards with satisfying thuds. He closed his eyes, the wind protesting against him, and then he jumped through the air and down towards the sea. He did not surface upon going under the waves. His stomach rumbled as he swam easily through the water. Fish surrounded Kaelem, and upon sensing danger they dispersed in all directions, but their predator was faster. Gliding to the bottom of the sea he caught a Tub Gurnard and made its death instantaneous. He swam back to the shore and sat down next to his trousers, watching the waves lapping the sand.

It was early evening and everyone had gone home for supper. He ate the fish with enjoyment. The flesh was succulent and delicious, and its blood caressed his throat as it made its way down his oesophagus. It was then that he saw her. With brown, stylish hair, a slender body and sharp features there was no mistaking the girl who had been teasing his sister. Hatred filled Kaelem's mouth, the taste of the fish changed to a metallic sense of anger. How dare she come into his realm, how dare she do what she had done to Ali. As she entered the sea Kaelem subconsciously reached for his athame. Without knowing it he was suddenly swimming silently after her, underwater in his merman form. He knew what he was doing, knew that he needed at least one soul for the Haukea. They had trained him for two relentless years, he needed something to show them it was not all in vain. He didn't know what they would do to him if he didn't deliver, especially Bethamy - who was unpredictable and tainted.

***

Her toes touched the warm water. A hot spell had come over the town and taking a late night dip had seemed like a good idea to cool down and get some exercise. Swimming without a care she was not to know that something sinister was about to happen. She sensed nothing until it was too late. A hand clasped around her arm and dragged her down. Water swirled over her head and her eyes started to throb. She kicked upwards, and for a relieved second she reached the surface, spluttering out salt water with distaste. Her heart rate pumped furiously, but a stronger force pulled her back down with a small scream. Her voice vanished in another wave of water, as did her last chance of freedom. She wasn't strong enough to break through the surface again and she knew she was quickly running out of air. She kicked out desperately, but her legs were useless, they went through water and didn't give herself enough of a force to rise upwards. The world began to spin and turn as her lungs ran out of oxygen. She opened her eyes to see a bright light above her. Her face came alight with its glow as she closed her eyes from the relentless stinging. All she saw was the red light behind her eyelids as she lost the rest of her senses. Sickness crept into her mouth and head; she felt her body become light as she fainted, as her existence faded inside her.

***

Kaelem felt her fear, her body weakening. His emotions were running wild. He was strong and powerful, yet he also had some kind of sympathy for the girl. As he took her life with each breathless second in his grip, remorse overtook him, shadowing his supremacy. He rose to the surface and carried her to shore.

***

She felt as though she were flying, only knowing she wasn't dead when cold sea spray splashed her feet. She took in great gulps of air, savouring the sensation as she had never tasted anything like it before. She looked up and saw she was in the arms of a boy. He had piercings up the whole of his left ear, black hair and green, no, blue eyes. She felt the cool sea air brush against her face and closed her eyes, savouring life, steadily getting her breath back. But when they got to the sand she realised her saviour was carrying a knife.

"I'm sorry," he said. "I need your soul, for purposes I cannot yet explain." He paused, but looking into her frightened face he could not help but see beneath the cruel one that his sister had once seen. "You should have left her alone. She was so scared, so sad." Anger came over Kaelem when he saw that she was confused.

"Ali," he stated. "You can't respect her. Not even now, when you can feel the fear - you don't care. She's nothing to you but another way to boost your self-esteem. You're sick." He swiped down the double-edged knife into her chest. She started to breath harshly as the stones on the athame glowed. Blood seeped out of the wound Kaelem had created, staining her white bikini. Her soul flowed out of her and into the athame. When Kaelem pulled it out the girl's body went limp and fell forwards. Kaelem caught it in his arms. Lifeless eyes stared hauntingly up at him, sending a shiver through his body. His athame was dripping with her blood, his hands were stained crimson. He backed away, frightened. This was something the Haukea had never warned him about, that she would bleed, that she would become like this. It was as if he had murdered her. The lifelessness in her vessel, the dullness in her eyes – taking into account all his distaste and talk with the Haukea, he was still shocked and somehow scared. Her body fell onto the sand as he ran from her, ran to his house, ran to his sister.

CHAPTER TWENTY

"Whose blood is that Kaelem?" She tried to sound calm but when her brother didn't answer Aolani repeated herself, hysteria clamouring into her tone, "Kaelem, whose blood is that?!"

He was shivering as he tried to focus his eyes on her. It was as if he was just acknowledging that she was there, but his blue eyes seemed to quiver too. "It isn't mine," he answered, shaking his head. "It isn't mine."

Aolani took a breath, a sick feeling rising in her throat, contorting her stomach. "Then whose is it?"

"She won't bother you anymore," he cried, breaking down in tears. He leaned towards his sister for comfort. Aolani heard a small clang and looked at the floor to see he had dropped something. She bent down to pick it up.

"Don't touch it!" he screamed. "You'll put your fingerprints on it."

She drew her hand away sharply, as if it had cut her. She turned her gaze towards her half brother, and he saw fire in her eyes. "What do you mean? What have you done Kaelem?" Her voice trembled, synchronising with her brother's body. She wanted to cry, she had no idea what else to do, but she found she wasn't upset for the reasons she thought she was.

Kaelem spoke again, "I was supposed to. They said it would be for the best. I didn't know I was going to have to hurt her." He drew in a sharp breath, remembering the struggle, and felt tears crawl down his face again, but he didn't wipe them away.

He saw that his sister was frightened and scared. Kaelem backed away in shock when he noticed the fear in her eyes, the fear of him. He had never seen her like this before. She was only nine, but she had a strength beyond her years.

"I had to," Kaelem whispered. Her big eyes never left his, full of anger, full of hate of what he had done, full of terror and confusion that he even had the capability of performing such an act. "She isn't dead." He took a step towards her. Aolani's foot went back in response.

"You're insane," she muttered.

"I just - I didn't think the process to get her soul would be so disturbing."

"What did you do?"

"Her soul's in there," he pointed to the athame, "we're preserving it. She'll be -"

"We're?" Aolani replied. "What have you got into Kaelem? What did you really do whilst you were away?"

Kaelem reached out to her, trying to convince her the act was for the best, like the Haukea had with him. But she was more stable, more connected to her own morality, less easily moulded into being something she was not, a spirit that had lived a hundred lives, always knowing exactly who and what she was.

"They need her Ali, to save the human race. She will be free again when the time comes. Then you will see why this has to be done."

As soon as Kaelem's hand contacted with Aolani's skin she started. "Get off me! I don't know you, I don't know you." She kept saying it over and over again, putting her head in her hands.

"She is still alive, only her vessel is…"

She ducked out of his grasp, putting her hands over her ears, and ran.

***

The sound of a key in the door's lock brought Kaelem back to his senses. Slowly he turned his head towards the sound, then down at his athame. He bent, picked it up, and ran upstairs. He placed it on his bedside table and went into the bathroom as his dad greeted anyone who was listening with a friendly, "I'm back!"

Kaelem replied with a feeble, "Hi."

As Kaelem washed his hands the water turned a dirty crimson. Watching it he suddenly felt a wave of sickness and nearly passed out. He didn't go into the sea that night. He wanted never to go near it again. He clumsily stumbled back to his room, grabbing on to things to keep his balance. He fell onto his bed and cried himself to sleep.

Knocking. Kaelem opened his eyes and focused on his digital clock. The red numbers flashed ten thirty-two. He crawled drowsily out of bed and opened his door to come face-to-face with Dillon's worried expression. "I didn't want to wake you, but Ali's not back yet, and I was wondering if you knew where she was?" Kaelem was still for a second - she hadn't returned? To Dillon he explained that she was staying the night at a friend's, deliberately adding that he didn't know which one in case he phoned them. Dillon sighed with relief. "She should have told me."

"I'm sorry Dad, it was my fault, I would have told you, but I just felt so tired…"

"It's okay, at least she's safe. That's the main thing." Kaelem returned a guilty smile, and shut the door in Dillon's face.

He sat on his bed, scared for her safety; she was only nine… *but on the other hand, going after her might make things worse. She may only want some space, to get away from me*, he choked.

His eyes subconsciously made contact with his athame. When his brain registered what he was seeing he reached out a hand and picked up the knife. Studying it he marvelled that someone's soul was trapped inside it. A thought came to him: *she needs company.*

As if possessed he straightened his back and went downstairs. He reached for the door handle and Dillon stepped in front of him, blocking his path. "Where are you going at this time of night?"

Kaelem explained that he wanted some fresh air, and walked quickly past his father and out into the cold night.

***

The man exited the club with anger bubbling from him. He was not drunk, but something had definitely made him violent. Although he was a large man, with knowledge about how to fight properly he didn't abuse his strength, power and advantage.

Kaelem followed the man, being as stealthy as possible to get the right timing. But the man sensed his presence and swung aggressively round to face Kaelem. For a second Kaelem was an innocent boy again, and shrunk back, scared the man was going to attack him.

"What," the man said bluntly.

"I'm sorry. I…need directions," Kaelem replied. The man scoffed and walked away from Kaelem. Kaelem ran up to the man and slammed his athame into his back. The man arched and a scream echoed in the night, though it did not come from this man, it's sound was too high-pitched. The jewels on the handle glowed as the soul was sucked inside. The man tried to hit Kaelem, but Kaelem stopped his attacker's arm with his hand. He felt it heat up. The man jerked his arm out of Kaelem's grasped as a burn mark started to appear. For a moment Kaelem was taken aback, he had forgotten about his fire ability, the Haukea never mentioned it after the incident in the throne room, and the only other times were accidental, much like this was. That 'incident' still plagued his mind, but he no longer connected it with powers that he could use in real situations.

The jewels had now stopped glowing and so Kaelem pulled his knife out of the man's back. The vessel went limp and fell. Kaelem heard running footsteps and turned his head towards them. For a second his breathing stopped; his sister was coming towards him. Kaelem ran from her, but in his hurry and fright that his sister had seen what he had done, he tripped.

"Kaelem," he heard his sister next to him. A yell for help rang in their ears from where he had just come.

"Ali. I…" he began sympathetically.

"What's wrong with you?"

Kaelem's face hardened at her question. "Nothing's wrong with me Ali. I told you, this is the first step. We need them to help give us a better future."

"For who, Kaelem? What are you talking about? How could you be involved with something like this?" Distress blurred her words.

"They are strong minded and smart. They will be trained and used to help create a safer world," Kaelem replied lightly.

"But you killed him."

"No. I haven't," he said sharply. "Like I explained before: I took his soul. It's in here." He held out the athame, and Aolani stepped back from it.

"Are you going to kill me, too?"

"I didn't kill him!" he shouted defensively.

"Kaelem, I can't deal with this. I can't. Oh, what are we going to do?"

"What do you mean?" Kaelem asked.

"They think he's dead! They're going to want to find who did this. Just like…" She stopped herself and swallowed back the words, trying to calm down. "This isn't right. I'm going now Kaelem. Away from you. I don't want to see you for a while. I feel sick, this just isn't right."

"Please Al…"

"No. Go to where you belong." Aolani's head moved subliminally towards the sea. She walked away from him, her footsteps tapping the concrete beneath her feet. Suddenly the sound changed beat and stopped; she hadn't gone far before she had keeled over, expecting to vomit. Kaelem ran to her. "Go away," she said weakly. "Please, leave me alone." Her voice caught. She moved her gaze away from Kaelem.

"You'll soon see what I mean," he said, and walked away. His fear hadn't lasted long, but he was still worried over his sister's safety. In the shadows he made sure she got home okay, his soul tearing apart inside of him with each of her solemn steps. As soon as Dillon let her in he made his way towards the sea.

CHAPTER TWENTY-ONE

Kaelem sat on the pier's edge looking out at the sea. The wind lightly blew his hair from his face. The full moon reflected in the calm water. He looked up and saw it for its reality, transcending white down onto the world and presenting a dim and haunting light to the night.

He closed his eyes, trying to imagine the wind blowing away his pain. He was here for the first time alone. His sister was no longer near to him, her comforting smile was gone, and he knew it wasn't going to be all right. He was sick and she was trying to make him better, but he had thrown her help back in her face. Kaelem whispered to the full moon that he would try, for her, not to do the Haukea's bidding. Perhaps his sister was right in thinking that taking the souls assigned death to them, but when he opened his own eyes they showed doubt. He had been around them too long, and their 'logic' had embedded itself into Kaelem.

He looked down at the athame he was subconsciously playing with. It had caused so much emotional pain for his sister, but in the long run wouldn't it be better for them?

Confused and angry he stood up and threw the athame as far as he could. He watched its shadow disappear when it fell below the water.

"I hate this!" he screamed after it. His rage made his breath harsh and fast. He turned away and ran to the pier steps, then back towards the beach. Sand billowed up into his face as he ran to the sea. The girl was there again, an obscured image watching his breakdown.

Kaelem went into the water and swam, going under, deeper and further, his emotion carrying him, callously, away from everything. He didn't want to resurface; he couldn't stand seeing his sister's sad and disappointed face again. He only stopped once he had reached the seabed. Here his heart missed a beat due to disbelief and fear from what he saw half buried in the seabed, but the blue stones clearly called to him with their extraordinary colour. He picked it up and held it close to him. *I'm sorry. I have to do this.* He rose to the surface.

"I'm sorry Aolani. I need more souls. You'll understand soon. Please don't be ashamed of me." The wind blew into his face, making it suddenly became much noisier as he went above the waves and swam back to shore.

***

Two weeks had passed since Kaelem had left his sister, and he hadn't returned home. But now nostalgia came to him in a wave of cold sensations. An awful feeling crept along Kaelem's skin. He opened his eyes reluctantly, slowly, hoping his surroundings wouldn't show themselves in the form he dreaded. Kaelem was gravely disappointed when his eyes were blinded by light refracting from ice. A familiar voice greeted his coming back to wakefulness. "Hello Kaelem," It said, dripping in cockiness.

"Do you watch me as I sleep or something?" he asked Bethamy.

She only smiled. "The athame please, and tell me you have souls." Kaelem nodded, and handed the knife to her. "The bodies?" Bethamy asked. Kaelem felt a jolt go through him. "I never told you, did I?" she sounded concerned. "That is my fault, I'm sorry. The excitement detached from my thinking. Apparently I gave you more credit than you deserve.

"Come. I must show you something before I send you back."

Bethamy led Kaelem down a huge corridor. At intervals large rooms spread from it. When Kaelem looked into one he was astounded; inside laid rows and rows of frozen bodies, preserved in ice. As they walked down the corridor he saw that each room stored the same contents. There must have been thousands of vessels.

"This is where we keep the bodies of the souls we take. Don't worry, we do have spare, sometimes the soul is a little, uncooperative, and certain precautions need to be done to eradicate the weak links, especially the ones which may lead to our downfall."

"What do you do with the old souls? They can't live forever, can they? Where are the souls stored after they have been removed? Why remove them at all?"

"Humans can't live in our climate, it is too cold and they would die. We want their bodies, to put the soul back into once we are ready. There is no use putting them into one of us, because our bodies wouldn't be able to stand the Earth's temperature and we don't want to have the hassle of casting spells all the time to make us immune. It is too tiring and dangerous. For these reasons we take out the human's soul using the athame and keep the soul in a special place. Somewhere the soul can't escape or move on. The bodies here are dead without their soul, so to make sure they don't decay we freeze them. Souls want to go back into something, to be something, or they will be lost. Wandering around with no purpose, the soul will try all it can to possess something. Therefore we had to come up with a solution so that they are stopped from doing this. I can't show you where they are, nor tell you how they are stopped at this moment, only I know those secrets. You never know who might find out and set them free. It's too important for our race, and the humans', to risk it."

Kaelem looked unsure.

"But don't worry. They will all be set free eventually." The statement sounded cynical, but once more Kaelem found himself agreeing to the mind of the Haukea Queen. Somehow it was the right thing to do. Somehow her reasoning was sane.

"So how do you get the souls to trust you, after all that you have done to them. Why would they want to fight for your side? And don't lie this time."

"You are right, of course we can't teach them through behaviourism. But they have seen our power, what it can do. When the soul first comes to us we put them in a Haukea's body so that they can feel the power for themselves. We show them how we can help their race evolve, and make the world better for future generations. Just like we showed you Kaelem."

"I still don't understand why they would trust you after you put them away in that place."

"They won't remember that part of their stay. You see souls go through many bodies, and once in a vessel they will only have knowledge of existing in that body. Only when they are free of a body can it have true knowledge of itself. Once the soul is put back into their human body the only thing they will have conscious knowledge of is their time spent in the Haukea's vessel. This is one reason why we chose sorcerers to put the soul into, because their power allows for the soul to remember being in it, even when they acquire another body. This is unlike human vessels, where the soul may only be vaguely aware of having a past life, or have understanding beyond their years. Anything else? Kaelem shook his head. "Remember for next time then: whenever you take a soul, ice-over its vessel and hide it. One of our sorcerers will be able to sense you freezing the body and will come to get it. They will then bring the body here. You won't have to do anything else apart from giving the athame to me."

Kaelem nodded in understanding. "I will," he consented.

"Stay here then, and wait for me to come back." Bethamy left, following the rooms ahead of them she disappeared into the distance, leaving Kaelem anxiously awaiting her return. She came back half an hour later, giving Kaelem back his athame. "Not bad.

"Now, let's see if you've been practicing your combat."

The two went to the weapons room. Bethamy chose a side-sword for herself, but offered nothing to Kaelem. She took the sword out of a black lacquered wood scabbard. A polar bear's head was engraved into the pommel, its mouth wide and fierce. The blade itself was smooth, and the steel hilt was elaborate: blue-black in colour with two arms. Bethany advanced towards Kaelem.

"Come on Kaelem. Hit me." She swung the sword round, coming closer and closer towards the boy, but Kaelem stood his ground, ready to evade her attack then quickly counter it. He leaned to the side as Bethany thrust it at his chest, then he struck out with his knee to the back of her thigh. Bethany avoided this, and before Kaelem could balance she had cut his arm. But he was accustomed to the pain she caused and had been taught not to show that he had been weakened, so he grabbed her arm with both hands without a flinch. He sensed heat rush through his body, then penetrate through his palms.

"Good Kaelem," she commented. Although she didn't like the Keahi inside of him, she wanted him to feel hate and violence towards his enemies, and use his strengths against their weaknesses. This was a perfect example of what she wanted of him. When the battle with the Keahi finally came around, he would be ready.

Kaelem took his right hand off her arm and struck her shoulder, then moved his arm round her neck and under her throat, but his left hand loosened on her arm, and she managed to cut him on the back of his leg and twist out of the burning grip around her throat. Kaelem limped slightly and pushed his elbow into her shoulder with force. Stepping round he brought her to the ground. With each frustrating blow Bethamy had given him the heat had roared more and more inside of Kaelem, and now it had spread up his whole arm. He threatened his opponent by looking her in the eye, and that was when he saw a change of light. He got to his feet quickly and kicked the two attackers behind him.

"Excellent, you remember well," she croaked. "But that is not always good enough. Be prepared for the unexpected, always." She threw her sword at Kaelem. He breathed in sharply and rolled to the floor. She smiled as the sword struck another guard behind Kaelem. Kaelem looked back at him in shock.

"What are you going to do?" Bethamy questioned.

"Is he on our side?"

Bethamy laughed at his question: it made a difference to him now. "Let's say he is. Heal him Kaelem. I want to see you heal him." Kaelem went up to the guard. He pulled the sword out and quickly placed his palms over the wound. Light emitted from his hands, and once again his energy was drained. When the man was fully healed Kaelem fell to the floor. Bethamy got up and took her sword back. She looked down at Kaelem and dug the side-sword into the ground near his head. "We need to work on that Kaelem. It's no good you being able to heal us in battle if it's going to weaken you."

"No," Kaelem replied obediently. "It isn't."

Bethamy smiled again and walked out, leaving Kaelem to clamber pathetically to his feet.

CHAPTER TWENTY-TWO

The next day Kaelem was allowed the leave the Haukeas' world. He went with new thoughts crowding his already throbbing head: the souls were okay, they were not harmed, and in the end they would aid in making the Earth a better place. But in his subconscious his father's influence was asking, '*for whom?*' However, when Kaelem saw a tall woman appear on his beach he did not hear this alien voice in his head. The woman's hair was pulled back into a loose bun, and a long skirt floated delicately round her ankles. A white halter-neck finished off the outfit, but its colour was soon to change. This woman was strong-minded; she had potential use.

***

Mya saw it happening. The ease with which Kaelem performed the act was amazing. He was stealthy and fast. He was calm; he had obviously done it before, and more than once.

She knew it was time for him to see Aka, no more people could die because of this. She now had proof that he needed help; he needed his father. There was no time to make their relationship closer, something had to be done immediately, or who knew how much further Kaelem would fall into the Haukea's world of thinking?

Mya ran as fast as she could to the woods, towards the point which was incanted, allowing Aka to be able to sense if a Keahi walked into the spot. She didn't know how he had got the sorcerer to do this, as the only people who had that type of power were the Haukea, but she knew better than to question her King.

***

The woman was too busy looking up at the cliff face to notice Kaelem draw up his athame behind her. He quickly brought it down into her back. She arched, letting out a small breath of surprise and pain, but her soul was quickly transferred inside the knife, and her vessel fell lifelessly to the ground. Kaelem put his foot on top of her; from it ice seeped out and spread across her whole body. He then turned from her and calmly waded into the sea. He washed his athame and hands. He breathed in the salty water and went further in. Soon his sister will see the advantages of what he had been asked to do.

The rain poured down. A thunderstorm was coming, stirred by the unusual heat created unknowingly by Kaelem. He put his arms up to it; treasuring the immense feeling of predominance it gave him. On the beach a Haukea was transporting the soulless body.

CHAPTER TWENTY-THREE

Kaelem entered the house on Dunmow Hill; after all that had passed he wasn't about to forget his promise to his little sister.

He heard the television when he walked through the door and so went into the living room. His stepfather was watching a low budget horror film, but there was no sign of Aolani.

"Have you seen the news lately Kaelem?" Dillon asked.

"No."

A long silence followed, becoming tenser with each loudening breath that came from Dillon. "I know what you have done." Kaelem jumped at his step-dad's sudden outburst. "Aolani shared it with me." Dillon paused, waiting for the harsh wind outside to die down so that Kaelem would be able to hear his next sentence. He continued more sympathetically; however the sympathy wasn't for Kaelem, it was for his daughter. "Don't be mad at her, she was scared, she shouldn't have to carry that burden."

Dillon watched the television screen instead of looking at Kaelem, but his stepson glared at him sharply. "I would never harm her." There was movement coming from upstairs.

"You should have stayed away Kaelem. They'll find out who did it eventually."

"And when that time comes, I will show them why I did it." There was no remorse in his voice.

"The Haukea have influenced you more than I suspected. I only hope you can realise what they are really planning before it goes too far. Your mother made the right choice in the end." Dillon finally turned to face Kaelem. "She understood, and never took another soul."

"My mum."

"She was a good woman, powerful with a strong mind. If it wasn't for Aka…"

"Aka?"

Dillon stopped himself.

"Go Kaelem, I don't want to see you again." He went back to surveying the film.

"But you don't understand." Kaelem heard a creak behind him, and looked round to see his little sister.

"Why can't anyone see?! You are all so sightless to what is happening around you."

"You are the one who has been blinded Kaelem."

Dillon's stepson screamed with frustration at his reply, and grabbed his arm. "It isn't fair why me why didn't you tell me before now who I am I would have had more time to understand it all. I hate you." Kaelem felt his hand heat up, and the element penetrated onto Dillon's arm.

"Kaelem," his sister called to him, a distant voice, scared. In a flash of lightning Kaelem turned round and saw once again the expression on her face that no longer told him she cared about her brother. But he had read it wrongly. He let Dillon go, and his step-dad collapsed, clutching the red burn that would later turn into a scar, a reminder, forever letting him know the mistake everyone had made in not telling Kaelem about his true identity.

"You need help." Aolani ran to Dillon. "He's your dad."

"No," Kaelem replied, "he's yours." He went to walk out of the house, when he turned round. He knew now that he cared too much about her, he knew that it was him who was causing her grief, and that she didn't understand why he was taking the souls. He was going to make her believe he had stopped, long enough for the reward that would come from it to be seen by her, because he knew that was the only way her hurt was going to leave her soul. Thunder screamed, Aolani's eyes widened in fear and distrust. She looked to her father for comfort, but he wasn't able to help her.

"I was here Ali," Kaelem said softly, "to protect you."

CHAPTER TWENTY-FOUR

Kaelem looked towards the girl's normal spot and waited until her shadowed form seemed comfortable. He didn't mind her staying there. In fact he wished her there, hoped that she would return each night to witness his transformation. For she was someone who knew who he was and wouldn't tell, he was certain she wouldn't betray him. There seemed to be a mutual agreement between them concerning him, signed with feigned rejection of what he was. He was glad of the unobtrusive company.

***

Mya observed that the boy now had his ear pierced, indicating that he was truly of the Haukea persuasion, yet he also had dyed his hair black. What were they trying to do, confuse the Keahi?

***

Kaelem went to the sea, but something was different, the atmosphere was tense. Then he saw her coming towards him.

For the first time Mya had left her spot. She was set-faced and her eyes were focused intently on him.

Kaelem breathed in sharply, recognising her for the first time as the girl in his form. It was the fear of the unknown that made him run - he didn't know what she was going to do to him, why she had the urge now, after all this time, to go up to him. What worried him was also the fact that she had enrolled herself into his form and was following him around. What did she want? Was she an enemy? The way she was constantly glaring at him made Kaelem anxious, perhaps she had seen him take the souls? Did she know about the Haukea? There was so much ambiguity surrounding her, and he didn't want to find out the truth for fear of his freedom and life.

The sea was calm today, despite the apprehension surrounding the world, but instead of rushing through the water Kaelem found that his feet walked on top of it. Startled, he looked down and saw that where his feet had trod the water had been turned to ice. But he had no time to waste to adapt to the feeling, the astonishment. The ice became like stepping stones, summoned under his feet, aiding him wherever he wanted to go. Kaelem looked back behind him and saw that Mya was still in pursuit. She looked in pain as she entered the water. Kaelem blinked, and she was gone. Confused, he stopped running and looked at his surroundings, paranoid of any movement. He felt his heart beating fast against his chest, fuelled with adrenaline and fear. Something came from beneath him, and suddenly the ice was gone. Kaelem dropped into the salty water and quickly made his way to the surface, conscious of anything that could be Mya.

Something swam past him and then circled him. Although he could feel the power it possessed over him - steering his relenting body to the shore- a weakness emanated from the thing that was controlling Kaelem. All the same, for now it seemed to have overcome that, driven by something with more importance, something that even Kaelem was unable to retaliate against.

He remained lying on the sand for a while, with the sea lapping gently at his feet. He tried to get his breath back, but his mission was unsuccessful. He concentrated instead on what he would do if Mya came back, and, indeed, what had happened to her. He needn't have worried about the latter part though, for before he had time to react to her sudden reappearance, Mya grabbed him. His heart rate increased once more as he tried to fight her off, but he was too weak with grief.

"Follow me if you want to be released," she growled harshly. Kaelem obeyed out of shock and cautiousness of what she could be capable of doing to him.

It was a long walk, drawn out by the fact that Kaelem had no idea where Mya was taking him. He wondered how long she had been spying on him, planning this, waiting for the chance to catch him, watching him on the beach, going to his school… how much did she know about his life? Was his sister safe?

He felt betrayed; disappointed that the pact he had thought was between them had never existed.

"Hurry up," she said, "we still have a way to go," her voice sounded cold and hateful. Kaelem shuffled along more quickly.

"Where are we going?" he dared. He could see the corner of her lips form a smile, but she didn't reply to Kaelem's question.

The sun was low as dusk settled in; the trees that now surrounded them blocked out what little light was left. Leaves rustled below their steady feet and an unseen bird rose up in silent flight. Mya looked up. The sun had left them now to light another hemisphere, and the eerie moonlight had come to be their only guide.

"We're nearly there," she whispered - not to Kaelem, to the sky. He followed her line of sight upwards.

"What?" he asked.

"You'll have to wait. You can't know now, but it will become clearer soon. The bird is here, it is guiding us. You can't see it now, but you will. You will see what is under its disguise." She paused and turned her head to look at Kaelem, her face deathly serious. "Under all of our multiple disguises. For better or worse is the important thing however." She turned her sight away from Kaelem's startled expression and back up to the sky, leaving him trying to decipher what she was seeing, and hiding her smirk. He opened his mouth to declare he wanted to know what she meant, but then realised he was suddenly alone as he moved his sight down from watching the moon. Mya had gone. A twig snapped in front of him. He strained his eyes against the darkness and saw a black shadow creeping ahead of him, small and sleek. The smell of pinecones and wet leaves rose up, making his eyes sting and senses come alive in the humid air. The shadow sat down, looked behind, then carried on stalking ahead of him, every so often looking back at Kaelem. It wanted him to follow, and he did. The girl had left him, and he wasn't about to wait around for her return in another unfamiliar place, and anyway, he didn't trust her.

They hadn't walked long before the shadow stopped. Kaelem went up close to it for the first time and saw that it was a Siamese cat. He bent down to stroke it, but it began to change shape, getting larger as Kaelem watched. When it had finished its morph Kaelem saw that it was Mya.

"This is a taste Kaelem. Don't you see it yet?"

"All I see is you manipulating me," Kaelem replied under his breath, exasperated. She looked once more at the sky. "It's nearly here, the bird that led us here has spread its wings and flown away. That means he is coming." She looked at Kaelem and smiled.

A few minutes later a burst of flames came down from the sky and landed a yard in front of them. Kaelem stepped back, but Mya, still grinning, said, "he's here."

Scared, Kaelem asked, "Who?"

Mya responded to his question with mirth, but her appearance remained treacherous, "You'll soon know Kaelem."

"I'll soon know a lot won't I?" Kaelem commented sarcastically.

Mya began to walk towards the fire. "Come on," she said, ignoring his remark. But Kaelem stood motionless. "It is alright. It's going to be okay." She kindly held out her hand to him. Kaelem swallowed his distress and took it. Mya's countenance went back to being that of resentment. The flames began to get smaller, and a man emerged from them. His face was straight as Aka greeted Kaelem, greeted his son.

"Thank you Mya, your reward will be coming soon." He faced Kaelem. "Brace yourself: the first time can be a bit dizzying."

"What -" Kaelem didn't have time to complete his sentence before he was engulfed in fire. He closed his eyes, but it did not help him as he was suddenly lifted into the air and feeling as though he was flying through the sky. He felt a pleasant warmth surround him, and peeked a look, only to witness a blaze of fire covering his whole body, moving furiously in the force of the wind, spikes of flame licking his face. He quickly closed his eyes against the sting of the wind and the panic of what was going on.

It seemed like too long a time passed before he had the sensation of slowing down, and the wind finally gave up hounding him. He waited until his feet touched solid ground before opening his eyes. When he did he was glad to discern the fire around him had disappeared, but his eyes refused to focus on the environment. Nauseous and disorientated Kaelem tried to walk. His legs felt like jelly, and the world span before him so fast he collapsed, clutching his stomach. Someone put his hand on his shoulder and Kaelem tensed, expecting a coldness that brought inevitable sleep. But the contrary happened: he suddenly felt much better, and the airsickness seemed to have left, though a dizzy spell overtook him as he sat up.

"Welcome home Kaelem. You are safe." The voice was deep, comforting; somehow familiar. "Come," the voice said, "we need to introduce you."

Kaelem studied the man: he had black hair and tanned skin, he was tall, and smiling with emotion. Tears seemed to prick his eyes. Kaelem knew he had seen the face before, and recently, but he didn't know where from. Perhaps the man had been spying on him and he had subconsciously seen him on the street?

"Who are you?" Kaelem asked. The man looked away.

"You do not know how complicated the answer to that question is Kaelem. For you."

"I'm sick of everyone keeping secrets from me. Tell me what's going on. Tell me who I am!"

Aka looked back at his son, startled. "I am so sorry Kaelem, for having kept all this from you, for everything you have had to find out about your identity. But it was for your safety, believe me, we thought it was for the best. But we were wrong. We *are* wrong. It is all my fault, I will not deny that. I should never have been so selfish. I promise Kaelem, that you will know everything eventually. For now, however, I have to introduce you to the Keahi."

"Keahi? No! I don't want to. I can't. You're evil."

"We are evil? Really. And taking souls is not?" Kaelem glared at the man. He didn't say anything back. Instead Aka lead his son into a series of endless caves, extending off in multiple directions. Kaelem followed unconsciously, not realising he was being taken anywhere. They reached a dead end. The man said something, and the wall became double doors. The man took Kaelem's arm and led him through, to welcome a crowd of waiting and smiling faces. Kaelem looked behind him to see the doors slowly closing. Beyond them was darkness.

Kaelem contemplated the faces around him. The Haukea had always been scared of him, of his capabilities; the Keahi seemed intrigued. Kaelem didn't know why, but he felt safer with these people than he had ever been with the Haukea, even though they gave off a much more powerful presence and were also, supposedly, 'evil'.

Each time Aka saw his son he thought of the boy's mother, how neither were aware how close they were to one another. He would reunite them, but not now. Now Kaelem had to work to regain his fire skill, whatever that could be. He had shown little sign of it as a baby, only his immunity with burns and extreme heat. Unless that was the extent of his abilities. Not all Keahi were privileged enough to have active powers, as not all Haukea were, including their Queen. This led Aka to thinking about the Haukea side to his son: had he learnt his power? What was it? What had the Haukea poisoned his mind with already? Their hate for the Keahi was already shown through him, by the way Kaelem had reacted once Aka had told him who they were. But what about the humans? The Haukea had already included him in their plans, the fact that he had taken souls proved this. A half-breed is a powerful asset to have. Maybe he was a threat being here. If he was then Keahi powers may not be able to stop him. He hoped they had not made Kaelem a warrior. The questions and worries flittered through Aka's mind as he took hold of his son's hand, trying to suppress the nostalgic sensations of a more innocent time that were sure to cloud the judgement of his actions, and showed him to his room. "It is Mya's party. I will let you relax first before I hand to you the pressure of having to socialise with the other Keahi."

Kaelem was reluctant to go with him, but decided it was better than staying here in a room full of the enemy, rather than the company of one, who Kaelem didn't sense as being a stranger at all.

The room they entered was quite large, and painted in different hues of reds and oranges. It was more lively and homely than the one he had stayed in on Hau Houna. He felt he could belong here, as if he wasn't an outsider intruding on their lives. He didn't sense he was so vulnerable - not hated or watched because he was dangerous. *No*, he thought, *they're doing this to entice me. I can't give in; they want my world destroyed.*

The place was hot and furnished with comfortable chairs, a bed, and a wardrobe. As he went inside he saw it also included an ensuite shower.

"I hope you like it. I need to go now, but I will come back soon." *Whether he wants me to or not*, Aka thought. "Try to settle in," he added. Aka then left.

Kaelem heard the door closing, yet he didn't hear it locking. He got up and slowly pulled the handle. The door opened. He pulled it wider and put his head outside the door, but seeing Keahi walking casually down the corridor, he closed the door quickly, not ready to face them yet, not knowing what they could do. He went to 'his' bed and slumped down, wondering what he was doing here and wanting once again to go home. "How long will it be this time?" he asked himself.

***

"He is here Lily-Flower."

She smiled at this news. At last: something good. "Really. Can I see him now?" She sounded the happiest she had been for too long a time.

"Later. When he has settled in. I promise then that you will see him."

Her smile widened. "Thank you Aka."

"He has seen the Haukea."

Her smile faded. "You sensed him then."

Aka nodded. "Your boyfriend hid him well."

"This is my fault. I got scared when you left, I felt unsafe; you weren't there to protect me anymore. The Haukea came to collect his power, I had no other choice. They are capable of horrendous things Aka, if anything had happened to me, then there would have been no way of protecting Kaelem from their twisted thinking. That's why I left his powers in the hands of the Haukea. But I guess it didn't work, they still managed to take him, to use him." A strain came upon Lily-Anna's eyes, as if tears were trying to fall, but had evaporated.

Aka shook his head. "It was an accident Flower, I was never meant to fall in love with you," he touched his scar, "but some things aren't supposed to leave you. I shouldn't have taken you, not with Kaelem so vulnerable without your guidance. I was ignorant, I had lost faith in you, and for that I am deeply sorrowful. You never lied to me, I should have trusted your decisions and believed in your redeemed soul." He paused, then after reflection he changed his tone to fit with the next bit of news for his wife, so that the sentimentality towards their son wouldn't shroud the truth of what had happened to him - what he was doing willingly - and they could think practically of how to deal with the situation, "Mya informs me that Kaelem has already taken souls. We are not sure how many yet, but she said he doesn't seem bothered about it. Try to get through to him Flower, for I do not know how to stop it."

Lily-Anna's eyes focused on the floor. "I do." she spoke silently; bitterly.

"How?" Aka asked.

"I guess, to save Kaelem from this, and to save others from losing their lives, to save hundreds from grief, sadness and fear, it has to be done." She looked up at Aka's face. But it isn't easy. It involves the death of someone close to him."

Confusion swept Aka's features. Lily-Anna sighed. "The only way to stop a Haukea from taking souls is to make them realise that it doesn't matter what the outcome may be, what they are doing causes pain for those close to the soul. Once the Haukea has felt what it is like for the friends and family of the people whose soul is taken they will see the truth and won't be able to take another. They will then be more open to understanding that the Haukea are evil; that if they're already willing to cause this much grief to individuals they will have little conscience for turning the humans into slaves. I had hoped that Kaelem would sympathise with the souls in the vein that the soul he takes never gave consent to be involved in this, but unfortunately this connection doesn't seem to have happened; I guess he is trying desperately to prove he is still human and will do anything to save the race. I am trying to work through how to use this to save his soul, but the Haukea are clever with their words."

Aka was scared, but he knew he had to remain composed. "So. If nothing else works we, have to, kill Kaelem. We have to kill our son?"

"No. Not him necessarily. If he is to be redeemed, someone close to him has to die. He will feel the pain that he has caused in others, and see the truth." Lily-Anna swallowed, disgusted at what was coming out of her mouth.

"So. I will set your soul free, then he will be cured!"

She shook her head. "He has to have deep feelings about that person - he hates me remember? Even if he did love me, he hasn't known me long enough. He may be sad, but it will come from the wrong place in his heart, it won't have the regret of past promises never to be fulfilled, of a future that was once so strong, so bright, falling down into the dark abyss of oblivion. His regret will come from that which was never born, a relationship never founded, but it won't be enough to make a connection between that sadness and the huge hole that forms when someone you have known all you life, or love so much you would die for them…suddenly leaves you."

There was silence. Aka knew she was talking about him. He wanted to say sorry, but she had heard him say that word so many times it no longer meant anything to her. He needed to show her something else, something from his soul, spontaneous and special. But nothing would do. He would never regain the one thing he craved so much for, her trust, her love. Her.

"I have met other Haukea like me. They said that they too fell in love with a human they were meant to take the soul of. When they refused Haukea came and did it for them. They said from then on they haven't been able to take another. It wasn't the love for a human, because while they were with them they still took souls," she paused for a second, "and so did I."

Aka felt sick, but he tried not to be fazed by the information. "But what about us? I did not die."

When Lily-Anna next looked up at him he saw tears forming in her eyes. "Didn't you?" she asked regretfully. "Because to me it felt like you did. When I saw who you were, and that we could never be together, see each other again - it wasn't just that. I was beginning to go against them before you went. There was one difference between me, and Haukea like me: I'd had a child which I thought was human. I couldn't bare the thought they would take him, if he ever grew up to be strong or smart, or anything they could manipulate. It's not right, Aka, to deprive

152

people of loved ones whom mean more to them than the world. It isn't right to control someone else's destiny."

Aka nodded. "It is okay Lily-Flower."

They sat in silent thought. Lily-Anna was the first to speak again, "Are you going to teach Kaelem his fire power?" There was even a hint of excitement in her voice.

"Is it safe? What if he uses it for the wrong purposes?"

"It is more dangerous not to, especially if he can't control it or understand it. It may come out of him, and he might not have the ability to stop it." She stood up. "Show it to him Aka. He deserves to know his full potential. He has been in the dark about it for such a long time, with no knowledge of who he is - look where it got him. It is our fault. I should have spoken to Kaelem long before it got this far, before he got his powers back."

Aka smiled. "I love you." He knew he wouldn't get a response form the statement, but he couldn't help how he felt about her. He left after that, embarrassed, sadly knowing she no longer felt the same way towards him. As he closed the door Lily-Anna ran up to it and put her ear to the wall, listening to his careful footsteps fade away. She sighed: how did they ever get like this?

"Good luck Aka," she whispered.

CHAPTER TWENTY-FIVE

Aka knocked on the door. When it became obvious there would be no answer he casually opened it, yet a pang of sadness went through him, for Kaelem was sitting on the bed, back straight and eyes glazed over, staring at a stain on the wall. A single candle burned somnolently, as if taking on the characteristics of his son's mood. Kaelem's eyes widened when Aka stepped into the room and the flame brightened.

"It is okay Kaelem," Aka tried to reassure. As he sat next to his son Lily-Anna's words echoed through his mind: *No more secrets.*

Shadows flickered over their faces from the candle's flame. Orange colours coated everything surrounding it. Familiarity swept through Kaelem, reminding him of home: a place where he hadn't been for a long time. But this amber was brighter, it was alive. It glinted off Kaelem's earrings and into Aka's eyes. The Haukea thought him one of them now. Aka sighed, for he knew his son belonged to no-one. He was unique, and utterly alone.

"Do you - know who I am?" Aka asked his son.

"The Keahi's King: an evil leader whose interference will destroy my planet. I want to be released from here. I can't stay, you're going to manipulate me, and put Earth in jeopardy." Kaelem choked, suddenly remembering with fear what the Haukea had told him about what his relationship was to the Keahi's King. He looked at the man sitting beside him closely, trying to get into the right position so that the candlelight wouldn't shadow features that may mirror his own. "I want to go home now," Kaelem stated angrily. He stamped as far away from Aka as was possible in the vain hope he would not be spoken to, so that perhaps he would hear nothing more about these strange lands that he didn't ask to know about - having a similar experience to that with the Haukea was something he would not repeat willingly.

The flame from the candle seemed to rise up with frustration, swaying in the direction Kaelem walked.

"I can help you Kaelem. I can show you how to control the fire."

Kaelem's resentment paused, and in response the flame became smaller. "Promise me," Kaelem said desperately. "Look me in the eye and promise me that after this you will take me home." He wouldn't take any more chances when it came to his freedom.

Aka got off the bed and put his son's head in his hands, holding it in the light. "I promise," he answered sincerely. The immediate relaxation in Kaelem was obvious, and the flame straightened. Yet distance and distrust still gleamed in Kaelem's eyes and voice. *What did they do to you Kaelem?* Aka meditated.

"How do I control it?" Kaelem asked bluntly.

Aka suppressed a regretful laugh. "It will not be easy. You will have to work hard, practice. It may be frightening at first, I am not teaching you how to lock it up within you, I am showing you ways in which you can use the power to…"

"No," Kaelem suddenly interrupted. "I can't. You are like them, you're brainwashing me, making me do harmful things. I only want to control the fire, I want nothing to do with your personal vendettas."

Aka flinched slightly, embarrassed that Kaelem was comparing his support to the Haukea's motives, but the anger that had been brewing was soon calmed; he reminded himself that Kaelem was ignorant of the whole truth, and that this was his only chance of leading his son towards a more tolerant place where he could use his powers guilt-free to help people. "Kaelem, it is all right, I will not make you do anything for us. All I want is to help you control your gift. If you wish I can bind it, but wait and see, weigh up both the consequences and the importance of what can be achieved and destroyed with your power. This is not for my gain, but for yours. Are you ready to handle this responsibility? Do you want what it means to be in charge of something so powerful for the existence of life?"

Seeing the sincerity in his father's face Kaelem nodded. This man wasn't like the Haukea, he was softer, kinder, perhaps he was being tactful, but for once Kaelem had been given a choice to opt out, and this filled him with assurance.

"When would you like to start?" Aka wanted Kaelem to feel at ease, that they were doing this at a pace which suited him. He wanted his son to be proud of what he was - whatever that could be - but he suddenly felt anxious: did his power work differently due to what he was? Kaelem had never had the chance to show any development of his abilities from either side of his heritage.

Kaelem wasn't concerned, he had seen what he could unleash, and he grew excited at the prospect of obtaining control over himself again. "Now," Kaelem stated, knowing what the power could do, understanding that if he learned how to be in command of it, then an incident similar to that in the throne room could be avoided.

"Embrace it then. It is a gift if used rightly, a curse if you do not understand it." Aka thought of the Keahi in the dungeon, Kaelem thought of the Haukea.

"You can stay here if you feel more comfortable. You will not have to leave this room, okay? Do not worry Kaelem, nothing can harm you here." The tone was steadying and comforting; it was serious and full of love and protection.

"We are going to start small, figure out what it can do. Different people show their fire in different forms. I guess you saw this variety in power from being with the Haukea."

"I know what it is." Kaelem looked at his hands. A sudden flashback of fire bursting from them invaded his mind. He shuddered.

"Go on," Aka said.

"It came out of me. It - It took over and wouldn't go back." He looked up at Aka's face, troubled. "The feeling of power was extraordinary. More than what I experienced from my Haukea inheritance. But then it became frightening. I hurt people with it, and I didn't want to. Not like that anyway."

Aka smiled to reassure him, and breathed deeply to make his voice relax. "It is okay Kaelem. This is why I am teaching you, so that things like that do not happen again." He paused, then continued, "Where did the fire come from?"

"I made...My hands." He looked subconsciously back down at them again.

Aka beamed. "This is good. I can help you more, for that is where my power is rooted from. Do not panic if this does not work, you may need to find your own technique to control the fire. Can you conjure the flame for me? Nothing can be harmed here. Whether nothing materialises, or the fire screams out of control, you are safe. We are all safe." He picked up the candle and gave it to Kaelem.

"Look at the flame melting the wax. Imagine it burning inside of you. Then think of the fire rising to your surface, your blood boiling, your skin bubbling, until it becomes so pressurised that the fire explodes from your hands. If you want it to cease, just clutch your hand."

After an awkward silence where Kaelem just stared at Aka from the corner of his eye, too embarrassed to move, Aka stood. "Perhaps it will be easier to concentrate without me here." He walked out, a hint of happiness in his tone, anticipation roasting within.

Kaelem didn't move for a while, but with uncertain movements he eventually picked up the candle that Aka had left beside him. Kaelem placed it on the desk that stood in front of the bed. He stared at the flame for a couple of minutes, until his vision blurred the flame, making it seem like rays of light were shinning from it in multiple directions, just as the summer sun catches the blue water so perfectly it sparkles like diamonds. Kaelem sighed at the thought of the sea, the salty air. He longed for it. The flame suddenly came alive, emitting spikes of light as Kaelem faded into a trance. He closed his eyes and concentrated on the beautiful flame he could see in the darkness of his eyelids, and felt his hand begin to heat up. Excited, scared, Kaelem opened his eyes, only to be granted disappointment as his hand went cold. He rested on his bed, hypnotised by the smoky atmosphere and the solitary glow. His eyelids became heavy and he dozed off in to a frustrated sleep.

When Aka came in Kaelem was asleep. Blackness engulfed his son, created by the thick curtains that kept out the light, coming from the endlessly luminous sky. With four suns surrounding their planet it was unthinkable for Aki Houna not to be bright, yet the dark had come from the candle being extinguished, most likely this was due to Kaelem, but his son wasn't to realise that.

A ball of fire materialised in the dark, getting bigger and bigger. A body appeared next to it: Aka's body, holding the fire. Sparks suddenly flew from the ball, accelerating in different directions. Each purposefully lit one of the numerous candles in the room, which so far tonight had been left cold. "Provided you did not inherit my curse, I cannot wait until you show your full potential." Aka shook Kaelem awake. "I will show you an exercise that may help the fire come out," he said softly.

Aka left the room again after he had given his son the instructions, and Kaelem tried the technique.

To help him Aka had left the candles alight. Gothic metal played in the background to help Kaelem's emotion bring out his extraordinary power.

As Kaelem was sitting on the bed he thought of Aka's words about the flame burning inside of him. He just had to coax it out.

His right leg was positioned in front of his left, with his knees touching the bed linen in a crossed position. Kaelem's hands rested on his legs, crossed right over left, with palms facing upwards, his fingers outstretched. Kaelem looked down at his hands, curled his spine so he was bent over them and concentrated intently on what he was doing. His eyes closed as he blocked out all sounds except for the metal music playing in time with his mood.

Kaelem's back straightened as he softly lifted his arms, keeping his hands in the same position until they were in front of his face. Then he lifted his chin. He brought his hands in against his chest and folded his fingers into fists, trying to contain the heat. Then, simultaneously, his left arm stretched forwards as his right went back. He opened his eyes, looking down his right arm line. When it was nearly fully extended Kaelem moved his head to stare at the back of his left flexed hand, and unfolded his fingers.

It took all of his energy to heat up his hand, but once it came it grew into an extreme warmth, like fire. His whole arm trembled from the pressure, creating the sensation that he was about to explode. Kaelem concentrated hard, staring at the back of his arm, his whole body now shaking and his arms hurting, but still he was determined to prove to himself what he could do. What he could control. Suddenly his left hand shot fire, like lava, although his right did not; nevertheless he was too amazed to see the blaze come from him to care about that now. Still, the pressure had finally become too high so he clutched his fist to stop the flame, and collapsed from exhaustion and pain, his legs remaining in the same position as from the start of the exercise, his arms folding underneath his head as a pillow. Aka walked into the room and up to the boy, whispering, "Well done."

CHAPTER TWENTY-SIX

Aka picked up his son and carried him down to the cells. He walked with Kaelem in his arms, until reaching the most frequently used door in this part of the palace, then gently put Kaelem on the floor and unlocked the room. Lifting Kaelem back up they went inside. Upon entry Aka put on the thermal clothing as usual, knowing another set was unnecessary for Kaelem. His son did not need that kind of protection.

The woman in the chair turned round, and when she saw Kaelem's limp body in his father's arms she expected the worse. Pulling in a deep breath she rushed to her son.

"He is not dead. Just exhausted," Aka explained.

Lily-Anna glanced up at Aka gratefully before concentrating on her son. She stroked the hair out of Kaelem's face and stared at him in silence. A peacefulness seemed to emanate from Kaelem's body, making Lily-Anna's fears for him subside for a little while. "Sorry. It's just that I haven't seen him in person in such a … long time," Lily-Anna commented, her voice soft and relaxed.

"I know how you feel." They shared a look, knowing why he said it and it hurt her. "I did not mean…"

"You are the one who told me to bind his powers. That day you scared me, I was insecure. You are King of the Keahi, and our

161

son a potentially indestructible force. The power you could posses over the Haukea… it was too much to even think about. I may not believe in the monarchy's cause, but they are still my people."

Aka laid Kaelem down on top of Lily-Anna's bed of ice. Kaelem's face was suddenly troubled as his parents looked down affectionately at him.

"You do not need to explain yourself. I am sorry, I do not criticise your judgment; it was the right thing to do."

"What's going to happen now?" Lily-Anna asked, the worry coming back to her.

"I am going to take him back to Earth. He belongs there, all his friends and everything he knows is there. It would not be fair to drag him away from all that. He has been protesting to me to take him home."

"But what about his powers? At the moment he is around people similar to him, who know what he can do, it is no secret, but when he goes home there will be no one to sympathise with, no one that understands his true power."

Aka sighed at Lily-Anna's rant. "Yes, but here he may use his Haukea element against us to force us to take him home. I am granting him his wish out of fear Lily-Flower. You are right: he is too powerful."

"And he won't be on Earth?" Lily-Anna laughed, exasperated.

"Please Flower. I think this is the best thing we can do. The safest thing for him. I will keep a close watch on Kaelem to make sure that he is all right, that he will be of no threat to anyone. But honestly I think he will be healthier where he wants to be."

Lily-Anna nodded. "Can I say good bye to him first? I don't know if I will ever see him again." She broke down into tears when she saw her serene son. Aka went to her.

"Of course," he said softly. "Later I will leave you two alone together. You can speak to Kaelem with no interference from me."

Lily-Anna smiled through her tears. Her shoulders relaxed; her smile lit up her face. Aka hadn't seen her this happy since she first held Kaelem in her arms. "Thank you Aka. Thank you. I-I think that – after…he should see both of us, talk to us. Together."

"I would like that. And I hope Kaelem will too."

Lily-Anna continued to smile. Aka tried to hold back the strong feeling of love he felt for her. She looked so beautiful when she beamed like that. A sun of relentless fire coming from a place where only the coldest of winters rested.

"I will take Kaelem to you when it is time for him to leave. He still has not found his true potential for his power and he needs more time to control it. You will see him again." Aka picked Kaelem up and went out of the room as Lily-Anna watched, through tearful eyes, her son being taken away from her once again. "Bye," she whispered to Kaelem, and shuddered.

Aka walked to Kaelem's room and put him gently on his bed. He smiled at his son. "You can go home soon Kaelem. My promises are never in vain." He left the room before Kaelem regained consciousness.

Later, Kaelem sat up on the bed and put his head in his hands. Tears streaked his face. He had been caught again. Would there be another two-year gap until he saw his family and friends again? What were the Keahi going to do to him? He wanted to go home. He went to his window and opened the curtains. An incandescent light filtered through. At first all he could see was a barren wasteland, but as Kaelem's eyes adjusted he saw what the landscape really beheld. Even though it was dry and dusty he could see small patches of cold blue flowers. He unfastened his window, surprised to find that it could open far enough for him to escape through onto the infinite field. This was something at least; it was a refreshing thought that he had made it to a place where he wasn't controlled or followed.

The colourful blooms of flowers were easy to see in the otherwise baked earth, their stems struggling out from cracks, reaching towards the light from a dark abyss. As he went up to one patch of flowers a strange sensation crawled over his skin. The blue was mingled with orange and red. The flowers were tiny. Kaelem bent to touch the delicate miniscule petals. They felt cold, yet when his fingers brushed the red coloured petals a severe heat washed over them.

"I would be grateful if you did not tell anyone." Kaelem turned at the familiar deep voice. "These flowers are not supposed to grow here. Lily-Anna cast a spell on them, so that they could thrive. They were planted in her memory. I added the others to show our unity." He pointed to the orange and red petals." Other Keahi do not have access, or indeed a view, to this part of the palace. You and I are the only ones who have the privilege. I am hoping however that once the two races do become one again, whoever is leading the Keahi at that time can open up this land to everyone. It is so beautiful."

"I wish I had met my mother. I don't remember much of her. She was taken away before I could capture many memories, and we have no photographs of her."

Aka kept silent. He bent down to look at the flowers with Kaelem, then spoke, "Just because someone is gone from the land of the living, does not mean that they are dead." Kaelem looked round at his father.

"Come on," Aka said, "it is going to be a tough day tomorrow if you are soon to see your home. The more you practice, the sooner you will learn your power, and the closer home will be for you."

Kaelem followed Aka away from the flowers and back inside the palace.

CHAPTER TWENTY-SEVEN

The training sessions were going well. Kaelem knew he was handling his powers better now for he guided the fire with more control than he previously thought possible. He was able to conjure up the flames with just a single command, sent from his brain to his hand. Aka was noticing the difference in Kaelem's confidence too; he saw that his son was more relaxed with his abilities, now that he understood them. But he sensed both a sadness and a longing in Kaelem. He saw it in his son's eyes, and it broke his heart. He knew Kaelem would never, could never, see this world as his home, and Aka knew deep down that Kaelem was right in his thinking.

Aka walked into Kaelem's room smiling. "Hello Kaelem." His son greeted him back with a noise from his throat. "Would you like to go for a walk? Get out for a bit?" Kaelem nodded and followed his father outside. It felt good to be out of the binding walls of the palace.

Aka led Kaelem to the field, but his father took him further away from the palace than Kaelem had ever dared to go, and still they kept on travelling, engulfed in silence until the palace was only a shadow on the fiery horizon.

"I thought we could do some work out here for a change, to get you used to having to summon your power in different surroundings and other situations. You can become too comfortable with

continuity that you forget even the basics when it comes down
to a real circumstance; your body switches to autopilot, but when
the time surprises you there will be a lot more pressure, a lot
more to worry about in terms of being wary of what is going on
around you, and you may have nothing, not even time, to guide
you through your life-or-death decisions." The two sat opposite
each other. Aka closed his eyes and breathed in the outside heat,
leaving his son to contemplate and absorb this for a second.

I love it here, Aka thought. *It is so peaceful, so fresh. You can be
yourself out here. Free. No one asks anything of you. No one expects
you to save the world. It never gets dark here.*

Kaelem leaned back as fire engulfed Aka's body. A moment later
the flames sucked themselves back inside their vessel. Aka looked
up at the bright sky, Kaelem followed his gaze.

"We have four suns surrounding our world Kaelem. Four suns
to build our energy from, unlimited power and protection." Aka
paused, his features crinkled as if in hate, then his face smoothed
and, as if coming out of a trance-like state, said, "Let us start."
Kaelem looked back at his father. "First: conjure your fire."

Without hesitation Kaelem stretched out his left hand, and flames
burst from it.

"Good. Now try moving the flame ball towards me. Use your
mind, your connection to the fire. This is only a test. Some
people do not have telekinetic abilities over their powers, but you
may have the potential."

Kaelem stared at the ball of fire in his hand, concentrating hard,
focusing all of his energy into moving it. The flame flickered,
but the mass stayed in the same spot. Kaelem tried again, but to
no avail. He growled in frustration and threw the ball physically
instead. It flew through the air, creating a graceful arc of sparks
as it landed a hundred yards from where they sat.

"Kaelem. It is okay, do not worry. It will take time. Remember your first struggles to even summon the fire? Look at how far that has evolved. I can feel your power, your determination. One day you will be able to do things you never imagined possible. And I know that it will not be long until you can go home." Aka stood up. "I think we will leave other techniques for today. Practice Kaelem, and you will be able to progress onto higher things soon. You can do whatever you like for the rest of the day." Aka strode away from Kaelem, away from his palace. He looked once again up at the yellow sky as he wandered alone. "No. It never gets dark out here." He sighed. "But what will happen when Lily-Anna's light goes out forever? What will I do then? How can I cope with only half a soul left, a son committing the acts of the Haukea, and a deceased wife? This is not how it is supposed to be." He lay down on the scorched earth, one of the suns beating directly down upon him as he continued to marvel up at it. He reminisced over the good times he had spent with her, and how they escalated to a new high when their son was born. Then he saw them collapse in misery on that fateful day his father had died, setting of a chain reaction in which the Haukea came to destroy his and Lily-Anna's marriage. A tear clambered out of his eye and sizzled on the hot earth. Aka blinked. *Some rulers do not deserve the power our sky gives us. Some deserve the flame to extinguish.*

"It should never have happened in the first place Flower. I am so sorry." He sat up suddenly and clutched his stomach in grief. "I do not want you to leave me, and you never will. I will let you go Flower, I will not keep you waiting much longer for your release." Aka got to his feet, composed himself, and went reluctantly back to his palace and his duties as King.

***

Kaelem stayed where he was as he watched his father leave him. He then summoned the fire again, but as hard as he tried he

168

couldn't get it to travel. It just wavered on the spot, seeming to contemplate movement, but not bothering to do as it was told. Kaelem clenched his fist and the fire went out. He stood, making to go back to the palace, but thought against it and decided to traipse around the field instead. His father's words echoed round his head: *he could be himself out here. No worries.*

Kaelem sang to himself as he began to relax for the first time in ages. The lyrics were to a song he remembered liking as a child, they made him feel a bit happier. He spread his arms out, embracing the wide space surrounding him, his fingers stretching to their farthest limit as heat flowed through them. He smiled.

It was a long time before he made himself go back to the uncomfortable palace - his need for water was urgent.

Aka was in the entrance hall when Kaelem arrived, he was conversing with a group of serious-looking Keahi.

"I'm just going to take a bath," Kaelem stated, feeling depressed now he was back within confined spaces.

"Dinner will be ready in an hour," Aka replied. Kaelem nodded and went to his room. He closed the door and savoured the silence. Running hot water into the bath he breathed in the steam arising from it. He cupped his hands and dipped them in, capturing some water, liking the sensation as it trickled delicately through his fingers when he lifted them out of the tub. He threw what was left onto his face and felt bliss when the hot water touched his skin, making his senses come alive. Droplets made ripples in the clear water. He changed his form, noticing that the pain which once dominated his transformation had now subsided to mere twinges running through his body. Kaelem sunk down below the surface, loving the feeling of the water, wanting to stay underneath it forever. He imagined himself in the sea, the invigorating sensation of swimming fast and knowing he didn't have to stop. He missed this almost as much as home.

Forty-five minutes later he climbed out of the bath and got ready to eat with the King.

As he walked down the corridor someone called to him. He looked to where the voice was coming from, already knowing that it belonged to Xalvadora, a thirteen-year-old Keahi. She was sweet and innocent, and her features highlighted this. Although her face was rounded she had a slim figure and large, balmy eyes. He smiled at her. She had soon become the only one who he felt comfortable around, and what was even more amazing was that he knew the feeling was mutual. The other Keahi were wary of him, although not afraid, they just preferred to keep their distance. Kaelem could sense their eyes wandering to his earrings, the mark of their enemy, whenever they met him. They distrusted Kaelem because of this correlation to the Haukea. Oringo was the only other exception, but he became annoying after a while, always questioning Kaelem about his background, his powers, what it was like. It became exhausting and distressing. Kaelem tried hard not to even think about these things; therefore he tended to keep out of Oringo's way as much as possible without seeming rude.

"Where are you going? " Xalvadora asked.

"To have dinner. What about you?"

"Just wandering around. I'm bored."

"I'll come to see you when I've finished eating then. If that's okay?"

She brightened up at this, even though she tried to hide it. "Okay."

They walked apart. Kaelem became happier too that he had something to do after supper. He normally stayed in his room, alone and tired. He desperately needed something to keep his mind off things, and Xalvadora always made him feel at peace.

CHAPTER TWENTY-EIGHT

The dinner was like every other meal in the palace: it was eaten in a huge room that contained a long table and a lot of people. Kaelem always felt uncomfortable in the presence of these Keahi, and the feeling was mutual and obvious. These dinners were never a nice experience. The atmosphere was filled with tension and avoidance. He guessed his father forced these events upon them to get everyone used to each other. It wasn't working. It was like a formal gathering everyday, and Kaelem just wished it was over, or that he could take his meal to eat elsewhere. Nevertheless, nothing he could do would stop this assembly.

The food came: huge platters of rice, lentils and pulses, simmering in sauces and served with steaming vegetables. Kaelem sighed, feeling sick. "Don't you have any fish?" It was an innocent enough query as this seemed to be the only thing he could digest now. But there was a great shuffle as the whole hall looked in his direction with repulsion on their faces. The comment lay in the air until slowly people went back to their meal, but they now acted as if the food and forced conversation had been tainted. Kaelem lent in towards his father, deciding it was better to whisper his questions to him alone. "So there's no seafood then?"

"Kaelem, I am sorry you feel the need to…"

"Yes, you're right, I do seem to have an unplenishable appetite for seafood. Maybe you can tell me why?!" He stared at his father,

171

and after a few moments of silence in which his father didn't seem to acknowledge his outburst Kaelem rose from his chair and left the room.

Aka breathed the guilt out of his system - now was not the time to show weakness. *I should never have allowed myself to become so attached to Lily-Anna. It was an idiotic move that has put my whole race in jeopardy. I should have thought about my people first.*

Aka couldn't hide a slight jump when his eyes fell upon Oringo, standing in the doorway Kaelem had left open. He wasn't invited to these events. Oringo came up to Aka and whispered in the King's ear, "We can't help who we are attracted to Aka."

His eyes widened - had he said his thoughts out loud? "Sometimes we must let go of things we love Oringo, for the good of the masses." Oringo stood, a thoughtful and distressed expression on his face. "Is something the matter Oringo?"

Oringo jumped, not realising his emotions had seeped onto his features. A smile formed and he shook his head. "No. I just don't like the thought of sacrifice." Oringo exited the hall without a continuation of the conversation, closing the door as he departed.

***

Kaelem made his way to Xalvadora's room. When he knocked on her door he heard a quick scuffling coming from the other side, then the door was flung open. Although Xalvadora appeared flushed, she had obviously made an effort with her appearance, whilst trying to appear casual and at ease. Her black hair fell just above her shoulders in spirals, her slim lips shone a pale red, and her orange eyes glowed with warmth and anticipation. Kaelem could see himself reflected in them.

The room in which Kaelem entered was slightly smaller than his own, however it compensated by being much more personal. It was hers. It had always been hers. Art was spread across the walls - some if which Xalvadora had created - dancers of different shapes and sizes in multiple positions. Some danced solitary, sad and lonely; lively and celebratory, others were dancing in couples, leaping across the page, or twisting and intertwining in each others' presence. Some were abstract pieces that other Keahi had done for her. He looked around in wonder at all the colours and shapes, it made the room seem alive, and beautiful.

"They're amazing," he told her.

She appeared to blush at his compliment, her already red cheeks glowing even brighter. "Thanks." She watched Kaelem as he walked around the room; saw his expression was genuine about her art. She went closer to him, uncomfortably close. Kaelem sat down on a chair, and she took another seat, putting it next to his. She then leaned towards him. Kaelem moved away sharply, causing the chair to tip with the sudden motion, and it fell with an awkward clang. "What are you doing?" he asked.

Xalvadora wavered. "Sorry. I… Sorry." She stood up and went to her window, looking away from him.

"I can't," Kaelem said, "I do not have feelings for you in that way."

"Who do you love?" she asked gently, sadly.

"Pardon?"

"There must be somebody who you have left a hole in your soul for. Please. I want to know…what she's like."

"I don't know. I haven't even met her yet. I haven't even said 'hello' to her. It's probably only a stupid crush."

Xalvadora turned towards him, to show she was listening.

"I guess I'm too afraid to speak to her, what if she hates me? What if I say the wrong thing and offend her. What if she says nothing back?"

She reached out to touch his face, but Kaelem flinched back.

"I'm not trying anything Kaelem, I am just a friend trying to comfort you."

"Oh, Xalvadora, I'm sorry, it's not you I'm shying away from, I'm saving you. Trust me, you don't want to know what my skin feels like." Xalvadora smiled and held her palm up, then proceeded to make contact with his face. This time he let her: he had warned her.

"It's so cool, so smooth, it almost shimmers."

"Like a fish's scale," he replied nervously. She smiled again, confusion sweeping over her eyes, yet her fingers continued to gently stroke Kaelem's skin. "Stop. You don't know what it means, and until you do you can't touch it. You may not want to, it may destroy you."

"Kaelem I -"

"If you're so entranced by me, maybe this will change your mind, then you can understand why everyone treats me the way they do!"

"Your earrings? I know where you are from Kaelem."

"But do you know the reality of it?" He lifted his foot, and took her hand, pressing it to the sole. She cringed when she felt the freezing cold penetrate into her palm. She took it from Kaelem's grip, and clutched it.

"I know what it means, that you are part Haukea, that you are the enemy, and I don't care." Her eyes shone with determination and truth.

Kaelem breathed out and collapsed onto her bed. "I'm sorry Xalvadora."

"I may not understand what you are going through, but I want to help. I believe in you." her voice was soft and genuine.

They talked for the rest of the evening. It was good. The events that had preceded this seemed to be wiped away, and for once Kaelem was with someone who had no other alternate motive than to simply be with him for company, a feeling that was much missed since Jeb had gone from his life. But what made this even more special was that there was no secrecy: she knew what his capabilities were, she knew that he was a potential danger to her, yet there was also no fear that he would do the things the rumours told, there was no suspicion that he was a spy, sent in by the Haukea, to surreptitiously destroy the Keahi.

Kaelem and Xalvadora talked about random things. This was a sweet release from the conversations Kaelem had reluctantly become used to concerning his power, his life. He felt he could speak to Xalvadora about anything and not be judged, and it was great. He smiled and laughed so much that he never wanted to leave the stability of her bedroom. But the time eventually came, and so they said goodbye to each other. As Kaelem trudged back to his room he found he wasn't sure how he felt, all he knew was that it was a glorious feeling compared to all the other emotions he had experienced these last two or three years.

This didn't last long however, and soon enough he felt the depressed feelings edging their way sadly into his head. He felt faint and sick at the thought of yet another day of training followed by more training in a seemingly never ending cycle. He crashed his head in to his pillow and cried out, already longing for the company of Xalvadora to lift him back up again. To save him from his self destructive world.

***

Kaelem awoke at six, the dream that he'd had lingering in his head, wanting him to unravel its secrets. He had felt as though he were flying.

It had started in the courtyard of his school, Alma was there. She came up to him and put her arm around his waist before leaning in to tell him something, but there the dream went sour as she drew away, speaking Spanish, into a crowd of women. Then, once again, the dream shifted into something happier: Xalvadora's face appeared, bright and friendly. She took his arm and led him to where a figure stood looking into a lake that had formed beyond the school's entrance gates. She grabbed the hand of this women and joined the two together. The other's hand felt soft and cold in his grip. He looked into her face and was ecstatic to see Bethamy looking back at him, possessing an aura as beautiful and enchanting as their first meeting, before she had been made Queen. The grips on one another's hands tightened mutually and the two jumped into the water together. They swam underneath the waves, Kaelem holding onto Bethamy tightly, as if she would dissolve into her new self again without him, but it was also so she could breathe, as if Kaelem's hand were acting as her lungs, diffusing oxygen into her bloodstream. They were gliding, free, in ecstasy.

Kaelem woke up, a sick, unnerved feeling in his stomach.

CHAPTER TWENTY-NINE

Kaelem's eyes widened as the fire spurted from his left hand. A smile crept onto his face.

***

As usual darkness wrapped itself around Kaelem's room as he practised. The procedure was the same as always, but he had slowly gained more control over the fire, and as it came out of both of his hands he started to laugh. He had become accustomed to the energy it sapped out of him, and now he no longer needed all of it to conjure the flame. Kaelem felt stronger now than he had ever been. Everything seemed to be easier and faster to achieve. Except for one thing.

Kaelem began to dance in the company of the flames along with the music. Still sitting in the same position on his bed he twisted his body, wrapping his arms around himself, feeling the extreme heat delightfully burning him. Kaelem untwisted himself, and stretched his arms out to the side, making his palms face upwards as fire protruded from them, reeling up towards the ceiling.

He held his head high, lifted his chin, and closed his eyes. The great power he possessed gave him a sense of invincibility, as if he could rule the world. He breathed deeply, the smoke intoxicating his lungs. When he was at the height of exhilaration he opened his eyes and circled his arms above his head, creating patterns with the flames: a circle of protection created by his own fire, making him safe and indestructible. Kaelem focused on the unlit candles; eerie statues in the dark, awaiting to play their role. Kaelem put his hand up and concentrated on one of them; however the fire refused to leave his palm. He clenched his fist. Kaelem decided to try something different, experimenting, figuring out how his powers might work. Not attempting to conjure the flame until the last minute he thrust his right hand at it. As if angered by his constant summons a huge fire ball came out of his skin, forced its way to the surface, through the epidermis, and carried on towards the candle, leaving in its wake a trail of light and smoke. It set two wicks alight and ended its journey.

Kaelem tried again, riveted. This time he tried to move the fire slowly, to light the wick with precision, with meaning, rather than relying on luck. He created a new flame ball and glared at it, but it was more resilient than it had ever been. He threw the fire carefully and willed it to stop in the air. To his surprise and relief it did as it was ordered and hung motionless in mid-air. Kaelem stood up, but as he did his gaze was averted for a second and the flame dropped to the floor, extinguishing upon impact. Kaelem tried throwing and stopping the flame again, but this time the telekinesis did not work, and the fire hit his wall. Kaelem sighed with annoyance and walked sluggishly over to the candles he had managed to light, putting them out using the thumb and index finger of his left hand. He then slumped back onto his bed, reflecting on how stupid the whole thing was.

***

The next training session was two days later. Aka could only hope it was enough time for Kaelem to clear his mind a bit, for although the Keahi King didn't want to load too much onto Kaelem at once – his son already had too much to deal with, and he doubted two days could heal what needed to be mended - the time of relaxation had come to end, and sinister things were drawing closer each day. They had no time, so Father and Son were meeting outside again.

"Move the fire Kaelem."

Kaelem inhaled and breathed out slowly. He threw the flame in his hand, and though he stared at it intently it ignored his plea, carrying on towards a direction it chose.

"You have to gain the fire's trust. Treat it like it is living. Respect it, and it will respect you. Remember, it is from you, but it also has a mind of its own." Aka put his palm out. Fire burst from it and floated upwards. It drew Aka's name in the air. Kaelem's father laughed like a child who had written a secret with a sparkler. "Try one of your other techniques for getting the fire out, maybe that too will make a difference?"

Kaelem thrust his palm forwards. The ball of fire emerged slowly, at first seeming to be a bump rising from his hand, then as flickers of flame gave away its true identity it turned into a glowing orange ball, penetrating out through Kaelem's skin, and then dislodging itself. When it had broken contact with its summoner, the fully formed flame-ball made its way in a straight line ahead of him.

"Interesting," Aka whispered. Kaelem's mind then asked it to stop, and it halted mid-flight. He went up to it, remembering to keep his gaze on the ball. He touched the fire, but to his horror it sucked itself back inside of him. Kaelem screamed. Aka got up and went to his son. "It is okay. It is supposed to do that, do not worry. I am very pleased with the progress that you have made. It will not be long now until you can see your family again."

"Yes," Kaelem replied sadly, "but what will they think of me now? I don't know if they will accept me back."

"I will always be here for you Kaelem, if you ever feel lost or alone; I am part of your family too. You know where to find me."

"But it isn't the same. I don't know if I can trust myself. I still feel that the Haukea are right, even though I have been around you for this long. I feel drawn to both sides."

He sensed Aka tense up, but his father's voice didn't give away his emotion. "It is okay for you to feel this way. After all, you are born from both races, it is understandable you feel duty to both, and for that I am sorry."

Kaelem walked away from Aka at this, wanting to be alone. "I'll see you tonight." Kaelem informed.

"Wait. Drink this first, it will help with your concentration." He gave Kaelem a vial with a blue liquid inside. It tasted refreshingly cold. Kaelem looked inquisitively at his father: Why would something so unusually cold as this be in a place of fire? Aka smiled and turned away.

Kaelem ran. He ran across the seemingly never ending field, away from civilisation, from the palace, his father. He became alone, with only his thoughts to comfort him.

Kaelem eventually stopped from exhaustion. He collapsed, breathing harshly: it felt as if ice were enveloping his body. As he fainted Aka appeared by his side in a wealth of flames. "You can go home after you meet your mum." Fire engulfed them both.

CHAPTER THIRTY

Kaelem's eyes fluttered open. He sat up, and his eyes fell on a woman, awe spread across her familiar face. He backed away in fear when he recognised her as the woman who had been haunting his dreams. She was real, and she was here.

He rushed to the door, but it wouldn't open. He let out a small scream of panic. "What do you want with me?!"

Lily-Anna took her gaze off him, hurt. She remembered the day her spell was interrupted by Aka; had it really made this much of an impression? "Kaelem. That wasn't me in your dream."

"Then how do you know about it?"

"I was trying to comfort you, for what was going to happen next, so that you would trust me. But my projection was sabotaged. I am not evil. I promise you I am not that."

Kaelem's breath began to return to normal, and his heart rate decreased as he sat back down, but he still kept his distance from the woman.

He realised with a sick feeling in his stomach that he was displaying the same actions as the hated Keahi had exhibited to him: judging him by what they perceived him to be, not for who he actually was. The woman smiled at him, but this unnerved Kaelem "Why am I here, with you?"

She looked down, her eyes sad. "I need to tell you something. Whether you believe me or not I don't know, but be certain that it is the truth." Kaelem looked at her, confused. "I am Lily-Anna, your mother."

Kaelem felt sick. "But…you're dead."

"I cannot explain this to you yet. I think we should talk with Aka here too."

Lily-Anna knocked gently on the door, feeling weird that she was knocking for someone outside of the room. She knew Aka had not been listening to their conversation, for he respected her privacy - she was not a normal prisoner - he also regarded and respected the fact that she needed time on her own with her son. Yet at the same time she knew he would hear her call, he would be waiting in anticipation for the three of them to be together again, maybe even to gain one tiny second of pure happiness. But then the realisation would set in: that the wife was a zombie by the husband's own hands, and the son a killer for his enemy, from which the mother had escaped.

And so the door opened with Aka's shape looming in the doorway, tall and handsome. Lily-Anna breathed out, trying to dispel the feelings she kept for him. It was too complicated.

"Your stupid interference has worked. He's afraid of me." The anger rose in her as she saw a fleeting look of gladness sweep Aka's features like a passing cloud. The two looked towards Kaelem. He stood shivering in the corner, unsure of what to do. He wanted to escape this hell of not knowing what he was, of being a part of something bigger than he was capable of understanding. He curiously shifted his eyes between the two people standing before him. They had the answers he wanted, all of them. But a piece of him was scared of what explanation they would give. If indeed they were his biological parents, and they were fighting over him, what must their secrets reveal about his true self? What had made them so bitter towards each other, if they ever loved each other at all? And was it all his fault? "Probably," Kaelem whispered to himself, watching the floor to see if it would open up and drag him away from all the havoc. He was disappointed.

"Sorry," Aka commented.

"Kaelem - sit down, and we will explain everything to you from the beginning." She paused. "No more secrets."

CHAPTER THIRTY-ONE

The three of them sat in a triangle, the parents exchanging glances, the son distant from their silent knowledge. Aka nodded to Lily-Anna, indicating for her to tell the story first, or at least her version of it.

They turned to face Kaelem, who sat in anticipation, slightly scared of what the truth was going to be.

"Firstly, I should explain my role within the Haukea," Lily-Anna started. "I am a sorceress, a rarity in our world, just as being a shape shifter is on the Keahi's." She shifted her gaze onto Aka for a second. "One of my duties to them was to go to Earth and collect souls." Kaelem felt a shiver of recognition go down his spine, but his mother didn't pause. "Sorcerers are the only Haukea who can survive going to Earth, because we hold the power to keeping ourselves cold, and we cannot, as I see now as unfortunate, use our powers on anyone but ourselves. Not anymore, anyway."

"As with your Healers. How come you can't use your power on others anymore?" Kaelem inquired innocently. Lily-Anna looked fleetingly at Aka. "I didn't realise how much you didn't know about your past."

"I am sorry Lily-Anna, for not informing him, but I thought it would be best if he heard it in the presence of us both."

She nodded, and quickly smiled when she spotted the look of dismay on her son's face. "It doesn't matter. You are here now, and will soon know everything.

"Our kind used to be able to perform spells on others, but that was soon to be a past never revisited again." She told the story of the lost friendship between Haukea and Keahi, of the Angels, and how the Healers' vial had come to be in their possession, with Aka commenting that it was supposed to be for the Keahi.

"Wait. There is one thing I want to know. Why now, after all this time, is a battle commencing?"

Both his parents looked strained. "I am guessing Bethamy did not tell you?" Aka asked Lily-Anna. She shook her head. Aka turned to his son. "The battle that is upon us is not unique; the Haukea tell us that our races must clash together on the Neutral Land, the field which was cursed by the Angel, once a year. We do not know how it has come to be, but on this day a gateway opens that grants them entry to this part of our world. It is a strange circumstance: any other day they cannot penetrate our planet's guards.

"As the field is technically Keahi land we have no choice but to attend, for though we believe in a fair fight, the Haukea have threatened to scourge our land if we do not comply to meet them there – even though they do not give us much warning for when the battle is to commence – and then it is certain doom for the Homo sapiens and our world. It is true they cannot turn it to ice, but the combined power of their sorcerers can make our land a few degrees colder, which in time will make our lives very uncomfortable, and kill off our supply of food. Therefore on this day we fight as much to stop them destroying Aki Houna than we do to save the humans."

"Then how did the Haukea get to your world before the war split the two races apart?" Kaelem inquired.

185

Aka looked to his wife, who replied, "It used to be open to us. When my people first came into contact with Aki Houna we were greeted kindly, and the planet's defences allowed us entry. When the war began we found we could not get through its resistance, exempting that one day a year when the barriers which protect the Neutral Land is open to us. What puzzles me is that this day is at my queen's pronouncement. I'm sorry I can't give you any more explanation than this." Lily-Anna stopped to give her son time to understand all she was saying, or reject any more information, but Kaelem nodded his head for them to carry on – he would contemplate on it later, they finally seemed willing to tell him information, and he wanted to absorb it all now before they changed their minds – and so his mother carried on, "I want to give you a comforting link between the life you are living now, and the life you thought you had. So I will start at the very beginning of Aka's relationship and mine.

"I was on assignment in India, collecting a particular soul who possessed great power." Kaelem looked at Aka, but Lily-Anna shook her head. "We had been watching her for some time, little knowing that Aka had been watching me. We weren't to understand who he was anyway, for he was not king at that time, and the Keahi had kept him secret."

Aka then spoke, "Though even its hottest areas were cold to me, I loved Earth and the freedom it gave me. As I shunned the identity I had on Aki Houna, it became my retreat. I first saw Lily-Anna when I had finally decided to run away for a while; my father and I weren't on the best of terms, and I had reached my limit – or at least what I thought was my limit." He shuffled in his seat.

Lily-Anna reminisced over their first meeting, "We were in the state of Tamil Nadu. I remember sensing something different about him and thinking he might be a useful soul. He was over the moon when I approached him."

"Could you blame me?" Aka asked. "You were so beautiful, so unique. Like the language Tamil."

Lily-Anna smiled and continued, "We talked for hours, he explained that he had run away from duties at home, which convinced me not to take his soul - I didn't want to put him into the same situation he had just escaped from - but I knew our time together couldn't last; I would have to disappear once I took the soul of Anuva. But Aka's presence was so strong. It surrounded me, I craved it. I wanted him. And so we became closer, I let myself become closer to him. Until at last the time came when I stated I had to move, that I was going to England and wouldn't be coming back. However, my tactics were stupid, perhaps purposely so: we looked each other in the eye. He declared he would be coming with me. I couldn't resist; I was happy, ecstatic he desired me as much as I did him. For that one true second I forgot my duties, I refused who I was and I agreed we would leave India together." Lily-Anna paused, taking a few seconds to think on how that decision had set in motion the changes to her lifestyle, and the perceptions she would question regarding her own race; how ignorant she had been of everything surrounding her at the time, and how she wouldn't, in spite of everything, have changed what she said that day to her future husband.

She came out of her reflection to see Kaelem anticipating her next burst of exposition, and so she continued, "Once we had found our own house, booked the flight, and organised all the moving details it was a few months later, and the Haukea were getting restless: they had found out I was seeing someone, and though they knew it wouldn't last forever - for if he requested my hand in marriage it would become my duty to tell him about my Haukea heritage - they were worried about it affecting my mind-set, which made me nervous they would form an investigation because I still hadn't extracted Anuva's soul from her body. However, their doubts were diminished when the day before the move I acquired her soul and presented it to the Haukea. I continued taking souls and living with Aka in the South of England for two years after that. Then the day came when Aka asked me to marry him. I told him my duteous truths - he still didn't tell me of his birthright. He was compassionate about my story, of course now I know why he wasn't fazed. We married soon after our engagement." She concluded with the events that took place on the day she found out Aka's exact identity.

Kaelem sat in silence, trying to make the connection between the baby in the bathtub, his twelve-year-old self, and the person who was standing listening to the past. It felt weird to think he could not remember this infant who had once morphed so easily, little knowing, and little concerned, with his uniqueness. As he contemplated the wealth of information, all he could do was nod acknowledgment and gratitude to his mother as his father led him out of the room, his legs feeling like jelly. Kaelem looked back, pieces of their conversation being retold vividly in his head about a past he did not remember. Lily-Anna smiled at him in response. Kaelem flickered one back. Lily-Anna sighed - it was enough. She watched her son being separated from her once again and felt that same helplessness as before, of not knowing when she would next see him, or even if she would ever meet her son again. It tore her apart.

When father and son were alone, Aka said, "She came to her senses Kaelem. She saw what was happing, that the Haukea are wrong in the acts they commit, and I think you will too. I will help you through this."

Aka realised it was the worst thing he could have said, and his thoughts were confirmed by an outburst from Kaelem, "It's the right thing to do. They just don't see it yet, and neither do you!"

Aka stayed calm, intending to win his son's trust back again, because he knew the longer Kaelem was lost in the

Haukea's reasoning, the harder it would be for him to gain redemption.

But there was also a selfish reason for his actions: to find out what methods and language the Haukea had used to teach his son about their mission. He wanted to understand Kaelem's exact thoughts on the Haukea's warped sense of morality; he needed to get under his son's skin to gather knowledge of why the race thought taking souls was the right way to go about saving Earth. Both races' views on the matter surrounding humanity's existence were strong, and neither side were about to admit they were in the wrong, because both believed their actions were right. However, Aka's personal vendetta shrouded tact. "They will turn all the humans into slaves Kaelem. They do not want to save the Earth, they only want power, and at the moment that is exactly what they are gaining. They are already making you do their bidding; soon they will have complete possession over you. They are exploiting your power and using their blood running through your veins to advocate trust. You have experienced so much destruction inside you already, imagine the impact they will create on humans, the chaos they will cause when people become their puppets. The Haukea do not care about the race; their only concern with Earth is how long it will take until they can dominate it."

"But why?" Kaelem replied, ignoring the usual babble about him being controlled. "Why do they feel the need to rule them?"

"I told you: they just want power. Now is not the time to explain this part of the battle's history, but due to a significant difference between the morals of the leaders of our worlds two centuries ago, the Haukea royals can only heal themselves, whilst the Keahi regal bloodline has the power to heal others."

"How does that prove anything?"

"Kaelem, I am of royal blood, therefore your healing power comes from the Keahi side of you. If it were Lily-Anna's blood, then you would be able to heal yourself and nothing else."

"But they can't help how their powers work. That doesn't make them good or bad," Kaelem protested.

"Not now, no. But when they were first presented with them, they had the choice. They are evil Kaelem."

"That still doesn't justify who they are now, what they have evolved to be, the individuals within the whole. Are you saying that your wife is evil?"

Aka knew Kaelem wasn't going to change his mind, and arguing with him meant that he was going to succeed in distancing himself with his son, and creating another enemy for the Keahi to battle. Worst of all, he knew that his son was correct about the healing power. They weren't an evil race, it was just the monarchy who were corrupt; all the same it was obvious by Kaelem's strong opinions that he had spent enough time around Bethamy to forge his own thoughts concerning the royals' ethics.

Realising how strong the Haukea's influence was if they nearly made the Keahi King question their morality for the better, Aka breathed deeply, organised his thoughts, and said, "Let us go Kaelem. Before we kill each other."

CHAPTER THIRTY-TWO

"Come Kaelem." Aka reached out for his son's hand. When he had taken it they walked outside, into the field.

"Say goodbye. You will not be seeing it for some time." Kaelem smiled, and the two became engulfed in fire. Once again they flew through the air.

Kaelem closed his eyes; the fire no longer bothered him, but the height was still unnerving. He clutched desperately to his father, afraid of falling.

They landed safely in the woods, where a Siamese cat greeted them with a soft purr.

"Take him where he needs to be Mya." The cat seemed to nod her head, then she turned, tail high up in the air, and strutted proudly towards Kaelem's destination.

"I will see you again Kaelem. But you will have to decide whether we meet as enemies, or as allies.

Aka left in a burst of flames. Kaelem watched, then realised he was supposed to be following Mya. He looked around him and could just make her out through the trees. He ran.

***

The door was unlocked when Kaelem finally got home. Mya had gone away once they had reached his doorstep so he entered alone. "Hello?" he called as he stepped through the hallway. Uncertainty tinted his tone, but he got a reply:

"I'm in your room," it was Aolani's voice. Kaelem went quickly up the stairs and stood still; the door to his room was different. He pushed it and found that it was stiff and heavy. When he entered his room and let go of the door it slammed shut with a weighty bang. His time away had created a suspicious nature in Kaelem, and this was now triggered off when he saw that no one was in the room to greet him.

"Ali?" He called tentatively. He heard a click. "Ali!"

"I'm sorry Kaelem. It's for your own good, so you don't hurt anyone else."

"You fitted a lock to my door. I am not a criminal Aolani. I am your brother."

"I'm beginning to doubt that," she responded quietly.

Kaelem felt the fire heat up his hand.

"Dad informed me what else you are capable of doing, and fitted a fire door," she said, knowing Kaelem's intentions. "You'll have to stay there a while before you get through."

Kaelem banged on it, and she jumped back, frightened.

"I-I'm go…Get you a drink."

"Don't leave me Ali. Aolani!" He slammed his weight against the door. When it became clear this wasn't going to achieve anything he slumped against it, and put his head in his hands. "Welcome home Kaelem," he said sadly to himself.

Aolani raced downstairs, her heart rate elevated and her body shaken. She was secretly glad to be away from him, he had changed. He scared her now. How could they possibly live through this? The man in that room was not her brother. It couldn't be. She felt sad with nostalgia, and proceeded to get the chocolate powder, knowing Kaelem's favourite drink of the past. When the milk was found and warming on the stove she noticed how deathly quiet it was. Maybe her brother was planning something, perhaps his escape. If she went back up to his room, would he harm her? The milk bubbled in protest from the flame underneath and Aolani quickly removed it. She mixed the milk in with the chocolate, and as the steam rose tears fell from her eyes and fused with the drink.

She took a long, deep breath to brace herself for anything as she opened the door to Kaelem's room. But when she walked in all she saw was Kaelem asleep on his bed. She smiled and felt weightless. Her fear faded for a second as she realised he was her brother. She turned, in relief, to lock the door.

"You don't have to do that."

She jumped at the sound of his voice, spilling some of the hot liquid onto her hand, but she continued to turn the key. Once the lock was secured she went up to Kaelem. "I made you some hot chocolate." Aolani gave the mug to Kaelem and he gulped it down, leaving behind a moustache of milk. Aolani tried to hide a smirk.

"What. What?" At first he was blunt, then his confusion made him hesitant. His sister pointed to her top lip, and Kaelem hurriedly wiped the liquid away. He spotted Aolani's hand; it had gone red, burnt from the spill.

"You're hurt," he stated.

She looked at her wound. "It doesn't matter."

He took her wrist. "I can help." He focused his energy into her hand. Aolani withdrew for a second, then trusted him and clutched her hand in his. As the bright light came Kaelem felt himself getting weaker as all of his energy was sucked into his sister, but only when the room became blurred, and his head dizzy, did he stop. Upon breaking the connection he collapsed onto the bed.

"Kaelem!" His sister panicked.

"I'm fine," Kaelem replied faintly, but he was unable to focus on his sister.

"Kaelem, if you can do this type of thing, why don't you use the power you possess to help people? Why did you show that other side of you on the beach with the boy? That was not even a part of the brother I once knew. He didn't hurt people. Those stories you used to tell me on the pier; there was always a feeling of safety there because I knew that if the monsters came to take me, you would protect and fight for my life. I guess I was wrong."

"Ali. I'm not really harming anyone. I have spoken to the Keahi about it too, they have the same view as you, but I believe it is good what I am doing for the Haukea, for humans." He tried to keep his vision clear on her. "I feel that you all need to be convinced it is right, not me to be preached to about it being wrong."

Trying not to be phased by Kaelem putting humans in a different category to himself, Aolani asked, "Kaelem, what happens to those souls after they have entered your knife?"

"I'll see you tomorrow." Kaelem avoided the question and closed his eyes, turning himself away from her to face the wall, remembering the conversation with Bethamy, and the lost souls. His insides stung from the thought that his sister believed he was no longer her shield.

***

It was nine-thirty in the morning when Aolani knocked on the door. She waited, but no answer came from the other side. She put her ear to the door, holding her breath to try and pick out the faintest signs of movement. Nothing. She timidly opened the door to find him asleep on his bed. She put the tray of hot food and salty water down and locked the door. She then moved the tray to Kaelem's bedside table, but a hand grabbed her arm as she was about to stand up, and a voice whispered in her ear:

"Please tell me I'm not here again."

After a few steadying breaths she managed to talk, "Kaelem, you're home. I've brought you breakfast."

He stared suspiciously at the food, then back at his sister. "I'm sorry." He let go of her arm. "I just got so used to waking up in another place, I didn't want to be there this time. I didn't want to wake up cold, get told things I never asked to know, to be put in another situation I couldn't escape until they sucked out everything that was left of…"

"It's okay," Aolani reassured him, "I'm here. You're home." After a moment of silence Aolani spoke again, "Did you get any sleep last night?"

He sat up. His eyes looked red and sore. "Let me go."

"I thought you wanted to stay."

"Not here." He looked out of his window.

"I don't think I can let you go. Kaelem, if I do, you will take another…soul. I don't want you to kill whatever bit of humanity you have left in you. Those Haukea; they have brainwashed you, somehow. What they are doing - it isn't for the best. Do you really think they care about us? In the end they will rule us. We will all become…"

"Their slaves," Kaelem finished. Aolani glared at him. "I know," Kaelem continued. "The Keahi told me that too. I keep telling you: nothing you can say will make me change my mind. I am not losing myself, I am evolving into something greater than what I was, a saviour. Now let me go!"

"No." She found herself becoming disgusted with what her brother was telling her, with what he had come to believe. Who were these Haukea, and why *her* brother?

"Are you scared of me Ali?"

She paused for a second, taken aback at the sudden vocalisation of a question that had been tolling her mind ever since he had come back. This was the chance to tell both Kaelem and herself what she really felt, "Sometimes."

"I don't want you to be scared of me Ali, you have no need to be. I will never harm you."

"Shut up," she replied.

"What?"

"I said shut up, stop it, don't change the subject, it's not going to help you."

"I am your older brother Ali, I am supposed to protect you. I can't, if I cannot even save you from myself. I promise I will not harm you."

"Maybe, but you will kill other people."

"Ali!"

"I know, you just took the soul from the vessel. Kaelem...I'll see you this evening."

She made to depart the room, leaving Kaelem feeling sick that she no longer trusted him, when he said, "Wait."

Aolani stopped and went to his side. "What," She stated.

"Don't leave me."

"I have to."

"Why?"

"Because I can't stand this, knowing what you have done. I can't stay here. You asked me if I am scared of you: yes, I am. I can't help that." Kaelem looked at her, but he wasn't upset - he was angry. He had changed, he was no longer the boy he once was; he wasn't upset with her anymore, because he knew that one day he would prove everyone wrong. He rose up and Aolani took a step back, startled at the look in his eye.

He pushed past her and she fell to the ground, landing awkwardly, as he ran towards his freedom. Aolani turned her head towards him, and with tears streaking down her face, her voice distorted with pain, she called out to her brother, "You promised you wouldn't hurt me."

CHAPTER THIRTY-THREE

Kaelem continued to run, coming to his senses only when he felt the cold sea spray splash his ankles and cool droplets stroke his face. But he did not stop. Keeping his black shirt on he took off his trousers at the same time that he morphed; he had to keep moving, no more time to be wasted undoing stupid buttons. He had to free his mind. His tears were drowning him, his sorrow taking the oxygen from his lungs. The last words she spoke were plastered in his mind, never to be lost, suffocating in their sadness. He had hurt her, he had broken his promise, killed his own soul to obtain others. He was an animal. He yelled, and forced his way deeper towards the darker water. He tried to forget everything, his head was filled with voices telling him contradicting things, all right, all wrong, and in the process he had lost things, had forgotten what was significant to him, left behind his true judgements to be replaced with the thoughts of what others wanted him to believe in, but they were not him.

Aolani was right when she had announced he was no longer her brother, for the Kaelem that used to exist was gone.

He went deeper, still hoping the pressure would force things out of his mind. The sea- bed came into view a moment later, emerging from the depths like fresh air. He lay down on his stomach, face in the sand, basking in the cold water surrounding him, and for a blissful second he had no worries. His head was clear, and he breathed with relief, his lungs no longer feeling heavy. Kaelem concentrated on this feeling of freedom. He made himself suppose it was only him: he had no sister, no powers, nothing. He was Kaelem, and that was all. But who was Kaelem? It wasn't long before his worries crept back into his mind, like a predator so stealthy he didn't realise what was happening until it was too late to get rid of the weight.

"No," he said desperately, trying to make the memories disappear, but they were persistent. It was dragging him down and bringing along the thought of Aolani, the controversial duties to the Haukea, how his father and mother perceived him. Kaelem got up from the bed, but still kept close to it so no-one could find him. He swam on, getting faster, sleeker, streamlining himself to glide through the water easily. He closed his eyes to feel the rush of the powerful current hitting him forcefully, trying to make him turn to its path, but he sped on, feeling great, as if he were escaping from entrapment. He never wanted to stop, never wanted to go back.

The voices were resurfacing; Bethamy's tainted words, always poisoning his mind at his greatest moment to bring him back down, to believe in her cause, to make him turn around and retrace his steps to the way he came, and finish his duties.

The water was getting shallower, and soon his body was touching the sand and feeling the wind from above the waves. He found his trousers and went back to his human form.

Putting on the trousers Kaelem walked onto dry sand. He took the athame out of his pocket. Grabbing it with hate and clutching it with passion he was both slightly relieved it was still there and slightly wishing it had been swept away.

A man walked by with his Jack Russell. His weathered face smiled at Kaelem, but instead of offering his friendship Kaelem drew his athame. He sensed the man had a powerful brain, he was smart,

CHAPTER THIRTY-FOUR

They stood on the sand facing each other, a soulless body between them, separating them. Fear no longer dominated Aolani's eyes, instead a deep anger gleamed through.

"Ali…" Kaelem began.

"No. I won't, I can't hear any more of your explanations. I've had enough, I thought you wanted to protect me, I gave you chances to prove yourself, but in replace of my forgiveness you destroyed everything." Her features and voice became sharper, questioning, and full of frustration over being aware of things she had no control over. "Why aren't you here anymore? I needed this one stable thing in my life something to cling to that would never change that would never harm me but even that was too much to ask for wasn't it? Even from my own brother. Where did you go Kaelem what happened to your own soul why can't you see the truth about what you have become, about what you do, it's too much to handle, I need to get away from you." She took a shuddering breath as her eyes glanced at the man lying on the sand. She felt sick. Looking back at her brother she shook her head. "No more, I can't be here anymore. I-I can't be your friend anymore. I just-I don't-I'm not prepared to understand, and I don't think I want to if it means agreeing with this type of *abomination* to human life." She turned around and walked away, seeming unsteady on her feet. With a sinking feeling in his stomach Kaelem watched. Fire exploded from his hands, engulfing them in flames. He ran them through his black hair, the roaring force of the fire screaming in his ears.

"I never wanted you to leave. I am so sorry you had to see this," he whispered.

Once his sister was no longer in his sight Kaelem dared himself to move. He froze the body, and in a dream-like state wandered in the opposite direction to the way his sister had gone, lost and alone.

He had cut himself off from the only thing that was real and genuine in his life; the one thing that had made some kind of sense was gone, and it pained him to know that it was because of him that they had both lost their rocks. She was gone. She was gone.

He hated the Haukea for their logic, if those things lead towards taking away everything in his life that connected him to all the goodness he once was, how right could they be? Ali was right: what had he become? Who was he really? For he had been offered chances of redemption from his sister, only to propel them back at her with no thought of what it would turn him into, no thought of how they would hit her. She knew what the Haukea were moulding her brother into and so had tried to help out of love. But what was evolving inside of his body was more powerful then the two of them could control, and it was still there. What did she know? She hadn't seen through his eyes.

Kaelem found himself walking subliminally through the woods. A spectacular blaze shot from the sky faster than a comet and landed in front of him. The fire was sucked inside a form which was that of his father. Aka reached out to his son. "Why are you here Kaelem?"

"I don't know. I'm so confused. I don't know what to believe, what to trust anymore. Aolani's gone, but the poison is still inside me. It's taking over, I can feel the strings - and I like it." Blood still showed on Kaelem's hands. Aka held them.

"It has gone too far; I didn't intended your life to be like this Kaelem. I was a blinkered fool to think my actions would not have lead to something irreversible. I would never have wished this on you. On anyone." Sadness and grief shadowed Aka's eyes, for a second he said no more. And then something else flickered through Aka's eyes, and he burst into speech, "I will not let it come to that, I will not."

"What do you mean?" Kaelem asked, afraid.

"It is okay Kaelem. I will not let that happen. There has to be another way."

With that fire erupted from his father and the flames launched into the air.

CHAPTER THIRTY-FIVE

Kaelem walked back to the beach with a dreadful awareness that nothing connected him to what he once was. His previous life had become meaningless, like a word he didn't, couldn't, understand, yet meant everything. He knew nothing separated him anymore from his duties to the Haukea and the human world. They had merged together; slowly the Haukea's presence was reacting to his own, and like a reaction it was infecting his old human one. But wasn't there another element inside of him too? What of the Keahi? Could they be surreptitiously influencing him as well? What if his body couldn't handle everything it now held? What would subsequently happen to him? What would he think then? Would he ever be just Kaelem? Perhaps Kaelem had gone, had become the word he didn't understand and had no hope of regaining. He was so confused.

It was whilst he was in this dazed state that Opal unexpectedly greeted him. "Hello," she said dutifully.

"Hi," he replied solemnly, already too puzzled to bother to question her presence here.

"We need you now. We're going to attack soon." As usual she cut straight to the point.

"Do I have to be included in this? The Haukea dictate that a battle should commence on the Neutral Land each year, but why should I care, when both races have torn me apart?"

Opal looked down at her feet, her features softened and the rift between them was forgotten for this moment. Her face was sincere, yet her voice was still emotionless. "It's hard for you. I know. We've put you through so much. But some things are at our queen's discretion to tell. She will not answer. Yet. Only when you are ready. In the end it will be worth it. Respect her. She compliments you. But she is still wary you will turn to Keahi. She doesn't want them to know. She waits. For your choice. Yet you are allowed to fight for her. Beside her. I envy you…" she cut off, seeming confused that she had revealed an embarrassing secret.

"But how do I convince everyone my decision will be for the best without losing them? My sister hates me, I've injured my stepfather, and the Keahi, including my father, are trying to stop me from taking souls because they believe it is doing more harm than good." He looked boldly into her eyes. "Who is stopping me from joining them? Why are *they* more erroneous than you? You gave me all these new feelings and thoughts - what is stopping everyone around me from abolishing them in the same way? You both keep the complete secrets of your worlds, my inheritance, from me, so why are your half-truths so much more gracious than theirs? Which clan can truly save the human race? What if I'm starting to believe that they could be right!?

She put a hand on Kaelem's shoulder to calm him, her face once again became that of a warrior, sworn to protect her land and people. Though her staccatoed tone still seeped through in parts, for the first time she spoke passionately, fuelled by Kaelem's outburst, urging him to comprehend how important his privileges were to the cause she was fighting for, "If you believed that, then you wouldn't be here. That frozen body would contain a soul, a soul which would have gone about it's daily business of doing nothing but duties for itself. Instead of fulfilling a destiny of hope for both its land. And the Haukea's. You know it's right. You just need other people to see it too. Soon after this war has been won they will bow down to you in gratitude. This is why it is so vital that you join us in this battle. Without you we will not succeed. All your power. All of our preparation. Binding together to create a future you will be able to look upon with an eye of pride, knowing you were a part of it. What are the Keahi going to do for this Earth? Have you ever seen them actively doing anything to protect them? If you aid us now, soon you will be able to show your sister her fears were in vain. You are a hero." Her smile was sly. "She will beg for forgiveness. They will finally see what your eye has always beheld - true freedom."

Kaelem felt relief at the very prospect of this, but his eye was blind to the fact Opal was using similar behavioural techniques to what they had drilled into him from the start, and once again another vine came to tangle him up in the lies of the Haukea, discreetly, one by one, making it harder for Kaelem to come back to his once stable mind.

Opal's eyes shifted for a second, but before Kaelem could process the importance of it a hand touched his back, and he fell asleep.

***

Blinking his eyes open he shouted, "You could at least warn me before you do that! It's not a secret who you are anymore!" He screamed out in frustration. Then, seeing who was standing in his room, he added tonelessly, "Hi Bethamy." He reached for his athame. "Here."

"Thank you. Kaelem, it's time. The gateway is about to be opened onto the Neutral Land, and both sides are ready for the attack. Are you ready?"

"Do I have a choice?"

Her laugh was sickly as she grabbed his hand and took him into the throne room, where all the Haukea sorcerers and sorceresses were gathered. "They are our warriors, and so are you. You are one of us, and our enemy is the Keahi. Make sure this is embedded in your mind, there is no room for hesitation in battle, remember all that you have been taught Kaelem. The fact that you gave us souls, even after our opposition told you to cease what you believe is right, is proof that you think our cause more worthy than theirs."

"I suppose so…"

"Then you will fight with us, for us. For Earth, for your mother."

Kaelem nodded, his eyes suddenly shining, no longer dulled with confusion. "Yes."

His mother. He felt revenge flowing through him, something telling him he had to punish Aka for what he did to her, yet the poison made him forget the couple's relationship as it had truly been; the purity of it before the Haukea interfered.

"I'm ready." He exclaimed, and they all cheered for him. "I'm ready!" he shouted, making himself believe in the Haukea, and betraying what he really wanted: the two sides united.

I'm ready.

CHAPTER THIRTY-SIX

They stood in a large, desolate field where the wind smelt of decay and the landscape was dark and dead. The long, trampled grass covering the place was black and brown, reflecting its catastrophic mood. An eerie silence fell upon the field, for not even the crows came here: there was nothing left to feast upon once the corpses had decomposed. The scenery was hopeless and those who came to this place came for a hopeless reason. Once roses had been carefully pruned, adding to a beauty which once emitted with such a stunning vibrancy, a place where the Haukea and Keahi could meet up every year to celebrate, the clash of elements producing a refreshing rain - but that had long passed. At first the roses had thrived, taking possession of the field. Then the rain stopped coming. With nothing to fuel them their destruction ended. Only their thorns were left now, leaving scars on the dry earth, cutting any pitiable thing that had somehow survived to try and get a taste of life again.

Today a sinister and sad presence had come, not to care for the land as they once might have, but to infest it with yet more blood. The Haukea and Keahi were back.

Feet trod on the thorns, overpowering the spiky rulers of this wasteland who were unable to defend even themselves anymore. Tension rose from both sides as they moved sombrely towards each other.

An aura of colour similar to the aurora borealis surrounded each sorcerer: spells of protection against the searing heat they would soon have to withstand. Yet the power would not completely stop the pain of the heat, for they could not be certain how long these would have to last, and it was best to have a weak tribute to the spell than having it desert them altogether half-way through battle when they would not have the advantage of casting before they were blistered beyond redemption.

Kaelem walked slowly with the Haukea, scared about what was going to happen, anxious about the outcome. He looked at each body and sensed the apprehension within, mingled with excitement: though this battle happened once a year, these Haukea had trained their entire lives for this opportunity. They were obsessed with it, for today not only had the time finally come when their ultimate weapon joined their ranks, they were the ones who got to fight side-by-side with it - whether he wanted that destiny or not.

He was beginning to doubt if he would be able to fight with them as the Keahi came into view. Seeing familiar faces surprised and offended when they met his gaze sent a pang of guilt and treachery through his spine. He smiled weakly, until he realised it wasn't appropriate. He quickly concentrated on his feet instead. When he looked up again his eyes fell onto Aka, and he remembered his father stating that the Haukea really wanted to turn humans into slaves, and one of the reasons the battle was taking place was to stop this. How could the Keahi have been lying if they were willing to go to war to help? Or was it the Keahi that in fact wanted the power? Kaelem shook his head, he was confusing himself.

Then something wonderful and terrifying happened. Nearly all of the Keahi, except for Aka and a few others who possessed amazing fire-power, turned shape. Among them he recognised those he had been forced to have dinner with. Their bodies twisted and changed, some growing, some shrinking, some changing into powerful and muscular animals, some into small birds that flew above him with grace and agility.

"This is it," someone gasped behind Kaelem. "I can't believe this is happening." But after that nothing happened for a while, they just stood looking at each other, tense, but somehow peaceful.

"The calm before the storm," another Haukea commented. "Treasure it forever, because it won't come again."

Kaelem sensed the flickering of Keahi eyes on him, each one taking its turn to acknowledge what side he had finally chosen, and Kaelem felt ashamed, as if he had betrayed them. How could he possibly attack? But there was one set of eyes that didn't look. They stared off into the distance, filled with the grief and weight of knowledge that he was responsible for each Keahi life: Aka. Slowly his eyes focused on something: they focused on Bethamy. She saw what his people were doing and laughed. It was horrible. It was out of place, and it was sadistic. "It's over Aka. He's ours."

"He is not anyone's!" Aka's voice boomed furiously across the field so everyone could hear. There came a great noise as each warrior turned to face the two opposing leaders. "He is deciding his own destiny, and if that happens to be with the Huakea, so be it. But I am not going to be holding back just because he is my son. He has chosen what he wants, and if that is against me, against my people, and our beliefs, then I have no choice but to treat him indifferently as the enemy. My first concern is to protect my land and the families forged within." He didn't even glance at Kaelem as he said his speech, but Kaelem was staring at his father, hurt and afraid.

"So you're going to kill him?" Bethamy asked mockingly. A creepy silence flowed through all the living bodies that had dared to enter the place of destruction.

"If need be."

Kaelem inhaled sharply. Bethamy smiled, then walked out of her line and up to Aka. Her fingers wrapped around an ornate silver hilt, and as she drew her sword the sound echoed as if it were the only thing that could be heard. The blade glittered like snow, a frost rose from it, seen by the naked eye.

Bethamy and Aka were the only ones who possessed weapons. Bethamy due to her power being useless in battle, just like her mother's, and Aka because they had made a vow of honour to only use the blades on the one whose blood was strong enough to touch it in a fair fight. Aka unsheathed his own sword. The weapon was not glamorous; it was not for show. The black blade, however, was unique: instead of the sun glinting from it, light was absorbed into it, and those who looked too long would begin to feel their own life diminishing into the sad and hopeless place without sun.

Quickly Bethamy swung her sword, cutting Aka's cheek. Blood froze on the blade and crept from the fresh gash in Aka's face. The red liquid trickled down, making random pathways towards his lips, and crystallised. Aka breathed harshly through the cold pain. Everyone else held their breath for what was to come next. From the Keahi a shout was made. Fire escaped as ice came quickly to counter-attack, freezing the fire into ice-balls, then melting it to water. Suddenly the field was no longer silent; it was filled with roars and shouts, screams and spells. The air was alive and humid. Kaelem ran, horrified. A strong hand caught him by his shoulder and Kaelem stopped in fear. But the sound of Bailey's voice made him relax a little. He whispered to Kaelem, words just audible above the roar of war, "You have a lot of power, I believe in what you can do, but please, don't draw out their deaths." Then he was away.

Kaelem watched Bailey move through the onslaught, driving some down to the ground, until he was lost within. Seeing the innate and unhesitating way Bailey had attacked the Keahi Kaelem knew he belonged to neither. He witnessed acquaintances from both sides trying to kill each other without even wondering what sort of person they could be, they were just the enemy. He knew then that he was azygous. This wasn't his battle, so how come he was fighting it for both sides? He spun around and walked quickly. Fire and snow and ice were flying everywhere, some hit him, but nothing did Kaelem any harm, on the contrary, he gained strength from each blow as the element became absorbed inside of him.

He wanted a third choice, to be captured a third time, to be captured by himself and told how to live as a human. He wanted to live as he had once done, in ignorance of these other worlds, of his other life. He didn't want to be involved in this war, he only wanted to go home and wake up knowing that none of this was real. But as flames came towards him, struck him, became part of him, Kaelem knew that this was reality and he was stuck with having to choose between one or the other, because he couldn't fight for both. Sadly he realised humanism was not an option. His thoughts led him to thinking about his sister, how he had hurt her as a result of something he had no control over, had no say in. This was their life, not his; their war, not his. Emotions built up in him of anger and depression. He felt the heat rising inside of him, and as he walked footprints of ice showed where Kaelem had been. It froze the trampled thorns, and cracked as people ran subconsciously over them.

If getting his old self back meant destroying everything in this place that connected him otherwise – so be it; he didn't want to be associated with anything on this field. He proceeded to hit the Haukea with burning fists and kick the Keahi with freezing feet. Some fell to the floor, never to return to consciousness, whilst others were strong enough to hit back and escape him.

Nevertheless, Kaelem was relentless as he ran through the field, knocking people down; causing scars to others. The fight was no longer concentrated on the two opposing sides, but on Kaelem's sudden onslaught. The fighting stopped as panic swept across the field. Souls ran from their immune enemy, for unlike their original fight they could do nothing to counter-attack. The sorcerers' only knew magic associated with cold, and though the animals had the power to inflict physical pain on Kaelem, they had to get near him first, plus they were still vulnerable to the cold no matter what form they chose.

Bethamy turned her attention onto Kaelem, disgusted at the cowardliness of her people. The shape-shifters crept forward, surrounding Kaelem in a condensed group, a circle whose diameter was slowly getting smaller. Bethamy stood inside the ring with Kaelem, and raised her sword…

"What do you think you are doing?" Aka screamed at her. "Stop!" A gap appeared to let him through.

"So," she said back sardonically, "you do care if he lives or dies. He isn't just another enemy after all, is he?" They glared at each other.

"No," Aka replied. "It is much more complicated than that, but I do not suppose someone owning such a narrow mind as you could contemplate a soul with multiple duties and emotions having to face each sentiment alone, knowing that no one else could dare understand them."

In their fury against one another Bethamy and Aka had forgot to check on the reason for their argument.

Kaelem meanwhile looked around him, devising a plan to get through the animals surrounding him. He decided to take advantage of the shapeshifters being momentarily distracted by the conflict between the two leaders. Kaelem decided to take on the principle that with his heightened emotions he should be better at moving his fire with telekinesis, and controlling the ice coming from his feet. In the calm Kaelem could at last concentrate on what he was doing, and what needed to be done after.

As the ice froze the ground beneath him, Kaelem managed to make it slither away. No-one noticed - the Keahi would have no time to brace themselves or retaliate.

A shout suddenly rose in the air. Then, as if a bomb had gone off, the ice expanded. Like an infection it spread from Kaelem to cover the whole of the area which he had been trapped in, and the ground the circle of animals had been standing on. The universal code of screams was expressed from a hundred animals as it froze their feet. The Keahi sank to their knees in weakness and pain. Some tried to escape, tried to transform into birds to fly away, but it took too much energy, and so they lay, half of one thing, and half of another. Kaelem felt a bit of empathy rising for these poor creatures - they reminded him of his own turmoil. But he didn't waste long this time in self-pity as he pushed his way through the Keahi.

He was then confronted by Haukea, wondering what was happening within the circle, and whether they were safe from Kaelem yet. But he didn't care for them - not once his eyes spotted Bailey. He focused on the scene and tried to contemplate what it meant: Bailey was protecting someone from Kaelem, he held her fragile figure in his arms, and she was not Haukea.

Kaelem looked angrily at them, and knew he couldn't let this continue. His mother was a zombie because of a similar union, and he had been created. What if their passion became irresponsible like his parent's? What if she became pregnant? He wouldn't let another person be born like he was: half Keahi, half Haukea. He couldn't allow an innocent child to go through the pain of not knowing where they belong or who to fight for – to not have clarity of their own beliefs. They were selfish to think it would work, to think their child would be happy.

"No. Not again," he whispered as he stalked up to them. Bailey and the girl backed away from him together. When Haukea came to block Kaelem's way to protect their best fighter, they found fireballs being launched at them, and decided to retreat for now – they would back Bailey up if the situation became desperate for him.

"No!" Kaelem shouted to the couple. "You can't. It won't work. Just look at my family."

Bailey stepped in front of the woman, his huge bulk hiding her fearful eyes from Kaelem's.

"I won't let it happen again," Kaelem stated. "Never again." The fire in his hands grew larger and larger, when it was at its peak pressure Kaelem launched it at Bailey. The Haukea shifted, but the woman came from behind Bailey and took the impact instead, absorbing its energy. She looked up into Bailey's eyes, and they hugged each other for comfort. "It won't work," Kaelem said again. He flung fireball after fireball at them, whilst the others just watched in stunned horror and awe. Some hit Bailey, and though he stood his ground, he gradually became weaker and weaker, until he could no longer stand. Eventually he fell, clutching his love.

"Keisha, I won't leave you." She smiled. While she was distracted, Kaelem kicked her, ice freezing her form. She fell to the floor, and Kaelem held her down with his foot on her back, his ice forming itself into Keisha's own private sarcophagus.

"Stop!" someone yelled, but Kaelem refused, and fear kept anyone from doing anything else.

Bailey never let go of her hand as the ice enveloped her, and he became one with it. Never once did he look away from her eyes as life faded from them, a smile remaining, forever enchanting him.

Bailey cried for the first time. Kaelem took his foot off her, allowing Bailey to lift Keisha in his arms, looking like he was never going to let her go.

Kaelem stepped back, breathing harshly with anger and loss of power. He realised what he had done, he looked about him with clearer eyes at all the faces, the bodies, most of them fallen by his own hand, and then at Bailey, the strongest and toughest man he had ever known, holding his love, face buried in her long, loose black hair. Kaelem's eyes were now fearful as he looked around him for help, but all stepped back from him. The war for now was forgotten for there was a new threat. Bethamy was the only one who stepped forwards. "I'm sorry." Bethamy raised her sword once again, as if to strike down on Kaelem, but instead she aggressively struck the earth near Bailey.

"How could you?" she spat angrily. "You have betrayed us Bailey, you have made an alliance with a Keahi." She turned to Kaelem. "Next time don't centre your anger on the Haukea." She left the scene calling a name: Saxton.

"I didn't mean…I was confused. I…" The swarm of Haukea and Keahi all looked at him, petrified. "I'm sorry," he said.

A noise came behind him, and when Kaelem looked he saw his father staggering slightly towards him. The Keahi that had been in the circle were now suspended above the ice in shields of fire, slowly recovering. They were back in their human form. Kaelem thought he spotted Mya, and quickly looked at Aka for a second, then down with remorse at Bailey. But there was still a type of anger that remained, a rage towards Aka because if it weren't for him this would never have happened.

216

Kaelem stretched out his arms to the side, the palms of his hands facing towards the ground. Fire burst from them, causing the ground to burn. Slowly he began to turn, then spun faster and faster, the wind rushing in his face, screeching at him to stop, his bare feet spilling un-meltable ice. He stopped, bringing his hands over his head and clapping them together. What he had made was a burning circle of fire around himself, streaks rose up to join at a point above his head, whilst the floor was covered with ice up to the circle of fire. A force field no-one could enter. For the first time after getting his powers he felt completely safe from danger. He became oblivious to everything around him, but he no longer cared: nothing could hurt him. He wanted to stay in this sanctuary forever, and never come out.

CHAPTER THIRTY-SEVEN

Aka reached out to Kaelem through the fire. His thermal clothing kept some of the cold from getting to him, but he still couldn't hide a slight shiver. He burst into flames, and once the fire had spread to his fingertips it ignited Kaelem. Aka took flight to the sky, his son alongside him, trying to understand the meaning in all that had come to pass in the melancholic field, as those below watched. Bailey and the deceased were the only ones who were indifferent to this departure.

They landed in the Keahi dungeon. Shouts rose from behind the doors as father and son made their way silently down the long corridor, to room two hundred and six.

"Is it over?" Anxiety was etched onto Lily-Anna.

"No. It's postponed," Aka replied.

Kaelem looked at his mother wide-eyed; not a word could reach his trembling lips. She blinked at him, her own eyes becoming sore with seeing so many mixed emotions bursting from such a small space: despair, terror, questioning and vengeance clouded his chatoyant eyes, turning the blue a slight hue of green. Her heart beat painfully against her chest at the sorrow of how her son had come to live and be deceived by all around him, including her.

"Kaelem. I'm going to fix it, I understand what needs to be done, I have always understood. Repression is not something that should be harboured; I hope you still have forgiveness left in you, but at this moment in time you must go with your father. Clarity will soon reign in your soul, I promise. I love you." Something burst from her eyes, something which tried to penetrate Kaelem: a promise that someday he would understand and know everything. Kaelem nodded slightly, and Lily-Anna gave him a tired smile.

Seemingly unaware of this transaction Aka lead his son out of the room, then further down the corridor, rather than towards the dungeon's exit. They walked in silence. Reaching their destination Aka pushed open a door to their left. No-one occupied it. He guided his son into the cell. Aka gave one last glance at Kaelem before exiting and locking the room.

He sighed and put his head in his hands, standing outside the room, listening to Kaelem trying to break through the door, listening to him asking to be let out. He remembered his son as a child: small and delicate, laughing on the swings, holding his and his wife's hand as they walked through the woods, fascinated and awed by all around him. Aka remembered the fear when he cradled Kaelem in his arms, that if he blinked the dream would be gone and Kaelem would disappear. Aka went back to Lily-Anna.

***

"He needs help Flower. The Haukea have made him into something I don't think even they can control or know the motives of."

"What happened?" she asked, breathless with apprehension, a flash of her son's eyes penetrating through her.

"Something that I will make sure never happens again. He is powerful. I do not see any other option, it is time Flower."

"But she is my daughter!"

219

"And he is our son. I know we cannot choose, but if he is allowed to carry on like he is he will ruin the lives of many other sons, daughters, parents, friends and…"

"Yes. I understand," she added gently.

"I am sorry Lily-Flower. But today I saw him do something that was horrific. I never thought it would lead to this. But it has, and it is too late to stop it now. He cracked Flower, when he saw something that reflected our old love, that would mean another being like himself would be born. He hates who he is, and what we stand for. He killed Keisha, and numerous others. I am aware now of why this must be done, of how there is no other option. It saddens me that my son will have to experience the same anguish as you went through. For though he saw the pain on her love's face as the Haukea cradled Keisha, he did not feel it. That is the difference."

Lily-Anna nodded. "I hoped there would be another way, but I cannot find it. It's over. Our last chance is to summon his sister, we need to talk, to explain what is going on in her brother's head. Maybe she will think of something we haven't, something only a sister could know, to stop this pain."

Aka was silent for a second, seeming to be on the verge of saying something, but wondering whether or not to suggest it. Finally he came out with it. "I am going to give Kaelem the Keahi tattoo. Maybe it will help in bad times, to remind him he has a choice."

Lily-Anna looked away. "But it could also reinforce the hatred of his uniqueness. It is not our decision to make, his body is already converted by that which he cannot control. It is his vessel Aka, his decision, and so far he hasn't had much say in what he wants, nor had much choice in leading a 'normal' life if he wanted to. Marking him could make him more perplexed in our endeavours. It is in the same mindset as the Haukea when they pierced his ears."

"I think he needs to embrace his entire heritage so that he can become something which is stable yet powerful. I only want what is best for him Flower, I do not want him to suffer or feel disjointed from everything any more than he already is. Seeing him as he was today made me realise the extent to which people have left him ignorant of what his blood symbolises. Kaelem cannot see that he is able to be everything inside of him; I want to show him that it is alright for him to become all of them. The tattoo and the earrings combined are his birthright, are him."

Lily-Anna looked back. "I just hope that you are right, and it is more than you wanting him to become your heir to destroy the Haukea."

Aka was shocked; after everything she still perceived his intentions as selfish. "I love Kaelem because he is my son, a son born out of love, not out of need."

***

The room was relatively large, which surprised Kaelem because it was a cell. It had a window that looked out on the Keahi's barren land. He sat on the soft bed and contemplated, rubbing the irritation on his left arm. He sighed. Once again he had become branded, as if he was not human, as if he were just a weapon to be owned in order to win the war. But it meant nothing to him. He cared no more about who he was, nor of what had been drilled into him. For that brief moment on the field he hadn't needed to decide which side to protect. He had been on his own, and it was fine - it was perfect. He wanted to feel that freedom again. He didn't grieve for the lost; he felt empowered that he could do so much damage to the ones who held him captive. Maybe he was a weapon, but he was one with a soul, one that could think for himself. He had freewill.

He wanted his athame back; he needed to get to the Haukea.

CHAPTER THIRTY-EIGHT

"Aka," Lily-Anna choked. "I am afraid for my daughter. Yet it will not be long until the final decision concerning Kaelem has to be made, and she needs to come here to fulfil what is to be done. She is scared for him Aka, I can sense it. She needs answers, an explanation that is going to make everything comprehensible to her. She needs the truth; she wants to know what she can do to save Kaelem. I need to speak with her."

"I understand your anxieties Flower, but you need to be calm, this next step is going to be hard for all involved, and Aolani needs something strong to cling to. She needs to be reassured that in the end, whatever happens, it is going to result in her brother being well again. You have to be that rock Flower, or else risk her crumbling away. It is a frightening prospect for someone to handle. You need to soothe her fear before giving into your own."

"Yes," Lily-Anna replied defiantly.

"You know she will not be able to survive the journey here do you not? You wish me to bring you to her. I will take you to Earth then."

"I will guide the way," Lily-Anna commented. She chanted a spell on herself to make her immune to the inescapable heat that would penetrate her skin. Aka grasped his love firmly, and they flew together towards Aolani. They landed on a pier and witnessed her sitting on the edge, looking down at the water.

"I always wanted to take more of these journeys with you," Lily-Anna commented sarcastically. Though she had only experienced it once when Aka had first taken her to his kingdom it had seemed like a lifetime's trip. She felt a wave of nausea and dizziness wash over her.

"Are you okay? I know how much you loved it." He smiled. They shared a moment together, of memories long passed, and of thoughts that had been replaced with feelings of regret and tension. Walking together along the pier Aka kept Lily-Anna's balance by holding her arm, she leaned gently against him.

"Do you miss this?" he commented.

"What?" Lily-Anna answered with far less compassion in her tone, and projecting a lesser positive emotion than what she was feeling. She was a young woman again, taking a romantic walk on the beach with her husband, but the circumstances were far from innocent, and so she expanded her reply to his question with the feelings her soul cried out belonged to another Aka, "The sickening acknowledgement of secrecy?" There was the tension again, right on cue, whenever their relationship had a dwindling hope of being reborn. *He deserves this torture, yet I am killing the last chances we may ever have together.* She gave a quick glance at him, one he could not notice, and one which embedded for her everything that he stood for.

"Do you want me to leave you alone with Aolani?" Aka asked patiently.

"Yes. Thank you Aka, this does mean a lot to me."

"You know where to find me do you not?"

"Yes. The place where you took me when you first kidnapped me."

Aka felt a pang of shame and depression. He left her, knowing she would return; she had no choice as he was the only key to releasing her soul, but he wished that she would return for another reason. Lily-Anna then separated from Aka, her sickness now fading, and sat next to her daughter whilst Aka left silently.

Lily-Anna couldn't believe how much her daughter had grown. She hadn't seen her since Aolani was a baby, lying in her arms. Lily-Anna's heart felt heavy in the silent, serene night. Doubt swept round her as to whether or not she could ask her to perform this act, yet she knew she had to, and must not show this qualm in her presence. Aka's voice whispered in her head and it strengthened her.

Aolani turned towards her mother, though she was unconscious of who it was she was seeing. Lily-Anna smiled and Aolani turned her attention back towards the sea, then got ready to leave. Time was limited.

"Wait," Lily-Anna said softly. "I have news, about Kaelem. I know how to redeem him."

Aolani sat back down and gazed intently at the strange woman. Her skin was unnaturally pale, highlighting her cold blue eyes and hair, her left ear was pierced numerous times. Just like Kaelem's was now.

"I think to understand what I am about to say you need to know more of the truth. You need to know who I am, and why I am helping you and your brother." She took a steadying breath. "This is the truth Aolani: I am your mother, I am Kaelem's mother." She paused and waited for the reaction to come from Aolani. Her senses were going into overload.

It took a while for her daughter to answer, but when she did Lily-Anna knew that Aolani felt no conviction the one standing before her was her mother. It brought down with full force the consequences of the deceit her children had been dealt regarding their lineage. "Are you one of those who took Kaelem, who made him become this creature?"

"That is complicated."

"Then explain it to me, explain everything. I want to know, I want my brother back." The anguish and anger flowed out of her, stunning everything around them into a powerful silence, as if they had been forced into a bubble. After a moment sounds began to make themselves heard again, and with them came Lily-Anna's voice.

CHAPTER THIRTY-NINE

Kaelem closed his eyes and focused. He had to get back to the Haukea, but knew with dismay that they could not hear him down here. Haukea sorcery would not work, and the only other way he knew was by his father transporting him. He was stuck. Even if he did manage to get out of the dungeon he couldn't get off the planet.

But then, like a strange dream, he heard a scuffling at the door. When Kaelem put his hand on it he jumped: the door had suddenly opened and Oringo stood staring down at him.

"I've come to get you out. You shouldn't be here."

"Where should I be?"

Oringo smiled. "Away from this land."

Kaelem relaxed slightly, but suspicion kept him from fully trusting Oringo. "Why are you helping me? Aren't you afraid?"

"Your power is great. It's wasting away in here. I have to take you back to the Haukea. So that you may reign over all.

"I was not afraid. No. I was intrigued. You're not bad. Just confused. Being here is making your condition worse. Making you question where your loyalties lie."

"And where do they belong?"

A flash of annoyance swept over Oringo's face, but the answer came immediately and confidently, "With the Haukea."

Kaelem suddenly realised why Oringo wore his beanie: it was to hide the holes in his ears. "Why are you allies with them?" Kaelem queried.

"Power." Oringo's eyes shifted; there was more to it than that, something even more unhonourable. "Let's go," he added abruptly.

Within a matter of seconds Oringo went from a solid form to turning incandescent, then translucent, until finally disappearing altogether. Kaelem felt a hand grab him, transmitting an extremity of heat he had never felt before, apart from perhaps the enthralling, palpable power emitting from his father, but this was touchable power, it could almost have been his. It both frightened and thrilled him as he saw his body glowing as Oringo's did, and steadily he faded.

They started to walk briskly out of the palace.

In the entrance hall they saw Aka. Kaelem held his breath. Aka's eyes look weird, radiant. They seemed to fall for a second on the two of them, but Oringo carried confidently on, aware of the extent of his own power, and Aka turned away from them. Kaelem did not even dare to breathe out in relief.

After a few minutes of walking through a hamlet Oringo came to a stop. "This is where you will be transported to the battle field." Kaelem looked at Oringo quizzically. Oringo sighed. "You wonder why I chose the side of the Haukea. When these Keahi haven't even told you the basics of their community." Kaelem thought that neither had the Haukea, but decided against pointing this out. "We are on a planet Kaelem. There are Keahi living all over

227

it. This village and that palace are not the only places which exist here. The battle field is a place of neutral temperature for Keahi and Haukea. That is why the conflict is fought there. It was created when they were at peace. It symbolises a lack of hierarchy. No divisions. Therefore it's on the opposite side of the planet to the palace. We need to get there so a Haukea can transport you. Without jeopardising his strength. There are teleportation points. To go to certain areas of this planet. Just as there are transportation places connecting Earth to here. We need to move quickly. In case Aka can sense or know when someone uses these ports. Or enters that field. We will be safe once we reach Hau Houna. His senses are negligible there."

Kaelem stood on the spot Oringo pointed out and watched the world disappear then reappear in a different form in mere seconds. He wondered why he couldn't have used this mode of transport before, instead of flying on his visits here.

A boy came up to him not long after he had arrived. He was small and had white hair with a couple of strands of blue hair. His speech gave the illusion of being too old for his body, "Hello Kaelem, I will let you see this time the journey to our land, as part of your reward for what you have done for us. Your consciousness is our sign to you of trust. Do not disrespect it."

Kaelem's face clouded over with distaste. "You are the one who has been travelling me?"

The boy nodded. "Saxton at your service, by order of our Queen. All sorcerers have the ability to transport, but my power allows for me to put someone into a deep sleep. It was a matter of safety: we were not sure whether you had thoughts of turning your back on us."

He took Kaelem's hand, and turned to Oringo. "Thank you. The Queen has been most pleased with your contributions, and for now you are safe." The boy smiled, and to Kaelem's perplexity

Oringo shape-shifted into a fox. He didn't know Oringo was a warrior, what was he doing on that field, out of sight? Putting the Keahi into danger?

"We made a deal not to harm him on the battlefield - if he continues to do our willing. It's good to have a spy who won't betray us. Besides, injuries, fatalities, are easily made in the confusion of war." The statement was left hanging, waiting for someone to catch it, but it drifted of into the stale air.

Cold came to Kaelem suddenly. It swept through him, spreading from his fingers and flowing in his bloodstream and to his heart where it pumped freezing blood through the whole of his body. A blizzard of snow came out of the dusty ground and circled around the two as they gained altitude, flying with the flurry. As Kaelem looked down at the vanishing world, he became certain he could see the shadows of the fallen, and hear the echoes of the dying.

The two arrived in the same room as Kaelem had often awoken in from his cold slumber, but now his travelling companion was here, and to his relief Bethamy was not. Though disappointment came quickly when the boy led Kaelem to the throne room where Bethamy bowed sarcastically at the long awaited presence.

"Why?" Kaelem asked.

"Keisha: I could not have done a better job."

A flash of light gleamed, hypnotising Kaelem's eyes to the athame Bethamy was juggling. Anger broke the spell, and he become antagonistic over her carelessness of it. "I have come to collect my athame," he snarled.

"You're going to have to fight me for it. What if someone gets a hold of this, a Keahi, a human, do you think they would want you to have it back?"

"They can't hurt me." Kaelem stated cognately.

Bethamy stood. "Never underestimate anything Kaelem, it will be the last thing you do in war."

Kaelem went confidently up to his opposition, the stealer of his soul-taker, his emotions strong, possessively so, over the knife.

She drew her sword, striking him in the shoulder. The sharp blade tore his shirt, releasing blood, staining the white sleeve. He didn't care. He focused on the adrenaline and embraced it; let it cling to him as he grabbed the athame by its blade. The possession refused to cut him. Forcing it out of Bethamy's grip white heat seared through both him and the knife. Bethamy smiled: the revelation the war had given him still coursed through his veins, and she wanted him to stay in the trance. He had become dangerous, immune to the sympathies the Keahi might have once lain upon him, yet at the same time she knew she had to break through just enough so that he remained loyal to the Haukea. Now was the best time to mould him. "Come with me Kaelem, and see what you have done."

They went outside and rode a polar bear to one of the houses. Bailey was standing, trying to look unfazed, before a large crowd of taunting Haukea. Kaelem knew how much he was grieving, and was glad. Bailey deserved it. Let him feel what he could have created if he and Keisha had ever had a child.

Bethamy and a Haukea called Jadon separated themselves from Kaelem and spoke to the throng, "We are here to witness the exile of a man whose strength has aided us greatly, but whose heart was in the wrong place. What he did was dangerous and unforgiving, he acted without consideration for us; without conscience, and he has compromised himself. She could have been a spy; the love was something coveted, yet unreachable. It meant nothing to her." Jadon said

"If it had, all the worse," Bethamy spat. She circled violently toward Bailey and spitefully continued, "Apologise to us all for the danger you have created in return for craving something that never existed."

Bailey looked Bethamy in the eye and stated, "I have no regrets."

Bethamy glared back fiercely. She pushed him into the snow and called Kaelem over. "Burn him."

Kaelem pushed his hand down hard onto Bailey's left arm. The sufferer held his breath and closed his watering eyes, it was too late to cast a protection spell.

The burn was worse than Kaelem had ever conjured. It was full of hate, despair and disgust. He bent down to whisper into Bailey's ear and explained what his child would have had to deal with, what people would have perceived him to be, compared to how the child really felt. The things they would have made it do, the lack of freewill and connection. The words were worse than the pain, except that there was a type of understanding and sympathy in Bailey. He opened his eyes, and saw a spark of scarlet on the white background. Through everything he managed to say, "Not everyone is who they seem."

At last Kaelem released Bailey's arm. The skin was scorched and blistering. Dismissing the comment he spat on the wound, and a hissing noise emitted from it, as a wisp of smoke lifted into the air. Bethamy watched on gladly. "Take him away."

The transporter came, dragging with him a blizzard of snow that engulfed Bailey. His giant body became limp as the two disappeared in a snowstorm of lost dreams.

"You can go home now," Bethamy commented to Kaelem. He frowned, *Where was home?*

Bethamy saw the confused expression and a glimmer of pity seeped through for a second. "Earth," she replied simply. "Come, let's clean you up."

Kaelem realised only then that his white sleeve had turned red. It started to sting.

"Take off your shirt," Bethamy said once they had reached the bathroom. Kaelem did as she ordered. In the middle of wiping his arm clean with water she stopped suddenly. "When did you get this?" She sounded slightly panicked. Kaelem looked down at his arm; the tattoo had been revealed.

"It means nothing. It will be easier to fool them if they believe I am one of them. To them this is proof of that commitment." He pointed to his left ear. "Like these."

Bethamy nodded and continued to clean the wound with caution.

CHAPTER FORTY

"I was once part of the group who took Kaelem and convinced him to do those things. But I left long ago, when Kaelem was still a child."

"Is that why they kidnapped him, in exchange for you?"

Lily-Anna sighed at her daughter's question. "If only that were the case. You see, Kaelem's father is from a place the Haukea detest." Leaving out that Aka was ruler of the place seemed to be the best option at the moment: it was too much information to hint that her brother was a prince. She continued, "Therefore our relationship was despised, tainted. Even though he knew my identity I did not know he was Keahi until Kaelem was two years old; his father always wore his long hair down, to hide the symbol of the sun on his neck, and in my presence he never took off the long thin gloves he wore to cover the tattoo on his right wrist: the tree symbol of the Keahi." She touched her necklace. "When my people found out that he was Keahi they fretted that the child would become his weapon against them and that he would make me switch loyalties, they didn't know that the day Kaelem was born I knew I could no longer extract souls. The reason for this I will go into later, for it will reveal the key to Kaelem's repentance.

"Kaelem's father ordered me to expel our son's power so I could have peace of mind that he would not hunt us down, to portray that he loved me beyond reasons of control and domination."

Aolani's face showed confusion, so Lily-Anna explained in more detail, "When our powers flow through our veins they create an extra-sensory link to other members of the family, linked by blood. This means that those of the same blood lineage always know the location of one another.

"A year later I met your father." Lily-Anna paused. *Does Aolani know her father is aware of everything?* "I told Dillon about my life when I realised I was in love. It is the law for the Haukea to do this, but I didn't explain these things for *them*. Once they found out Kaelem was part Keahi I felt I had to prove to them I was still part of their cause, for fear they would execute him, because he gave me sympathy towards the humans. I shouldn't have pretended to them that I still agreed with what they were doing, but I was alone and scared. After I had you I was petrified the Haukea would destroy my family. That is why I stayed pretending to work for the Haukea: to show them I had no more sympathy for humans than I did before; however, each time the Haukea visited me I gave them another excuse for the lack of souls I had extracted. I took a few it is true, but I did it with a sorrowful heart, hoping that one day they would be free again. Of course the Haukea became suspicious of me, they thought I had disconnected myself from their cause, that Aka had got into my mind, and they believed I was spying for him. They began to monitor my actions closely, wary of alliances with the opposing side. Soon enough the Haukea came to take the vial which contained Kaelem's power."

"You still had it? Couldn't Kaelem's dad have tracked it down?" Aolani queried.

"It is only activated when it reacts in Kaelem's bloodstream, out of his body it becomes dead. Think of it as acting like a radar and batteries. Anyway, they were petrified that the Keahi would get Kaelem first, because he is their greatest threat." Lily-Anna sounded proud of this statement. "I had no choice but to give up his powers; I would not risk exposing Kaelem's innocence to the manipulation of the Haukea monarchy without me. At the same time Aka was feeling a shift of power. A lot of tension was rising, and he knew our two clans would combat together again soon. He was worried for Kaelem's safety." She glanced back at Aka's shadow, although he was out of earshot he had not left their presence. "I still do not know how he tracked me down. Even I do not know the extent to which his power reaches. He wanted to know where his son was, but there was no time for explanations, only a spell. Aka believed my sorcery was aiding the Haukea in the war to rule the humans, whilst in reality I had tried to tell Kaelem that he should not be troubled by the power he could receive, but just be wary of what others could do with it - for I knew I would no longer be there to consol and guide him. Aka interfered with the connection, he had misread my intentions and moulded it so that I would become a nightmare to Kaelem. It's ironic because he did that in case my influence created what he is today.

"Once the Haukea had realised I had disappeared they became anxious again: either I was in danger, or plotting against them.

"The only way in which I can be found is through Kaelem. The only way Kaelem can be found is through his power; it has a kind of magnetic quality, where the closer it is to him, the more forceful it becomes, wanting to be released into Kaelem. But instead of just using him to find me, they did what they were so scared of the Keahi doing: training Kaelem to win the Earth for them. They taught him to capture coveted souls, though Kaelem was not to know they were going to become resuscitated, brain-washed slaves. The royals have always been jealous of

235

the humans living on the land which they crave so much, yet I would never have thought it of Bethamy. Her mother was a strong manipulator, as were all the previous Haukea leaders, but there was something different about Bethamy. I can only dream of how it might have ended up had Annabel-Acacia not raised her daughter." Lily-Anna's brow furrowed, she seemed lost in thought. A moment later her eyes refocused. "But the war has become brutal, and Kaelem will have to choose in the end who he wants to side with, even though he is a part of all three. But this does not affect our particular mission."

Aolani sat in silence, trying to take in the load of information. It suddenly all made an illogical kind of sense. What was more she finally believed the woman before her was her mother. All she wanted to do was to take comfort in her mother's arms, to talk about mundane problems and material objects. But the topics that mothers and daughters were supposed to discuss would not heal this situation, and time was running out - she didn't want another soul on her brother's conscience. So instead she took a deep breath, expelled slowly, and asked, "How do I save Kaelem?"

Lily-Anna's insides were tearing up at her question, and looking at her daughter's innocent face she found it hard not to show her emotion on the outside. But Aka's words repeated in her mind. "There are only two ways, one of them brings life, ending in death, and the other brings death, ending in life. Kaelem must be redeemed before he can go, so it is not him that must pass over, therefore the option I have concluded upon brings death." Lily-Anna stopped, not knowing how to break the news to her daughter when she wasn't even sure how to tell the truth to herself.

"Then who?" Aolani persisted.

"Please -"

"Tell me!"

Lily-Anna swallowed, looked her nine-year-old daughter in the eye, and said, "It is you."

"Me?"

"But I am trying to find another way. I have to find a different path for you and your brother."

Aolani rose up onto her feet. Pain seared through her leg, but she looked blankly out at the sea. "Why does it have to end in death?"

"A Haukea only realises what they are doing is immoral, only stops what they are doing, when a human close to them is killed due to their actions. Some Haukea do settle down with humans. Love cannot be contained or controlled, and most of the race have nothing against Homo sapiens, they believe they are helping them out, so why should they be opposed to them? But sometimes special requests are inadvertently given to the wrong Haukea, and their families become their target. It's strange because these mix ups have only been happening recently, someone must be doing this on purpose, and I hope they have the strength to carry on.

"The Haukea's blinkers come off once they feel the pain, and conclude that if this is what it takes to 'save' the human race, then surely the Queen cares not for their well-being, but rather power over them."

"But no one died in your case," Aolani commented, unmoving, unblinking, staring at the sea. Pretending the woman talking to her was not the mother she had never met.

"No. But I had Kaelem, and at the time of the reveal I believed him to be human, I was haunted by the thought of his soul being taken, stored, used for purposes I didn't want him to know about.

That is why I believe there has to be another way, and I won't give up searching for it."

"We have to do this now, before anyone else is hurt," Aolani said finally.

"Aolani, no - I should never have given you this option. It is as immoral as taking a soul. It is the same."

"It's okay. I will be saving Kaelem's soul, and many others as a result. You wouldn't have given me this option had there been a chance there was another way."

Aolani turned to her mother, who stroked her daughter's face. "I have missed you," she whispered. "I hope on another plane we will have time to get to know one another." Lily-Anna called Aka to her side. He came gracefully. "I have a potion," she said to both of them. "I made it when my son's powers were transported to the Haukea. Even though I was exiled, I had a contact there who was able to get me my ingredients, and as I mixed them I prayed in anticipation of a day I hoped would never come." She drew out a vial from her dress. It held a cold white liquid which moved flawlessly, almost as if it were a gas. "Drink this Aolani, and you will feel no pain. It expires after forty-eight hours." Aolani took it and drank the substance without a second thought. It went smoothly down her throat and she suddenly felt relaxed and happy. In spite of this she looked at her mother and Aka a moment later with anxiety distorting her features. She cried: for taking that potion made her realise there was no going back, she couldn't let her brother down. It wouldn't be fair. Lily-Anna tried to comfort her daughter by stating she would find another way before the two days were gone, but Aolani knew what she had to do. She let the cold of her mother's arms numb her.

"This is not fair," Aka whispered. "Damn that monarchy."

CHAPTER FORTY-ONE

Aolani limped up to Kaelem, who was sitting alone on a tree stump. A magnificent growing life had been destroyed, cut down and left for dead.

As she walked closer to her brother he turned his head towards her. The sun touched his face, making his eyes glitter an unnatural bluish-green. "I can't lie to you Aolani: it has become more than just following orders." He didn't need to say anymore as he looked away from her and focused his gaze into his sweaty palms, stained red.

Aolani took a deep breath, knowing what she had to do, remembering her mum's words. The spell had been drunk, she had to go through with it, for her brother's sake, and the lives and hearts of all the others he was yet to affect, and had affected. He was to learn the meaning of grief.

She put a trembling hand on Kaelem's shoulder, and said gently, "It's all right. I have the solution."

She felt her brother tense up.

When the weight of Aolani's hand was lifted Kaelem turned his head to watch his sister shuffle away from him.

CHAPTER FORTY-TWO

Lily-Anna sat in her cold room hoping another way would be found for Kaelem to be redeemed, and contemplating on what was going to happen that night.

Kaelem awoke sensing something wrong. He went to sleep and searched for either his mother or father. It was Aka who received the call. He looked troubled. "It is tonight Kaelem. I am letting my wife go tonight." His voice sounded cracked, weird, as though he were talking to himself rather than to his son. For once the tension between them was gone; nothing else existed apart from this moment in time. But the moment swept away, like the ticking of a broken clock gradually resuming its rhythm. Kaelem drew away as the dread became too much to bear. He wanted more time with his mum; there was still so much information to know, and so much he wanted to find out about her. Now he would never have the chance to have the relationship he sought for, to have a conversation that wasn't weighted. He woke up and swam to shore.

Making his way through the woods he came across Aka.

"You should not be here," his father stated.

"I'm her son!"

"There are more pressing issues going on."

"What could be more important than this? No wonder she died at your hands: death means nothing to you."

Aka shook his head and grabbed Kaelem, transporting them both to Aki Houna.

"Try not to let anyone know you are here. You have become a sort of omen around here for danger and death."

They had walked a while before Kaelem asked, "What about Xalvadora?"

"She only wants what is best for you," Aka replied. He looked down at his son and smiled. "I think she likes you. A lot."

Kaelem averted the gaze, feeling as if he had let Xalvadora down. He was neither the boy she had first perceived him as, nor whom she wanted to perceive him as. So much had changed. Maybe she could never forgive him. Maybe their friendship was gone. Maybe there would be too many unspoken words that needed telling. Before he knew it Kaelem was in his old bedroom. "What…"

"Wait in here," Aka interrupted, and walked out of the room. Kaelem heard the sound of a key in a lock. He banged against the door, yelling to be let out, but the only other sound was that of fading footsteps.

***

He heard a click. The door swung open, revealing Xalvadora. She smiled at Kaelem.

"Why?" he asked, caught off guard.

"I don't know. I see your soul is good."

"That's ironic."

"You will see, it will all work out." She left, leaving the door ajar. Kaelem ran, unrelenting, until he arrived at room number two hundred and six. He saw that there was no use obtaining the key, for the door was already slightly open. He went in, and thankfully he saw that it was only Lily-Anna who occupied the room. She was sitting on the ice bed, her eyes glazed. "Kaelem," she greeted sadly once she saw who it was. He went to her.

"Why does this have to happen now? I need you. You are the only one who understands my methods, I have put everyone through hell, and you are the one person who knows why, who understands that after all this is over it will be for the better."

"You misunderstand Kaelem. I love you, I love my people, but I do not agree."

"Then there is no point, there is no sense to any of this. Why couldn't you have been there for me? Why did Aka have to ruin the one individual who could guide me? You can't go yet, not yet."

"Kaelem, it is because of who I am that Aka killed me, because I tried to save you from what my people have been brainwashed into believing. My advice is to not trust the Haukea Kaelem: the royals are manipulative. It's hard, I know, to understand, nevertheless you must try. She cares so much about you."

"What do you mean?"

For a moment she seemed conflicted between two explanations, but she chose only one. "Your sister is helping you Kaelem, you must go to her, stop her. We will find another way to make yourself see how wrong the acts you have been committing are. It isn't going to turn out okay. It never was. There is so much pain Kaelem, so much pain. But at least this way Aolani gets to live. I was thoughtless." She turned her eyes to the floor, they caught the light of a blue flame on the table, it illuminated the hurt in her eyes, the regret. She then looked back into her son's eyes and continued to speak:

"I have experienced what you are going through, the split loyalties, the confusion, and I learned the hard way what path I needed to take. I don't want you to have to deal with the burden of death, but it will become the only way if you do not understand that the Haukea only want power. They don't care about wellbeing. Please Kaelem, decide soon. Before your sister goes through with it. She loves you too much not to.

"What do you mean?" Kaelem panicked.

Lily-Anna closed her eyes, they moved rapidly beneath her lids, as if searching for something. Then they opened. "Go to the Mowdon service station bridge."

Kaelem turned to leave, but Lily-Anna held him back, and embraced her son for the last time. A voice whispered in his ear:

Remember Kaelem, Bethamy knows I took the Healers' vial. All she wants is to make everything right. Two hundred years is a long time to wait for justice, but now it is within our grasp, within you. Do not give up now. Please. Learn, and grow strong from that education. I cannot state any more than this for my tongue has been bound.

A cold flame on the wall flickered then burst into heat, the blue hue turning orange.

Lily-Anna, Mum, he would never forget her.

CHAPTER FORTY-THREE

Atisarga my love.

They were in the dungeon in which Lily-Anna had first died.

Aka held her, and Lily-Anna let him. She wrapped her arms around him, smelling the nostalgic scent of burning wood and mint, making her remember the good times they had spent together: their wedding day; Kaelem playing in the park, on the swings with her, pushing him higher, or on the slide, Aka catching his screaming body of happiness. Now was the time to tell Aka. He had to know, even if it meant he grieved longer. She couldn't go with him not knowing, it would break her lifeless heart, and so she whispered softly in his ear.

Aka laid her back down on the table, fingers lingering over the burn he had given her when Kaelem was just a baby. She was his to do as he willed. His eyes stung, and a single tear wept from his eye. It crawled gently down his soft dark skin with pale grief. It fell slowly onto the skin under which lay Lily-Anna's heart. Light swept over her stricken body until it had engulfed her whole form. It was unbearable light, blinding to witness, even to the dark cave whose sinister shadows cowered away from it. But Aka, still holding her hand tightly, watched. It went dark. Aka, disorientated, blinked, and as he did he felt lighter, and saw that his hands were holding onto nothing but the cave's stale air. The last words played in his ears, seeming like a broken love song.

His love's last memories: "I never let your heart leave my soul. I am with you, in the past, here, and when I am gone. You are sublime."

CHAPTER FORTY-FOUR

Aolani stood on the bridge, the concrete feeling stable beneath her trembling feet.

"When the time comes it won't hurt." She looked up at the starless night; swirls of cloud gathered, as if ready to break and mourn her loss.

At least there would be no more thunderstorms.

She closed her eyes, and breathed, listening out for the occasional hum of traffic, feeling nauseous as her stomach tied into knots, butterflies flitting between them, getting stuck, then freeing themselves again. Thoughts ran to Kaelem, hoping that he still had the power to forgive, to grieve. She thought she could hear his voice, calling to her, feel his warm hand in hers, leading her from the bridge. She liberated her eyes. "Kaelem?"

"I'm here Ali. I understand, you can be saved."

She smiled. "And will you be saved too?"

He didn't answer, and a chill filled the air around them. Kaelem swung round.

Oringo's expression was ravenous, contradicting his pleased tone, "I'll take her Kaelem, I can keep her safe." Oringo smiled, but it lacked all the innocence of Aolani's.

"No."

"Why, don't you wish her to be safe? No harm will ever be done to her if she comes with me."

"I don't understand, I'm leaving the Haukea, why are you doing this?"

The smile seemed to widen, like a joker's. "To fulfil my latest mission."

Kaelem's hand tightened in his sister's palm; he could sense her tension, her fear.

"If I take her, your repentance will be granted. She will be gone from your life. But she will still be alive."

Aolani's breath escaped her. "Maybe it's not such a bad idea Kaelem."

He felt her drifting towards Oringo, and his grip became almost vice-like in her soft hand. "No! It's a trick Ali, he doesn't want this; I'm worth too much to his precious Haukea. He knows that when you die I will leave them forever, and they will probably kill him for not being able to stop my atonement. This is his latest mission: to take you, and keep you from dying."

"But what will the harm be in trying?"

"Your sister has more brains than I gave her credit for Kaelem. I would listen to her. Come on. One more step towards accepting the inevitable. "

Kaelem ignored him and leaned forward to his sister's height. He whispered so that Oringo would not be able to hear their conversation, "I've been to their world, seen their capabilities, I even believe that what they are doing is right. Through all that I've done, I still find it hard to disbelieve. They will manipulate and harm you Ali. I can't let that happen, not ever. I don't want to hurt you. I never meant to break you. I want to protect you until your last breath, and I can't promise that on their world. I can't tell you it will be alright."

"You promised long ago you wouldn't hurt me," she said quietly, almost internally. Kaelem nodded sadly, not wanting to upset her, no longer angry with her: it was his fault after all.

"I know." He hugged her tightly, then stood up to face Oringo. "I am not letting you take her!"

Aolani gasped.

"But…"

"I'm going to do one right thing this time. You came here to take away everything that ever meant something to me, and I will fight to keep it. I will die without redemption for it."

Oringo smiled in his way. "Oh Kaelem. You said yourself though: *You're worth more to the Haukea than a dead body.* If you choose not to give her to me - I have other ways." Oringo went into his pyrophanous self. After a second Kaelem felt heat soar through himself, and a hand push him backwards, catching him unawares. He fell backwards, bringing Aolani with him, he opened his hand, and a terrifying high-pitched scream ran through his bones, sweeping all thoughts of his own self preservation aside. He turned quickly, vaguely seeing the melted metal bars, and flew himself to the floor as he watched his sister falling through the air. He closed his eyes and reached out in vain hope. "Aolani!" he shouted. He pushed himself onto his feet and in one fluid motion was rushing down the embankment to the motorway, where her still form lay waiting.

He held her tight in his arms, rocking her, just like he used to do when they were younger, when she was afraid of the thunderstorms; a stroke of lightning, a flash of white reflecting the fear in her eyes. But she had never been hit.

Light engulfed Kaelem's whole body, and enveloped his sister. The world became silent; her presence was the only thing that mattered. She opened her eyes, the wounds slowly healing, the blood trickling back into her body. Her startling blue eyes looked into her brother's face; and they smiled. "It doesn't hurt Kaelem. Nothing tonight could hurt me, except your downfall. One day you will know Kaelem, why this had to be. You told me, even tonight, you believe in the Haukea's mission, and my only wish is that you can now know all the truths of that mission through objective eyes. Your sight came back from darkness, and you won't be sad anymore, you will rise above your evils, and you will find peace once more with this world, and you will save it. I know you will. You are my brother, and my faith will always be in your goodness, it is still there, your innocence, somewhere. You will know once again what is right."

He embraced her. "I'm so sorry." Kaelem's voice was muffled by her jumper.

It was then Kaelem felt the tap on his shoulder. He jumped.

"It's alright, we can take her now." Kaelem looked up, the world bursting back into horrific sound. Standing above him was a paramedic. Kaelem looked back down at his sister, and had to swallow; blood had once more diffused into Aolani's hair, and her features had become distorted below her seeping face. It was his fault, nothing could change that.

"I am with you Aolani. I will always be with you, just as you will always be in my heart."

With careful movements, so as not to harm her anymore, Kaelem guided his sister back on the ground, and wept for all the lost souls.

GLOSSARY

I have carefully selected the names of my characters for a reason, some of them being due to my Hawaiian phase, a few of them because of my fascination with how, in some cultures, it is believed names determine what the child's personality or destiny is going to be.

'Translations' for the characters' names

Aka – Shadow
Alma – Nourishing/Spanish for 'soul'
Annabel-Acacia – Beautiful-thorn
Aolani – Heavenly cloud
Anuva – Knowledge (Indian) or A new beginning (Russian)
Bailey – able
Dillon – Faithful
Jadon – He will judge
Jeb (Jebediah) – Beloved Friend
Kaelem – Honest
Keisha – Her Life
Lily-Anna – Graceful Lily
Oringo – He who loves the hunt
Saxton – From the village/town of the Saxons
Xalvadora – Saviour

Yaegar (Lily-Anna's maiden name) – Derived from Jäger, given to those who were hunters, taken from the German word jagen, which means to chase or hunt.

Foreign Translations (Literal meanings)

Haukea – White snow
Keahi – Flames

Aki Houna – Fire World
Hau Houna – Ice World

Hale ali'i – Palace
Wai hau loko – Ice water lake

Atisarga – Farewell, surrender, granting permission

Terminology

Ctenoid scales – A type of overlapping scale seen on fish such as Perch and Bass. This scale has comb-like ridges on one side.

Fluke – The horizontal, boneless tail seen on mammals such as whales and dolphins.

Nictitating membrane – A third eyelid that is drawn across the eyeball to protect it, remove debris, and keep it moist, whilst also allowing for visibility. In diving mammals it is used underwater to protect the eye, for example when swimming fast; in some sharks it is used when striking at prey to protect the eye, and in polar bears it prevents snow blindness.

Placoid scales – These scales are similar in structure to teeth and are also known as dermal denticles. They slant toward the tail to reduce friction when swimming. If they are stroked head to tail they have a smooth texture, whilst the other way they feel rough and can be used to harm prey. They are seen on sharks and rays.

Pyrophanous – Something that is rendered transparent by heat

AFTERWORD

Forgive me if I ramble.

It started as a fantasy from a dream I had, got doused with water on the shores of Cyprus, and blossomed into the unrecognisable form you hold in your hands now.

It began secretly, somewhere to retreat in my teenage years, a place where things were easier to explain, where I could release my anxiety and be comforted. I then did the unthinkable: I allowed people to read it, to criticise it.

Maybe they would shove it in the shredder, or, perhaps, they would enjoy it.

Re-reading my book eight years after I started to pen it I could see that Kaelem's journey and my own through adolescence reflect one another, and I guess sometimes authors cannot be separate from their manifestations, that subliminally they become a part of each other.

I read, reflected, and realised that this book had become a kind of diary to me. I recognised the obsessions I went through, and some I am still going through: the names inspired by the Hawaiian language, the tattoos and piercing of which I was forbidden, save for the usual one-in-each-ear, candles, and my continued fascination with water, the seas, oceans, and all that they hold.

I could also see how the characters had changed due to my frustration with reading and seeing white as good and the darkness of the gothic as completely an evil force, of which at one time Aka was going to be yet another stereotype of.

But why do our semiotics always dictate that black=bad and white=good? What if these roles were reversed?

So Aka morphed into another stereotype I guess: that of the tortured good.

Good becoming evil, or evil to good, has long intrigued me. The effect and tension this creates between that character and the ones he cares for, needs, loves, inspired me to write the relationship between Kaelem and his sister Aolani, and perhaps reflects my fear as a teenager that everyone seemed to be growing up and changing around me, while I seemed to remain constant, though later I realised I had been growing up just as much as them.

Finally, reading through this has allowed me to see that as Kaelem grew, so did I. As my father pointed out in the forward: the writing became better, though I'm not sure if 'better' indicates 'good.'

So I guess Kaelem and I went through our teenage years together, gathering knowledge from what surrounds us, realising that everything is not black and white, and fighting to get back what we once took for granted: our innocence.

We took this journey together, and now I am sharing it with you. Thank you for reading my words, my life - so far.

November 2008, Cheyenne Kai